IN THE CLEARING BELOW
TWO MEN FACED DEATH . . .

Bill Lynch and Cassidy were walking toward each other, neither hurrying or touching their gun. Sixty yards separated them—fifty—forty—thirty.

"God almighty," Lanky whispered from the rimrock.

Twenty-five—twenty. Lynch's hands swung closer to his thighs, but Cassidy still moved toward him, erect, not changing his pace.

"They're the two fastest draws in the Southwest," Red said from the cliff above.

Perspiration beaded on the faces of the watchers on the cliff. This was worse than they had expected. Forty yards would have been close enough to start shooting.

"It's a case of pure speed now," whispered Red.

Fifteen yards—ten—eight—six—five—

And a flurry of smoke . . .

A HOPALONG CASSIDY NOVEL

THE COMING OF CASSIDY

Clarence E. Mulford

TOR

A TOM DOHERTY ASSOCIATES BOOK
NEW YORK

This is a work of fiction. All the characters and events portrayed in this book are either products of the author's imagination or are used fictitiously.

THE COMING OF CASSIDY

Cover art by Carl Cassler

A Tor Book
Published by Tom Doherty Associates, LLC
175 Fifth Avenue
New York, NY 10010

www.tor.com

Tor® is a registered trademark of Tom Doherty Associates, LLC.

ISBN 0-812-52291-5
EAN 978-0-812-52291-4

First Tor edition: September 1992

Printed in the United States of America

0 9 8 7 6 5 4

Introduction

IN JUNE 1991 Bantam published the first of Louis L'Amour's acclaimed Hopalong Cassidy novels, *The Rustlers of West Fork*. Since then, publishers tell me there has been a tremendous ground swell of enthusiasm for Hopalong and his friends. Readers around the country want to know more about these Bar-20 boys—and above all, want more of their books.

Consequently, Tor Books is bringing back the original novels, written by Clarence E. Mulford, the man who created Cassidy and company. It's a good thing too. These are really first-rate books, full of true grit and pulse-pounding action, the kind of books you can't put down.

If you liked Louis L'Amour's Hopalong Cassidy novel— *The Rustlers of West Fork*—you'll *love* this one. This is no imitation, but the real thing.

A lot of western writers—people like Richard S. Wheeler, Earl Murray, Al Dempsey and yours truly—when we get together for a few beers, we sometimes talk about books. We talk about the books that inspired us; the authors who made us love the West and even want to write ourselves. For whatever it's worth, it's a short list. And for a lot of us, the guy at the top is Clarence Mulford.

Clarence, old hoss, wherever you are, here's a Lone Star beer to you.

—Jackson Cain,
   author of *Hellbreak Country*
   and *Hangman's Whip*

Preface

IT WAS on one of my annual visits to the ranch that Red, whose welcome always seemed a little warmer than that of the others, finally took me back to the beginning. My friendship with the outfit did not begin until some years after the fight at Buckskin, and, while I was familiar with that affair and with the history of the outfit from that time on, I had never seemed to make much headway back of that encounter. And I must confess that if I had depended upon the rest of the outfit for enlightenment I should have learned very little of its earlier exploits. A more secretive and bashful crowd, when it came to their own achievements, would be hard to find. But Red, the big, smiling, under-foreman, at last completely thawed and during the last few weeks of my stay, told me story after story about the earlier days of the ranch and the parts played by each member of the outfit. Names that I had heard mentioned casually now meant something to me; the characters stepped out of the obscurity of the past to act their parts again. To my mind's eye came Jimmy Price, even more mischievous than Johnny Nelson; "Butch" Lynch and Charley James, who erred in judgment; the coming and going of Sammy Porter, and why "You-Bet" Somes never arrived; and others who did their best, or worst, and went their way. The tales will follow, as closely as possible, in chronological order. Between some of them the interval is short; between others, long; the less interesting stories that should fill those gaps may well be omitted.

It was in the '70s, when the buffalo were fast disappearing from the state, and the hunters were beginning to turn to other ways of earning a living, that Buck Peters stopped his wagon on the banks of Snake Creek and built himself a sod dugout in the heart of a country forbidding and full of perils. It was said that he was only the agent for an eastern syndicate that, carried away by the prospects of the cattle industry, bought a "ranch," which later was found to be entirely strange to cattle. As a matter of fact there were no cows within three hundred miles of it, and there never had been. Somehow the syndicate got in touch with Buck and sent him out to look things over and make a report to them. This he did, and in his report he stated that the "ranch" was split in two parts by about forty square miles of public land, which he recommended that he be allowed to buy according to his judgment. When everything was settled the syndicate found that they owned the west, and best, bank of an unfailing river and both banks of an unfailing creek for a distance of about thirty miles. The strip was not very wide then, but it did not need to be, for it cut off the back-lying range from water and rendered it useless to anyone but his employers. Westward there was no water to amount to anything for one hundred miles. When this had been digested thoroughly by the syndicate it caused Buck's next pay check to be twice the size of the first.

He managed to live through the winter, and the following spring a herd of about two thousand or more poor cattle was delivered to him, and he noticed at once that fully half of them were unbranded; but mavericks were cows, and in those days it was not questionable to brand them. Persuading two members of the drive outfit to work for him he settled down to face the work and perils of ranching in a wild country. One of these two men, George Travis, did not work long; the other was the man who told me these tales. Red went back with the drive outfit, but in Buck's wagon, to return in four weeks with it heaped full of necessities, and to find that troubles already had begun. Buck's trust was not misplaced. It was during Red's absence that Bill Cassidy, later to be known by a more descriptive name, appeared upon the scene and played his cards.

C.E.M.

THE COMING OF CASSIDY

Contents

I	The Coming of Cassidy	1
II	The Weasel	12
III	Jimmy Price	35
IV	Jimmy Visits Sharpsville	49
V	The Luck of Fools	64
VI	Hopalong's Hop	81
VII	"Dealing the Odd"	95
VIII	The Norther	108
IX	The Drive	122
X	The Hold-up	138
XI	Sammy Finds a Friend	157
XII	Sammy Knows the Game	175
XIII	His Code	192
XIV	Sammy Hunts a Job	209
XV	When Johnny Sloped	223

CHAPTER I

The Coming of Cassidy

THE TRAIL boss shook his fist after the departing puncher and swore softly. He hated to lose a man at this time and he had been a little reckless in threatening to "fire" him; but in a gun-fighting outfit there was no room for a hothead. "Cimarron" was boss of the outfit that was driving a large herd of cattle to California, a feat that had been accomplished before, but that no man cared to attempt the second time. Had his soul been enriched by the gift of prophecy he would have turned back. As it was he returned to the work ahead of him. "Aw, let him go," he growled. "He's wuss off'n I am, an' he'll find it out quick. I never did see nobody what got crazy mad so quick as him."

"Bill" Cassidy, not yet of age, but a man in stature and strength, rode north because it promised him civilization quicker than any other way except the back trail, and he was tired of the coast range. He had forgotten the trail-boss during the last three days of his solitary journeying and the fact that he was in the center of an uninhabited country nearly as large as a good-sized state gave him no concern; he was equipped for two weeks, and fortified by youth's confidence.

All day long he rode, around mesas and through draws, detouring to avoid canyons and bearing steadily north-ward with a certainty that was a heritage. Gradually the great bulk of mesas swung off to the west, and to the east the range grew steadily more level as it swept toward the peaceful river lying in the distant valley like a carelessly flung rope of silver. The forest vegetation, so luxuriant along the rivers and draws a day or two before, was now rarely seen, while chaparrals and stunted mesquite be-came more common.

He was more than twenty-five hundred feet above the ocean, on a great plateau broken by mesas that stretched away for miles in a vast sea of grass. There was just enough tang in the dry April air to make riding a pleasure and he did not mind the dryness of the season. Twice that day he detoured to ride around prairie-dog towns and the sight of buffalo skeletons lying in groups was not rare. Alert and contemptuous gray wolves gave him a passing glance, but the coyotes, slinking a little farther off, watched him with more interest. Occasionally he had a shot at antelope and once was successful.

Warned by the gathering dusk he was casting about for the most favorable spot for his blanket and fire when a horseman swung into sight out of a draw and reined in quickly. Bill's hand fell carelessly to his side while he re-garded the stranger, who spoke first, and with a re-strained welcoming gladness in his voice. "Howd'y, Stranger! You plumb surprised me."

Bill's examination told him that the other was stocky, compactly built, with a pleasing face and a "good eye." His age was about thirty and the surface indications were very favorable. "Some surprised myself," he replied. "Ridin' my way?"

"Far's th' house," smiled the other. "Better join us. Couple of buffalo hunters dropped in awhile back."

"They'll go a long way before they'll find buffalo," Bill responded, suspiciously. Glancing around he readily picked out the rectangular blot in the valley, though it was no easy feat. "Huntin' or ranchin'?" he inquired in tones devoid of curiosity.

"Ranchin'," smiled the other. "Hefty proposition, up here, I reckon. Th' wolves'll walk in under yore nose. But I ain't seen no Injuns."

"You will," was the calm reply. "You'll see a couple, first; an' then th' whole cussed tribe. *They* ain't got no buffalo no more, neither."

Buck glanced at him sharply and thought of the hunters, but he nodded. "Yes. But if that couple don't go back?" he asked, referring to the Indians.

"Then you'll save a little time."

"Well, let 'em come. I'm here to stay, one way or th' other. But, anyhow, I ain't got no border ruffians like they have over in th' Panhandle. They're worse'n Injuns."

"Yes," agreed Bill. "Th' war ain't ended yet for some of them fellers. Ex-guerrillas, lots of 'em."

When they reached the house the buffalo hunters were arguing about their next day's ride and the elder, looking up, appealed to Bill. "Howd'y, Stranger. Ain't come 'cross no buffaler signs, hev ye?"

Bill smiled. "Bones an' old chips. But th' gray wolves was headin' southwest."

"What'd I tell you?" triumphantly exclaimed the younger hunter.

"Well, they ain't much dif'rence, is they?" growled his companion.

Bill missed nothing the hunters said or did and during the silent meal had a good chance to study their faces.

When the pipes were going and the supper wreck cleaned away, Buck leaned against the wall and looked across the room at the latest arrival. "Don't want a job, do you?" he asked.

Bill shook his head slowly, wondering why the hunters had frowned at a job being offered on another man's ranch. "I'm headed north. But I'll give you a hand for a week if you need me," he offered.

Buck smiled. "Much obliged, friend; but it'll leave me worse off than before. My other puncher'll be back in a few weeks with th' supplies, but I need four men all year round. I got a thousand head to brand yet."

The elder hunter looked up. "Drive 'em back to cow-country an' sell 'em, or locate there," he suggested.

Buck's glance was as sharp as his reply, for he couldn't believe that the hunter had so soon forgotten what he had been told regarding the ownership of the cattle. "I don't own 'em. This range is bought an' paid for. I won't lay down."

"I done forgot they ain't yourn," hastily replied the hunter, smiling to himself. Stolen cattle cannot go back.

"If they was I'd stay," crisply retorted Buck. "I ain't quittin' nothin' I starts."

"How many'll you have nex' spring?" grinned the younger hunter. He was surprised by the sharpness of the response. "More'n I've got now, in spite of hell!"

Bill nodded approval. He felt a sudden, warm liking for this rugged man who would not quit in the face of such handicaps. He liked game men, better if they were square, and he believed this foreman was as square as he was game. "By th' Lord!" he ejaculated. "For a plugged peso I'd stay with you!"

Buck smiled warmly. "Would *good* money do? But don't you stay if you oughtn't, son."

When the light was out Bill lay awake for a long time, his mind busy with his evening's observations, and they pleased him so little that he did not close his eyes until assured by the breathing of the hunters that they were asleep. His Colt, which should have been hanging in its holster on the wall where he had left it, lay unsheathed close to his thigh and he awakened frequently during the night so keyed was he for the slightest sound. Up first in the morning, he replaced the gun in its scabbard before the others opened their eyes, and it was not until the hunters had ridden out of sight into the southwest that he entirely relaxed his vigilance. Saying good-bye to the two cowmen was not without regrets, but he shook hands heartily with them and swung decisively northward.

He had been riding perhaps two hours, thinking about the little ranch and the hunters, when he stopped suddenly on the very brink of a sheer drop of two hundred feet. In his abstraction he had ridden up the sloping southern face of the mesa without noticing it. "Bet there ain't another like this for a hundred miles," he laughed, and then ceased abruptly and stared with unbelieving eyes at the mouth of a draw not far away. A trotting line of gray wolves was emerging from it and swinging toward the southwest ten abreast. He had never heard of such a thing before and watched them in amazement. "Well, I'm—!" he exclaimed, and his Colt flashed rapidly at the pack. Two or three dropped, but the trotting line only swerved a little without pause or a change of pace and soon was lost in another draw. "Why, they're single hunters," he muttered. "Huh! I won't never tell this. I can't hardly believe it myself. How 'bout you, Ring-Bone?" he asked his horse.

Turning, he rode around a rugged pinnacle of rock and stopped again, gazing steadily along the back trail. Far away in a valley two black dots were crawling over a patch of sand and he knew them to be horsemen. His face slowly reddened with anger at the espionage, for he had not thought the cowmen could doubt his good will and honesty. Then suddenly he swore and spurred forward to

cover those miles as speedily as possible. "Come on, ol'
Hammer-Head!" he cried. "We're goin' back!"

The hunters had finally decided they would ride into
the southwest and had ridden off in that direction. But
they had detoured and swung north to see him pass and
be sure he was not in their way. Now, satisfied upon that
point, they were going back to that herd of cattle, easily
turned from skinning buffalo to cattle, and on a large
scale. To do this they would have to kill two men and
then, waiting for the absent puncher to return with the
wagon, kill him and load down the vehicle with skins.
"Like hell they will!" he gritted. "Three or none, you piruts. Come on, White-Eye! Don't sleep all th' time; an'
don't light often'r once every ten yards, you saddle-galled,
barrel-bellied runt!"

Into hollows, out again; shooting down steep-banked
draws and avoiding cacti and chaparral with cat-like agility, the much-described little pony butted the wind in front
and left a low-lying cloud of dust swirling behind as it
whirred at top speed with choppy, tied-in stride in a winding circle for the humble sod hut on Snake Creek. The
rider growled at the evident speed of the two men ahead,
for he had not gained upon them despite his efforts. "If
I'm too late to stop it, I'll clean th' slate, anyhow," he
snapped. "Even if I has to ambush! *Will* you run?" he
demanded, and the wild-eyed little bundle of whalebone
and steel found a little more speed in its flashing legs.

The rider now began to accept what cover he could find
and when he neared the hut left the shelter of the last,
low hill for that afforded by a draw leading to within a
hundred yards of the dugout's rear wall. Dismounting, he
ran lightly forward on foot, alert and with every sense
strained for a warning.

Reaching the wall he peered around the corner and stifled
an exclamation. Buck's puncher, a knife in his back, lay head
down the sloping path. Placing his ear to the wall he listened

intently for some moments and then suddenly caught sight of a shadow slowly creeping past his toes. Quickly as he sprang aside he barely missed the flashing knife and the bulk of the man behind it, whose hand, outflung to save his balance, accidentally knocked the Colt from Bill's grasp and sent it spinning twenty feet away.

Without a word they leaped together, fighting silently, both trying to gain the gun in the hunter's holster and trying to keep the other from it. Bill, forcing the fighting in hopes that his youth would stand a hot pace better than the other's years, pushed his enemy back against the low roof of the dugout; but as the hunter tripped over it and fell backward, he pulled Bill with him. Fighting desperately they rolled across the roof and dropped to the sloping earth at the doorway, so tightly locked in each other's arms that the jar did not separate them. The hunter, falling underneath, got the worst of the fall but kept on fighting. Crashing into the door head first, they sent it swinging back against the wall and followed it, bumping down the two steps still locked together.

Bill possessed strength remarkable for his years and build and he was hard as iron; but he had met a man who had the sinewy strength of the plainsman, whose greater age was offset by greater weight and the youth was constantly so close to defeat that a single false move would have been fatal. But luck favored him, for as they surged around the room they crashed into the heavy table and fell with it on top of them. The hunter got its full weight and the gash in his forehead filled his eyes with blood. By a desperate effort he pinned Bill's arm under his knee and with his left hand secured a throat grip, but the under man wriggled furiously and bridged so suddenly as to throw the hunter off him and Bill's freed hand, crashing full into the other's stomach, flashed back to release the weakened throat grip and jam the tensed fingers between his teeth, holding them there with all the power of his jaws. The dazed and gasping hunter, bending forward instinctively, felt his own throat seized and was dragged underneath his furious opponent.

In his Berserker rage Bill had forgotten about the gun, his fury sweeping everything from him but the primal desire to kill with his hands, to rend and crush like an animal. He was brought to his senses very sharply by the jarring, crashing roar of the six-shooter, the powder blowing away part of his shirt and burning his side. Twisting sideways he grasped the weapon with one hand, the wrist with the other and bent the gun slowly back, forcing its muzzle farther and farther from him. The hunter, at last managing to free his left hand from the other's teeth, found it useless when he tried to release the younger man's grip of the gun; and the Colt, roaring again, dropped from its owner's hand as he relaxed.

The victor leaned against the wall, his breath coming in great, sobbing gulps, his knees sagging and his head near bursting. He reeled across the wrecked room, gulped down a drink of whisky from the bottle on the shelf and, stumbling, groped his way to the outer air where he flung himself down on the ground, dazed and dizzy. When he opened his eyes the air seemed to be filled with flashes of fire and huge, black fantastic blots that changed form with great swiftness and the hut danced and shifted like a thing of life. Hot bands seemed to encircle his throat and the throbbing in his temples was like blows of a hammer. While he writhed and fought for breath a faint gunshot reached his ears and found him apathetic. But the second, following closely upon the first, seemed clearer and brought him to himself long enough to make him arise and stumble to his horse, and claw his way into the saddle. The animal, maddened by the steady thrust of the spurs, pitched viciously and bolted; but the rider had learned his art in the sternest school in the world, the "busting" corrals of the great Southwest, and he not only stuck to the saddle, but guided the fighting animal through a barranca almost choked with obstructions.

Stretched full length in a crevice near the top of a mesa lay the other hunter, his rifle trained on a smaller boulder several hundred yards down and across the draw. His first shot had been an inexcusable blunder for a marksman like himself and now he had a desperate man and a very capable shot opposing him. If Buck could hold out until nightfall he could slip away in the darkness and do some stalking on his own account.

For half an hour they had lain thus, neither daring to take sight. Buck could not leave the shelter of the boulder because the high ground behind him offered no cover; but the hunter, tiring of the fruitless wait, wriggled back into the crevice, arose and slipped away, intending to crawl to the edge of the mesa further down and get in a shot from a new angle before his enemy learned of the shift; and this shot would not be a blunder. He had just lowered himself down a steep wall when the noise of rolling pebbles caused him to look around, expecting to see his friend. Bill was just turning the corner of the wall and their eyes met at the same instant.

" 'Nds up!" snapped the youth, his Colt glinting as it swung up. The hunter, gripping the rifle firmly, looked into the angry eyes of the other, and slowly obeyed. Bill, watching the rifle intently, forthwith learned a lesson he never forgot: never to watch a gun, but the eyes of the man who has it. The left hand of the hunter seemed to melt into smoke, and Bill, firing at the same instant, blundered into a hit when his surprise and carelessness should have cost him dearly. His bullet, missing its intended mark by inches, struck the still moving Colt of the other, knocking it into the air and numbing the hand that held it. A searing pain in his shoulder told him of the closeness of the call and set his lips into a thin, white line. The hunter, needing no words to interpret the look in the youth's eyes, swiftly raised his hands, holding the rifle high above his head, but neglected to take his finger from the trigger.

Bill was not overlooking anything now and he noticed the crooked finger. "Stick th' muzzle *up*, an' pull that trigger," he commanded, sharply. "Now!" he grated. The report came crashing back from half a dozen points as he nodded. "Drop it, an' turn 'round." As the other obeyed he stepped cautiously forward, jammed his Colt into the hunter's back and took possession of a skinning knife. A few moments later the hunter, trussed securely by a forty-foot lariat, lay cursing at the foot of the rock wall.

Bill, collecting the weapons, went off to cache them and then peered over the mesa's edge to look into the draw. A leaden splotch appeared on the rock almost under his nose and launched a crescendo scream into the sky to whine into silence. He ducked and leaped back, grinning foolishly as he realized Buck's error. Turning to approach the edge from another point he felt his sombrero jerk at his head as another bullet, screaming plaintively, followed the first. He dropped like a shot, and commented caustically upon his paucity of brains as he gravely examined the hole in his head gear. "Huh!" he grunted. "I had a fool's luck three times in twenty minutes—damned if I'm goin' to risk th' next turn. *Three* of 'em," he repeated. "I'm a' Injun from now on. An' that foreman shore can shoot!"

He wriggled to the edge and called out, careful not to let any of his anatomy show above the sky-line. "Hey, Buck! I ain't no buffalo hunter! This is Cassidy, who you wanted to punch for you. Savvy?" He listened, and grinned at the eloquent silence. "You talk too rapid," he laughed. Repeating his statements he listened again, with the same success. "Now I wonder is he stalkin' *me*? Hey, *Buck*!" he shouted.

"Stick yore hands up an' foller 'em with yore face," said Buck's voice from below. Bill raised his arms and slowly stood up. "Now what'n blazes do *you* want?" demanded the foreman, belligerently.

"Nothin'. Just got them hunters, one of 'em alive. I reck-oned mebby you'd sorta like to know it." He paused, cog-itating. "Reckon we better turn him loose when we gets back to th' hut," he suggested. "I'll keep his guns," he added, grinning.

The foreman stuck his head out in sight. "Well, I'm damned!" he exclaimed, and sank weakly back against the boulder. "Can you give me a hand?" he muttered.

The words did not carry to the youth on the skyline, but he saw, understood, and, slipping and bumping down the steep wall with more speed than sense, dashed across the draw and up the other side. He nodded sagely as he examined the wound and bound it carefully with the sleeve of his own shirt. " 'T ain't much—loss of blood, mostly. Yo're better off than Travis."

"Travis dead?" whispered Buck. "In th' back! Pore feller, pore feller; didn't have no show. Tell me about it." At the end of the story he nodded. "Yo're all right, Cassidy. He'd 'a' stood a good chance of gettin' me, 'cept for you." A frown clouded his face and he looked weakly about him as if for an answer to the question that bothered him. "Now what am I goin' to do up here with all these cows?" he muttered.

Bill rolled the wounded man a cigarette and lit it for him, after which he fell to tossing pebbles at a rock further down the hill.

"I reckon it *will* be sorta tough," he replied, slowly. "But I sorta reckoned me an' you, an' that other feller, can make a big ranch out of yore little one. Anyhow, I'll bet we can have a mighty big time tryin'. A mighty fine time. What you think?"

Buck smiled weakly and shoved out his hand with a visible effort. "We can! Shake, Bill!" he said, contentedly.

CHAPTER II

The Weasel

THE WINTER that followed the coming of Bill Cassidy to the Bar-20 ranch was none too mild to suit the little outfit in the cabin on Snake Creek, but it was not severe enough to cause complaint and they weathered it without trouble to speak of. Down on the big ranges lying closer to the Gulf the winter was so mild as to seem but a brief interruption of summer. It was on this warm, southern range that Skinny Thompson, one bright day of early spring, loped along the trail to Scoria, where he hoped to find his friend, Lanky Smith, and where he determined to put an end to certain rumors that had filtered down to him on the range and filled his days with anger.

He was within sight of the little cow-town when he met Frank Lewis, but recently returned from a cattle drive. Exchanging gossip of a harmless nature, Skinny mildly scored his missing friend and complained about his flea-like ability to get scarce. Lewis, laughing, told him that Lanky had left town two days before bound north. Skinny gravely explained that he always had to look after his missing friend, who was childish, irresponsible and helpless when alone. Lewis laughed heartily as he pictured the absent puncher, and he laughed harder as he pictured the two together. Both lean as bean poles, Skinny stood six feet four, while Lanky was fortunate if he topped five feet by many inches. Also they were inseparable, which made Lewis ask a question. "But how does it come you ain't with him?"

"Well, we was punchin' down south an' has a li'l run-in. When I rid in that night I found he had flitted. What I want to know is what business has he got, siftin' out like that an' makin' me chase after him?"

"I dunno," replied Lewis, amused. "You're sort of gard-jean to him, hey?"

"Well, he gets sort of homesick if I ain't with him, anyhow," replied Skinny, grinning broadly. "An' who's goin' to look after him when I ain't around?"

"That puts me up a tree," replied Lewis. "I shore can't guess. But you two should ought to 'a' been stuck together, like them other twins was. But if he'd do a thing like that I'd think you wouldn't waste no time on him."

"Well, he *is* too ornery an' downright cussed for any human bein' to worry about very much, or 'sociate with steady an' reg'lar. Why, lookit him gettin' sore on me, an' for nothin'! But I'm so used to bein' abused I get sort of lost when he ain't around."

"Well," smiled Lewis, "he's went up north to punch for Buck Peters on his li'l ranch on Snake Creek. If you want to go after him, this is th' way I told him to go," and he gave instructions hopelessly inadequate to anyone not a plainsman. Skinny nodded, irritated by what he regarded as the other's painful and unnecessary details and wheeled to ride on. He had started for town when Lewis stopped him with a word. "Hey," he called. Skinny drew rein and looked around.

"Better ride in cautious like," Lewis remarked, casually. "Somebody was in town when I left—he shore was thirsty. He ain't drinkin' a drop, which has riled him considerable. So-long."

"Huh!" grunted Skinny. "Much obliged. That's one of th' reasons I'm goin' to town," and he started forward again, tight-lipped and grim.

He rode slowly into Scoria, alert, watching windows, doors and corners, and dismounted before Quigg's saloon, which was the really "high-toned" thirst parlor in the town. He noticed that the proprietor had put black shades to the windows and door and then, glancing quickly around, entered. He made straight for the partition in the rear of the building, but the proprietor's voice checked him. "You needn't bother, Skinny—there ain't nobody in there; an' I locked th' back door an hour ago." He glanced around the room and added, with studied carelessness: "You don't want to get any reckless today." He mopped the bar slowly and coughed apologetically. "Don't get careless."

"I won't—it's me that's doin' th' hunting today," Skinny replied, meaningly. "Him a-hunting for me yesterday, when he shore knowed I wasn't in town, when he knowed he couldn't find me! I was getting good an' tired of him, an' so when Walt rode over to see me last night an' told me what th' coyote was doing yesterday, an' what he was yelling around, I just natchurly had to straddle leather an' come in. I can't let him put that onto me. Nobody can call me a card cheat an' a coward an' a few other choice things like he did without seeing me, an' seeing me quick. An' I shore hope he's sober. Are both of 'em in town, Larry?"

"No; only Dick. But he's making noise enough for two. He shore raised th' devil yesterday."

"Well, I'm goin' North trailin' Lanky, but before I leave I'm shore goin' to sweeten things around here. If I go away without getting him he'll say he scared me out, so

I'll have to do it when I come back, anyhow. You see, it might just as well be today. But th' next time I sit in a game with fellers that can't drop fifty dollars without saying they was cheated I'll be a blamed sight bigger fool than I am right now. I shouldn't 'a' taken cards with 'em after what has passed. Why didn't they say they was cheated, then an' there, an' not wait till three days after I left town? All that's bothering me is Sam: if I get his brother when he ain't around, an' then goes North, he'll say I had to jump th' town to get away from him. But I'll stop that by giving him his chance at me when I get back."

"Say, why don't you wait a day an' get 'em both before you go?" asked Quigg hopefully.

"Can't: Lanky's got two days' start on me an' I want to catch him soon as I can."

"I can't get it through my head, nohow," Quigg remarked. "Everybody knows you play square. I reckon they're hard losers."

Skinny laughed shortly: "Why, can't you see it? Last year I beat Dick Bradley out with a woman over in Ballard. Then his fool brother tried to cut in an' beat me out. Cards? Hell!" he snorted, walking toward the door. "You an' everybody else knows—" he stopped suddenly and jerked his gun loose as a shadow fell across the doorsill. Then he laughed and slapped the newcomer on the shoulder: "Hullo, Ace, my boy! You had a narrow squeak then. You want to make more noise when you turn corners, unless somebody's looking for you with a gun. How are you, anyhow? An' how's yore dad? I've been going over to see him regular, right along but I've been so busy I kept putting it off."

"Dad's better, Skinny; an' I'm feeling too good to be true. What'll you have?"

"Reckon it's my treat; you wet last th' other time. Ain't that right, Quigg? Shore, I knowed it was."

"All right, here's luck," Ace smiled. "Quigg, that's better stock; an' would you look at th' style—real curtains?"

Quigg grinned. "Got to have 'em. I'm on th' sunny side of th' street."

"I hear yo're goin' North," Ace remarked.

"Yes, I am; but how'd you know about it?"

"Why, it ain't no secret, is it?" asked Ace in surprise. "If it is, you must 'a' told a woman. I heard of it from th' crowd—everybody seems to know about it. Yo're going up alone, too, ain't you?"

"Well, no, it ain't no secret; an' I am going alone," slowly replied Skinny. "Here, have another."

"All right—this is on me. Here's more luck."

"Where is th' crowd?"

"Keeping under cover for a while to give you plenty of elbow room," Ace replied. "He's sober as a judge, Skinny, an' mad as a rattler. Swears he'll kill you on sight. An' his brother ain't with him; if he does come in too soon I'll see he don't make it two to one. Good luck, an' so-long," he said quickly, shaking hands and walking toward the door. He put one hand out first and waved it, slowly stepping to the street and then walking rapidly out of sight.

Skinny looked after him and smiled. "Larry, there's a blamed fine youngster," he remarked, reflectively. "Well, he ought to be—he had th' best mother God ever put breath into." He thought for a moment and then went slowly towards the door. "I've heard so much about Bradley's gun-play that I'm some curious. Reckon I'll see if it's all true—" and he had leaped through the doorway, gun in hand. There was no shot, no sign of his enemy. A group of men lounged in the door of the "hash house" farther down the street, all friends of his, and he nodded to them. One of them turned quickly and looked down the intersecting street, saying something that made his companions turn and look with him. The man who had been standing quietly by the corner saloon had disappeared.

Skinny, smiling knowingly, moved closer to Quigg's shack so as to be better able to see around the indicated corner, and half drew the Colt which he had just replaced in the holster. As he drew even with the corner of the building he heard Quigg's warning shout and dropped instantly, a bullet singing over him and into a window of a near-by store. He rolled around the corner, scrambled to his feet and dashed around the rear of the saloon and the corral behind it, crossed the street in four bounds and began to work up behind the buildings on his enemy's side of the street, cold with anger.

"Pot shooting, hey!" he gritted, savagely.

"Says I'm a-scared to face him, an' then tries *that. There*, damn you!" His Colt exploded and a piece of wood sprang from the corner board of Wright's store. "Missed!" he swore. "Anyhow, I've notified you, you coyote."

He sprang forward, turned the corner of the store and followed it to the street. When he came to the street end of the wall he leaped past it, his Colt preceding him. Finding no one to dispute with him he moved cautiously toward the other corner and stopped. Giving a quick glance around, he smiled suddenly, for the glass in Quigg's half-open door, with the black curtain behind it, made a fair mirror. He could see the reflection of Wright's corral and Ace leaning against it, ready to handle the brother if he should appear as a belligerent; and he could see along the other side of the store, where Dick Bradley, crouched, was half-way to the street and coming nearer at each slow step.

Skinny, remembering the shot which he had so narrowly escaped, resolved that he wouldn't take chances with a man who would pot-shoot. He wheeled, slipped back along his side of the building, turned the rear corner and then, spurting, sprang out beyond the other wall, crying: "Here!"

Bradley, startled, fired under his arm as he leaped aside.

Turning while in the air, his half-raised Colt described a swift, short arc and roared as he alighted. As the bullet sang past his enemy's ear he staggered and fell—and Skinny's smoking gun chocked into its holster.

"There, you coyote!" muttered the victor. "Yore brother is next if he wants to take it up."

As night fell Skinny rode into a small grove and prepared to camp there. Picketing his horse, he removed the saddle and dropped it where he would sleep, for a saddle makes a fair pillow. He threw his blanket after it and then started a quick, hot fire for his coffee-making. While gathering fuel for it he came across a large log and determined to use it for his night fire, and for that purpose carried it back to camp with him. It was not long before he had reduced the provisions in his saddle-bags and leaned back against a tree to enjoy a smoke. Suddenly he knocked the ashes from his pipe and grew thoughtful, finally slipping it into his pocket and getting up.

"That coyote's brother will know I went North an' all about it," he muttered. "He knows I've got to camp tonight an' he can foller a trail as good as th' next man. An' he knows I shot his brother. I reckon, mebby, he'll be some surprised."

An hour later a blanket-covered figure lay with its carefully covered feet to the fire, and its head, sheltered from the night air by a sombrero, lay on the saddle. A rifle barrel projected above the saddle, the dim flickering light of the greenwood fire and a stray beam or two from the moon glinted from its rustless surface. The fire was badly constructed, giving almost no light, while the leaves overhead shut out most of the moonlight.

Thirty yards away, in another clearing, a horse moved about at the end of a lariat and contentedly cropped the rich grass, enjoying a good night's rest. An hour passed, another, and a third and fourth, and then the horse's ears flicked forward as it turned its head to see what approached.

A crouched figure moved stealthily forward to the edge of the clearing, paused to read the brand on the animal's flank and then moved off toward the fitful light of the smoking fire. Closer and closer it drew until it made out the indistinct blanketed figure on the ground. A glint from the rifle barrel caused it to shrink back deeper into the shadows and raise the weapon it carried. For half a minute it stood thus and then, holding back the trigger of the rifle so there would be no warning clicks, drew the hammer to a full cock and let the trigger fall into place, slowly moving forward all the while. A passing breeze fanned the fire for an instant and threw the grotesque shadow of a stump across the quiet figure in the clearing.

The skulker raised his rifle and waited until he had figured out the exact mark and then a burst of fire and smoke leaped into the brush. He bent low to look under the smoke cloud and saw that the figure had not moved. Another flash split the night and then, assured beyond a doubt, he moved forward quickly.

"First shot!" he exclaimed with satisfaction. "I reckons you won't do no boastin' 'bout killin' Dick, damn you!"

As he was about to drop to his knees to search the body he started and sprang back, glancing fearfully around as he drew his Colt.

"Han's up!" came the command from the edge of the clearing as a man stepped into sight. "I reckon—" Skinny leaped aside as the other's gun roared out and fired from his hip; and Sam Bradley plunged across the blanket-covered log and leaves.

"There," Skinny soliloquized, moving forward. "I knowed they was coyotes, *both* of 'em. Knowed it all th' time."

Two days north of Skinny on the bank of Little Wind River a fire was burning itself out, while four men lay on the sand or squatted on their heels and watched it contentedly. "Yes, I got plumb sick of that country," Lanky Smith was saying, "an' when Buck sent for me to go up an' help him out, I pulls up, an' here I am."

"I never heard of th' Bar-20," replied a little, wizened man, whose eyes were so bright they seemed to be on fire. "Didn't know there was any ranches in that country."

"Buck's got th' only one!" responded Lanky, packing his pipe. "He's located on Snake Creek, an' he's got four thousand head. Reckon there ain't nobody within two hundred mile of him. Lewis said he's got a fine range an' all th' water he can use; but three men can't handle all them cows in *that* country, so I'm goin' up."

The little man's eyes seldom left Lanky's face, and he seemed to be studying the stranger very closely. When Lanky had ridden upon their noon-day camp the little man had not lost a movement that the stranger made and the other two, disappearing quietly, returned a little later and nodded reassuringly to their leader.

The wizened leader glanced at one of his companions, but spoke to Lanky. "George, here, said as how they finally got Butch Lynch. You didn't hear nothin' about it, did you?"

"They was a rumor down on Mesquite range that Butch was got. I heard his gang was wiped out. Well, it had to come sometime—he was carryin' things with a purty high hand for a long time. But I've done heard that before; more'n once, too. I reckon Butch is a li'l too slick to get hisself killed."

"Ever see him?" asked George carelessly.

"Never; an' don't want to. If them fellers can't clean their own range an' pertect their own cows, I ain't got no call to edge in."

"He's only a couple of inches taller'n Jim," observed the third man, glancing at his leader, "an' about th' same build.

But he's hell on th' shoot. I saw him twice, but I was mindin' my own business."

Lanky nodded at the leader. "That'd make him about as tall as me. Size don't make no dif'rence no more—King Colt makes 'em look all alike."

Jim tossed away his cigarette and arose, stretching and grunting. "I shore ate too much," he complained. "Well, there's one thing about yore friend's ranch: he ain't got no rustlers to fight, so he ain't as bad off as he might be. I reckon he done named that crick hisself, didn't he? I never heard tell of it."

"Yes; so Lewis says. He says *he'd* called it Split Mesa Crick, 'cause it empties into Mesa River plumb acrost from a big mesa what's split in two as clean as a knife could 'a' done it."

"The Bar-20 expectin' you?" casually asked Jim as he picked up his saddle.

"Shore; they done sent for me. Me an' Buck is old friends. He was up in Montana ranchin' with a pardner, but Slippery Trendley kills his pardner's wife an' drove th' feller loco. Buck an' him hunted Slippery for two years an' finally drifted back south again. I dunno where Frenchy is. If it wasn't for me I reckon Buck'd still be on th' warpath. You bet he's expectin' me!" He turned and threw his saddle on the evil-tempered horse he rode and, cinching deftly, slung himself up by the stirrup. As he struck the saddle there was a sharp report and he pitched off and sprawled grotesquely on the sand. The little man peered through the smoke and slid his gun back into the holster. He turned to his companions, who looked on idly, and with but little interest. "Yo're damned right Butch Lynch is too slick to get killed. I ain't takin' no chances with nobody that rides over my trail these days. An', boys, I got a great scheme! It comes to me like a flash when he's talkin'. Come on, pull out; an' don't open yore traps till I says so. I want to figger this thing out to th' last card. George, shoot his cayuse; an' not another sound."

"But that's a good cayuse; worth easy—"

"Shoot it!" shouted Jim, his eyes snapping. It was unnecessary to add the alternative, for George and his companion had great respect for the lightning-like, deadly-accurate gun hands. He started to draw, but was too late. The crashing report seemed to come from the leader's holster, so quick had been the draw, and the horse sank slowly down, but unobserved. Two pairs of eyes asked a question of the little man and he sneered in reply as he lowered the gun. "It might 'a' been you. Hereafter do what I say. Now, go on ahead, an' keep quiet."

After riding along in silence for a little while the leader looked at his companions and called one of them to him. "George, this job is too big for the three of us; we can handle the ranch end, but not the drive. You know where Longhorn an' his bunch are holdin' out on th' Tortilla? All right; I've got a proposition for 'em, an' you are goin' up with it. It won't take you so long if you wake up an' don't loaf like you have been. Now you listen close, an' don't forget a word": and the little man shared the plan he had worked out, much to his companion's delight. Having made the messenger repeat it, the little man waved him off: "Get a-goin'; you bust some records or I'll bust you, savvy? Charley'll wait for you at that Split Mesa that fool puncher was a-talkin' about. An' don't you ride nowheres near it goin' up—keep to th' east of it. So-long!"

He watched the departing horseman swing in and pass Charley and saw the playful blow and counter. He smiled tolerantly as their words came back to him, George's growing fainter and fainter and Charley's louder and louder until they rang in his ears. The smile changed subtly and cynicism touched his face and lingered for a moment. "Fine, big bodies—nothing else," he muttered. "Big children, with children's heads. A little courage, if stead-

ied; but what a paucity of brains! Good God, what a paucity of brains; what a lack of original thought!"

Of some localities it is said their inhabitants do not die,
but dry up and blow away; this, so far as appearances
went, seemed true of the horseman who loped along the
north bank of Snake Creek, only he had not arrived at
the "blow away" period. No one would have guessed his
age as forty, for his leathery, wrinkled skin, thin, sun-
bleached hair and wizened body justified a guess of sixty.
A shrewd observer looking him over would find about the
man a subtle air of potential destruction, which might have
been caused by the way he wore his guns. A second look
and the observer would turn away oppressed by a dis-
quieting feeling that evaded analysis by lurking annoy-
ingly just beyond the horizon of thought. But a man strong
in intuition would not have turned away; he would have
backed off, alert and tense. Nearing a corral which loomed
up ahead, he pulled rein and went on at a walk, his brilliant eyes searching the surroundings with a thoroughness
that missed nothing.

Buck Peters was complaining as he loafed for a precious
half hour in front of the corral, but Red Connors and Bill
Cassidy, his "outfit," discussed the low prices cattle were
selling for, the over-stocked southern ranges and the crash
that would come to the more heavily mortgaged ranches
when the market broke. This was a golden opportunity to
stock the little ranch, and Buck was taking advantage of
it. But their foreman persisted in telling his troubles and
finally, out of politeness, they listened. The burden of the
foreman's plaint was the non-appearance of one Lanky
Smith, an old friend. When the second herd had been delivered several weeks before, Buck, failing to persuade
one of the drive outfit to remain, had asked the trail boss
to send up Lanky, and the trail boss had promised.

Red stretched and yawned. "Mebby he's lost th' way."

The foreman snorted. "He can foller a plain trail, can't he? An' if he can ride past Split Mesa, he's a bigger fool than I ever heard of."

"Well, mebby he got drunk an—"

"He don't get that drunk." Astonishment killed whatever else he might have said, for a stranger had ridden around the corral and sat smiling at the surprise depicted on the faces of the three.

Buck and Red, too surprised to speak, smiled foolishly; Bill, also wordless, went upon his toes and tensed himself for that speed which had given to him hands never beaten on the draw. The stranger glanced at him, but saw nothing more than the level gaze that searched his squinting eyes for the soul back of them. The squint increased and he made a mental note concerning Bill Cassidy, which Bill Cassidy already had done regarding him.

"I'm called Tom Jayne," drawled the stranger. "I'm lookin' for Peters."

"Yes?" inquired Buck restlessly. "I'm him."

"Lewis sent me up to punch for you."

"You plumb surprised me," replied Buck. "We don't see nobody up here."

"Reckon not," agreed Jayne smiling. "I ain't been pestered a hull lot by th' inhabitants on my way up. I reckon there's more *buffalo* than men in this country."

Buck nodded. "An' blamed few buffalo, too. But Lewis didn't say nothin' about Lanky Smith, did he?"

"Yes; Smith, he goes up in th' Panhandle for to be a foreman. Lewis missed him. Th' Panhandle must be purty nigh as crowded as this country, I reckon," he smiled.

"Well," replied Buck, "anybody Lewis sends up is good enough for me. I'm payin' forty a month. Some day I'll pay more, if I'm able to an' it's earned."

Jayne nodded. "I'm aimin' to be here when th' pay is raised; an' I'll earn it."

"Then shake han's with Red an' Bill, an' come with me,"

said Buck. He led the way to the dugout, Bill and Red looking after him and the little newcomer. Red shook his head. "I dunno," he soliloquized, his eyes on the recruit's guns. They were worn low on the thighs, and the lower ends of the holsters were securely tied to the trousers. They were low enough to have the butts even with the swinging hands, so that no time would have to be wasted in reaching for them; and the sheaths were tied down, so they would not cling to the guns and come up with them on the draw. Bill wore his guns the same way for the same reasons. Red glanced at his friend. "He's a queer li'l cuss, Bill," he suggested. Receiving no reply, he grinned and tried again. "I said as how he's a queer li'l cuss." Bill stirred. "Huh?" he muttered. Red snorted. "Why, I says he's a drunk Injun mendin' socks. What in blazes you reckon I'd say!"

"Oh, somethin' like that; but you should 'a' said he's a—a weasel. A cold-blooded, ferocious li'l rat that'd kill for th' joy of it," and Bill moved leisurely to rope his horse.

Red looked after him, cogitating deeply. "Cussed if I hadn't, too! An' so he's a two-gun man, like Bill. Wears 'em plumb low an' tied. Yessir, he's a shore 'nuff weasel, all right." He turned and watched Bill riding away and he grinned as two pictures came to his mind. In the first he saw a youth enveloped in swirling clouds of acrid smoke as two Colts flashed and roared with a speed incredible; in the second there was no smoke, only the flashing of hands and the cold glitter of steel, so quick as to baffle the eye. And even now Bill practiced the draw, which pleased the foreman; cartridges were hard to get and cost money. Red roped his horse and threw on the saddle. As he swung off toward his section of the range he shook his head and scowled.

The Weasel had the eastern section, the wildest part of the ranch. It was cut and seared by arroyos, barrancas and draws; covered with mesquite and chaparral and broken by hills and mesas. The cattle on it were lost in the chaotic roughness and heavy vegetation and only showed themselves when they straggled down to the river or the creek to drink. A thousand head were supposed to be under his charge, but ten times that number would have been but a little more noticeable. He quickly learned ways of riding from one end of the section to the other without showing himself to anyone who might be a hundred yards from any point of the ride; he learned the best grazing portions and the safest trails from them to the ford opposite Split Mesa.

He was very careful not to show any interest in Split Hill Canyon and hardly even looked at it for the first week; then George returned from his journey and reported favorably. He also, with Longhorn's assistance, had picked out and learned a good drive route, and it was decided then and there to start things moving in earnest.

There were two thousand unbranded cattle on the ranch, the entire second drive herd; most of these were on the south section under Bill Cassidy, and the remainder were along the river. The Weasel learned that most of Bill's cows preferred the river to the creek and crossed his section to get there. That few returned was due, perhaps, to their preference for the eastern pasture. In a week the Weasel found the really good grazing portions of his section feeding more cows than they could keep on feeding; but suddenly the numbers fell to the pastures' capacity, without adding a head to Bill's herd.

Then came a day when Red had been riding so near the Weasel's section that he decided to go on down and meet him as he rode in for dinner. When Red finally caught sight of him the Weasel was riding slowly toward the bunkhouse, buried in thought. When his two men had returned from their scouting trip and reported the best way to drive; his and their work had begun in earnest. One small herd had been driven north and turned over to friends not far away, who took charge of the herd for the rest of the drive while the Weasel's companions returned to Split Hill.

Day after day he had noticed the diminishing number of cows on his sections, which was ideally created by nature to hide such a deficit, but from now on it would require all his cleverness and luck to hide the losses and he would be so busy shifting cattle that the rustling would have to ease up. One thing bothered him: Bill Cassidy was getting very suspicious, and he was not altogether satisfied that it was due to rivalry in gun-play. He was so deeply engrossed in this phase of the situation that he did not hear Red approaching over the soft sand and before Red could make his presence known something occurred that made him keep silent.

The Weasel, jarred by his horse, which shied and reared with a vigor and suddenness its rider believed entirely unwarranted under the circumstances, grabbed the reins in his left hand and jerked viciously, while his right, a blur of speed, drew and fired the heavy Colt with such deadly accuracy that the offending rattler's head dropped under its writhing, glistening coils, severed clean.

Red backed swiftly behind a chaparral and cogitated, shaking his head slowly. "Funny how bashful these gun-artists are!" he muttered. "Now has he been layin' for big bets, or was he—?" the words ceased, but the thoughts ran on and brought a scowl to Red's face as he debated the question.

The following day, a little before noon, two men stopped with sighs of relief at the corral and looked around. The little man riding the horse smiled as he glanced at his tall companion. "You won't have to hoof it no more, Skinny," he said gladly. "It's been a' awful experience for both of us, but you had th' worst end."

"Why, you stubborn li'l fool!" retorted Skinny. "I can

walk back an' do it all over again!" He helped his companion down, stripped off the saddle and turned the animal loose with a resounding slap. "Huh!" he grunted as it kicked up its heels. "You oughta feel frisky, after loafin' for two weeks an' walkin' for another. Come on, Lanky," he said, turning. "There ain't nobody home, so we'll get a fire goin' an' rustle chuck for all han's."

They entered the dugout and looked around, Lanky sitting down to rest. His companion glanced at the mussed bunks and started a fire to get dinner for six. "Mebby they don't ride in at noon," suggested the convalescent. "Then we'll eat it all," grinned the cook. "It's comin' to us by this time."

The Weasel, riding toward the rear wall of the dugout, increased the pace when he saw the smoke pouring out of the chimney, but as he neared the hut he drew suddenly and listened, his expression of incredulity followed by one of amazement.

A hearty laugh and some shouted words sent him spinning around and back to the chaparral. As soon as he dared he swung north to the creek and risked its quicksands to ride down its middle. Reaching the river he still kept to the water until he had crossed the ford and scrambled up the further bank to become lost in the windings of the canyon.

Very soon after the Weasel's departure Buck dismounted at the corral and stopped to listen. "Strangers," he muttered. "Glad they got th' fire goin', anyhow." Walking to the hut he entered and a yell met him at the instant recognition.

"Hullo, Buck!"

"Lanky!" he cried, leaping forward.

"Easy!" cautioned the convalescent, evading the hand. "I've been all shot up an' I ain't right yet."

"That so! How'd it happen?"

"Shake han's with Skinny Thompson, my fool nurse," laughed Lanky.

"I'm a fool, all right, helpin' *him*," grinned Skinny, gripping the hand. "But when I picks him up down in th' Li'l Wind River country I was a' angel. Looked after him for two weeks down there, an' put in another gettin' up here. Served him right, too, for runnin' away from me."

"Little Wind River country?" exclaimed Buck. "Why, I thought you was a foreman in th' Panhandle."

"Foreman nothin'," replied Lanky. "I was shot up by a li'l runt of a rustler an' left to die two hundred mile from nowhere. I wasn't expectin' no gun-play."

"He's ridin' up here," explained Skinny. "Meets three fellers an' gets friendly. They learns his business, an' drops him sudden when he's mountin'. Butch Lynch did th' shootin'. Butch got his name butcherin' th' law. He couldn't make a livin' at it. Then he got chased out of New Mexico for bein' mixed up in a free-love sect, an' pulls for Chicago. He reckoned he owned th' West, so he drifts down here again an' turns rustler. I dunno why he plugs Lanky, less'n he thinks Lanky knows him an' might try to hand him over. I'm honin' for to meet Butch."

Buck looked from one to the other in amazement, suspicion raging in his mind. "Why, I heard you went to th' Panhandle!" he ejaculated.

Skinny grinned: "A fine foreman he'd make, less'n for a hawg ranch!"

"Who told you that?" demanded Lanky, with sudden interest.

"Th' feller Lewis sent up in yore place."

"What?" shouted both in one voice, and Lanky gave a terse description of Butch Lynch. "That him?"

"That's him," answered Buck. "But he was alone. He'll be in soon, 'long with Bill an' Red—which way did you come?" he demanded eagerly. "Why, that was through his section—bet he saw you an' pulled out!"

Skinny reached for his rifle: "I'm goin' to see," he remarked.

"I'm with you," replied Buck.

"Me, too," asserted Lanky, but he was pushed back.

"You stay here," ordered Buck. "He might ride in. An' you've got to send Bill an' Red after us."

Lanky growled, but obeyed, and trained his rifle on the door. But the only man he saw was Red, whose exit was prompt when he had learned the facts.

Down on the south section Bill, unaware of the trend of events, looked over the little pasture that nestled between the hills and wondered where the small herd was. Up to within the last few days he always had found it here, loath to leave the heavy grass and the trickling spring, and watched over by "Old Mosshead," a very pugnacious steer. He scowled as he looked east and shook his head. "Bet they're crowdin' on th' Weasel's section, too. Reckon I'll go over and look into it. He'll be passin' remarks about th' way I ride sign." But he reached the river without being rewarded by the sight of many of the missing cows and he became pugnaciously inquisitive. He had searched in vain for awhile when he paused and glanced up the river, catching sight of a horseman who was pushing across at the ford. "Now, what's th' Weasel doin' over there?" he growled. "An' what's his hurry? I never did put no trust in him an' I'm going to see what's up."

Not far behind him a tall, lean man peered over the grass-fringed bank of a draw and watched him cross the river and disappear over the further bank. "Huh!" muttered Skinny, riding forward toward the river. "That *might* be one of Peters' punchers; but I'll trail him to make shore."

Down the river Red watched Bill cross the stream and then saw a stranger follow. "What th' hell!" he growled, pushing on. "That's one of 'em trailin' Bill!" and he, in turn, forded the river, hot on the trail of the stranger.

Bill finally dismounted near the mesa, proceeded on foot to the top of the nearest rise, and looked down into the canyon at a point where it widened into a circular basin half a mile across. Dust was arising in thin clouds as the missing cows, rounded up by three men, constantly increased the rustlers' herd. To the northwest lay the mesa, where the canyon narrowed to wind its tortuous way through; to the southeast lay the narrow gateway, where the towering, perpendicular cliffs began to melt into the sloping sides of hills and changed the canyon into a swiftly widening valley. The sight sent the puncher running toward the pass, for the herd had begun to move toward that outlet, urged by the Weasel and his nervous companions.

Back in the hills Skinny was disgusted and called himself names. To lose a man in less than a minute after trailing him for an hour was more than his sensitive soul could stand without protest. Bill had disappeared as completely as if he had taken wings and flown away. The disgusted trailer, dropping to all-fours because of his great height, went ahead, hoping to blunder upon the man he had lost.

Back of him was Red, whose grin was not so much caused by Skinny's dilemma, which he had sensed instantly, as it was by the inartistic spectacle Skinny's mode of locomotion presented to the man behind. There was humor a-plenty in Red's make-up and the germ of mischief in his soul was always alert and willing; his finger itched to pull the trigger, and the grin spread as he pondered over the probable antics of the man ahead if he should be suddenly grazed by a bullet from the rear. "Bet he'd go right up on his head an' kick," Red chuckled—and it took all his will power to keep from experimenting. Then, suddenly, Skinny disappeared, and Red's fretful nature clawed at his tropical vocabulary with great success. It was only too true—Skinny had become absolutely lost, and the an-

gry Bar-20 puncher crawled furiously this way and that
without success, until Skinny gave him a hot clew that
stung his face with grit and pebbles. He backed, sneezing,
around a rock and wrestled with his dignity. Skinny, holed
up not far from the canyon's rim, was throwing a mental
fit and calling himself outrageous names. "An' he's been
trailin' *me*! Hell of a fine fool *I* am; I'm awful smart today,
I am! I done gave up my teethin' ring too soon, *I* did." He
paused and scratched his head reflectively. "Huh! *This* is
some populous region, an' th' inhabitants have pe-culiar
ways. Now I wonder who's trailin' him? I'm due to get
cross-eyed if I try to stalk 'em both."

A bullet, fired from an unexpected direction, removed
the skin from the tip of Skinny's nose and sent a shock
jarring clean through him. "Is that him, th' other feller, or
somebody else?" he fretfully pondered, raising his hand
to the crimson spot in the center of his face. He did not
rub it—he rubbed the air immediately in front of it, and
was careful to make no mistake in distance. The second
bullet struck a rock just outside the gully and caromed
over his head with a scream of baffled rage. He shrunk,
lengthwise and sidewise, wishing he were not so long; but
he kept on wriggling, backward. "Not enough English,"
he muttered. "Thank th' Lord he can't massé!"

The firing put a different aspect on things down in the
basin. The Weasel crowded the herd into the gap too suddenly and caused a bad jam, while his companions, slipping away among the boulders and thickets, worked
swiftly but cautiously up the cliff by taking advantage of
the crevices and seams that scored the wall. Climbing like
goats, they slipped over the top and began a game of hide
and seek over the boulder-strewn, chaparral-covered plateau to cover the Weasel, who worked, without cover of
any kind, in the basin.

Red was deep in some fine calculations of angles when
his sombrero slid off his head and displayed a new hole,

which edged at him with Cyclopean ferocity. He ducked, and shattered all existing records for the crawl, stopping finally when he had covered twenty yards and collected many thorns and bruises. He had worked close to the edge of the cliff and as he turned to circle back of his enemy he chanced to glance over the rim, swore angrily and fired. The Weasel, saving himself from being pinned under his stricken horse, leaped for the shelter of the cover near the foot of the basin's wall. Red was about to fire again when he swayed and slipped down behind a boulder. The rustler, twenty yards away, began to maneuver for another shot when Skinny's rifle cracked viciously and the cattle thief, staggering to the edge of the cliff, stumbled, fought for his balance, and plunged down into the basin. His companion, crawling swiftly toward Skinny's smoke, showed himself long enough for Red to swing his rifle and shoot offhand. At that moment Skinny caught sight of him and believed he understood the situation. "You Conners or Cassidy?" he demanded over the sights. Red's answer made him leap forward and in a few moments the wounded man, bandaged and supported by his new friend, hobbled to the rim of the basin in time to see the last act of the tragedy.

The gateway, now free of cattle, lay open and the Weasel dashed for it in an attempt to gain the horses picketed on the other side. He had seen George plunge off the cliff and knew that the game was up. As he leaped from his cover Skinny's head showed over the rim of the cliff and his bullet sang shrilly over the rustler's head. The second shot was closer, but before Skinny could try again Red's warning cry made him lower the rifle and stare at the gateway.

The Weasel saw it at the same time, slowed to a rapid walk, but kept on for the pass, his eyes riveted malevolently on the youth who had suddenly arisen from behind a boulder and started to meet him.

"It's easy to get him now," growled Skinny, starting to raise the rifle, a picture of Lanky's narrow escape coming to his mind.

"Bill's right in line," whispered Red, leaning forward tensely and robbing his other senses to strengthen sight. "They're th' best in th' Southwest," he breathed.

Below them Bill and the Weasel calmly advanced, neither hurried nor touching a gun. Sixty yards separated them—fifty—forty—thirty—"God Almighty!" whispered Skinny, his nails cutting into his calloused palms. Red only quivered. Twenty-five—twenty. Then the Weasel slowed down, crouching a little, and his swinging hands kept closer to his thighs. Bill, though moving slowly, stood erect and did not change his pace. Perspiration beaded the faces of the watchers on the cliff and they almost stopped breathing. This was worse than they had expected—forty yards would have been close enough to start shooting. "It's a pure case of speed now," whispered Red, suddenly understanding. The promised lesson was due—the lesson the Weasel had promised to give Bill on the draw. Accuracy deliberately was being eliminated by that cold-blooded advance. Fifteen yards—ten—eight—six—five—and a flurry of smoke. There had been no movement to the eyes of the watchers—just smoke, and the flat reports, that came to them like two beats of a snare drum's roll. Then they saw Bill step back as the Weasel pitched forward. He raised his eyes to meet them and nodded. "Come on, get th' cayuses. We gotta round up th' herd afore it scatters," he shouted.

Red leaned against Skinny and laughed senselessly. "Ain't he a damned fool?"

Skinny stirred and nodded. "He shore is; but come on. I don't want no argument with *him*."

CHAPTER III

Jimmy Price

ON A range far to the north, Jimmy Price, a youth as time measures age, followed the barranca's edge and whistled cheerfully. He had never heard of the Bar-20, and would have showed no interest if he had heard of it, so long as it lay so far away. He was abroad in search of adventure and work, and while his finances were almost at ebb tide he had youth, health, courage and that temperament that laughs at hard luck and believes in miracles. The tide was so low it must turn soon and work would be forthcoming when he needed it. Sitting in the saddle with characteristic erectness he loped down a hill and glanced at the faint trail that led into the hills to the west. Cogitating a moment he followed it and soon saw a cow, and soon after others.

"I'll round up th' ranch house, get a job for awhile an' then drift on south again," he thought, and the whistle rang out with renewed cheerfulness.

He noticed that the trail kept to the low ground, skirting

even little hills and showing marked preference for arroyos and draws with but little regard, apparently, for direction or miles. He had just begun to cross a small pasture between two hills when a sharp voice asked a question: "Where you goin'?"

He wheeled and saw a bewhiskered horseman sitting quietly behind a thicket. The stranger held a rifle at the ready and was examining him critically. "Where you goin'?" repeated the stranger, ominously. "An' what's yore business?"

Jimmy bridled at the other's impudent curiosity and the tones in which it was voiced, and as he looked the stranger over a contemptuous smile flickered about his thin lips. "Why, I'm goin' west, an' I'm lookin' for th' sunset," he answered with an exasperating drawl. "Ain't seen it, have you?"

The other's expression remained unchanged, as if he had not heard the flippant and pugnacious answer. "Where you goin' an' what for?" he demanded again.

Jimmy turned further around in the saddle and his eyes narrowed. "I'm goin' to mind my own business, because it's healthy," he retorted. "You th' President, or only a king?" he demanded, sarcastically.

"I'm boss of Tortilla range," came the even reply. "You answer my question."

"Then you can gimme a job an' save me a lot of fool ridin'," smiled Jimmy. "It'll be some experience workin' for a sour dough as ornery as you are. Fifty per', an' all th' rest of it. Where do I eat an' sleep?"

The stranger gazed steadily at the cool, impudent youngster, who returned the look with an ironical smile. "Who sent you out here?" he demanded with blunt directness.

"Nobody," smiled Jimmy. "Nobody sends me nowhere, never, 'less 'n I want to go. Purty near time to eat, ain't it?"

"Come over here," commanded the Boss of Tortilla range.

"It's closer from you to me than from me to you."

"Yo're some sassy, now ain't you? I've got a notion to drop you an' save somebody else th' job."

"He'll be lucky if you do, 'cause when that gent drifts along I'm natchurally goin' to get there first. It's been tried already."

Anger glinted in the Boss's eyes, but slowly faded as a grim smile fought its way into view. "I've a mind to give you a job just for th' great pleasure of bustin' yore spirit."

"If yo're bettin' on that card you wants to have a copper handy," bantered Jimmy. "It's awful fatal when it's played to win."

"What's yore name, you cub?"

"Elijah—ain't I done prophesied? When do I start punchin' yore eight cows, Boss?"

"Right now! I like yore infernal gall; an' there's a pleasant time comin' when I starts again' that spirit."

"Then my name's Jimmy, which is enough for you to know. Which cow do I punch first?" he grinned.

"You ride ahead along th' trail. I'll show you where you eat," smiled the Boss, riding toward him.

Jimmy's face took on an expression of innocence that was ludicrous.

"I allus let age go first," he slowly responded. "I might get lost if I lead. I'm plumb polite, I am."

The Boss looked searchingly at him and the smile faded. "What you mean by that?"

"Just what I said. I'm plumb polite, an' hereby provin' it. I allus insist on bein' polite. Otherwise, gimme my month's pay an' I'll resign. But I'm shore some puncher," he laughed.

"I observed yore politeness. I'm surprised you even know th' term. But are you shore you won't get lost if you foller me?" asked the Boss with great sarcasm.

"Oh, that's a chance I gotta take," Jimmy replied as his new employer drew up alongside. "Anyhow, yo're better lookin' from behind."

"Jimmy, my lad," observed the Boss, sorrowfully shaking his head, "I shore sympathize with th' shortness of yore sweet young life. Somebody's natchurally goin' to spread you all over some dismal landscape one of these days."

"An' he'll be a whole lot lucky if I ain't around when he tries it," grinned Jimmy. "I got a' awful temper when I'm riled, an' I reckons that would rile me up quite a lot."

The Boss laughed softly and pushed on ahead, Jimmy flushing a little from shame of his suspicions. But a hundred yards behind him, riding noiselessly on the sand and grass, was a man who had emerged from another thicket when he saw the Boss go ahead; and he did not for one instant remove his eyes from the new member of the outfit. Jimmy, due to an uncanny instinct, soon realized it, though he did not look around. "Huh! Reckon I'm th' meat in this sandwich. Say, Boss, who's th' Injun ridin' behind me?" he asked.

"That's Longhorn. Look out or he'll gore you," replied the Boss.

" 'That'd be a bloody shame,' as th' Englishman said. Are all his habits as pleasant an' sociable?"

"They're mostly worse; he's a two-gun man."

"Now ain't that lovely! Wonder what he'd do if I scratch my laig sudden?"

"Let me know ahead of time, so I can get out of th' way. If you do that it'll save me fifty dollars an' a lot of worry."

"Huh! I won't save it for you. But I wish I could get out my smokin' what's in my hip pocket, without Longhorn gamblin' on th' move."

The next day Jimmy rode the west section harassed by many emotions. He was weaponless, much to his chagrin and rage. He rode a horse that was such a ludicrous excuse that it made escape out of the question, and they even locked it in the corral at night. He was always under the eyes of a man who believed him ignorant of the surveillance. He already knew that three different brands of cattle "belonged" to the "ranch," and his meager experience was sufficient to acquaint him with a blotted brand when the work had been carelessly done. The Boss was the foreman and his outfit, so far as Jimmy knew, consisted of Brazo Charley and Longhorn, both of whom worked nights. The smiling explanation of the Boss, when Jimmy's guns had been locked up, he knew to be only part truth. "Yo're so plumb fighty we dassn't let you have 'em," the Boss had said. "If we got to bust yore high-strung, unlovely spirit without killin' you, you can't have no guns. An' th' corral gate is shore padlocked, so keep th' cayuse I gave you."

Jimmy, enraged, sprang forward to grab at his gun, but Longhorn, dexterously tripping him, leaned against the wall and grinned evilly as the angry youth scrambled to his feet. "Easy, Kid," remarked the gun-man, a Colt swinging carelessly in his hand. "You'll get as you give," he grunted. "Mind yore own affairs an' work, an' we'll treat you right. Otherwise—" the shrugging shoulders made further explanations unnecessary.

Jimmy looked from one to the other and silently wheeled, gained the decrepit horse and rode out to his allotted range, where he saturated the air with impotent profanity. Chancing to look back he saw a steer wheel and face the south; and at other times during the day he saw that repeated by other cattle—nor was this the only signs of trailing. Having nothing to do but ride and observe the cattle, which showed no desire to stray beyond the range allotted to them, he observed very thoroughly; and when he rode back to the bunkhouse that night he had deciphered the original brand on his cows and also

the foundation for that worn by Brazo Charley's herd on
the section next to him. "I dunno where mine come from,
but Charley's uster belong to th' C I, over near Sagebrush
basin. That's a good hundred miles from here, too. Just
wait till I get a gun! Trip me an' steal my guns, huh? If I
had a good cayuse I'd have that C I bunch over here right
quick! I reckon they'd like to see this herd."

When he reached the bunkhouse all traces of his anger
had disappeared and he ate hungrily during the silent
meal.

When Longhorn and Brazo pushed away from the table
Jimmy followed suit and talked pleasantly of things common to cowmen, until the two picked up their saddles and
rifles and departed in the direction of the corral, the Boss
staying with Jimmy and effectually blocking the door. But
he could not block Jimmy's hearing so easily and when
the faint sound of hoofbeats rolled past the bunkhouse
Jimmy knew that there were more than two men doing
the riding. He concluded the number to be five, and perhaps six; but his face gave no indication of his mind's
occupation.

"Play crib?" abruptly demanded the Boss, taking a well-
worn deck of cards from a shelf. Jimmy nodded and the
game was soon going on. "Seventeen," grunted the Boss,
pegging slowly. "Pair of fools, they are," he growled. "Both
plumb stuck on one gal an' they go courtin' together. She
reminds *me* of a slab of bacon, she's that homely."

Jimmy laughed at the obvious lie. "Well, a gal's a gal
out here," he replied. "Twenty for a pair," he remarked.
He wondered, as he pegged, if it was necessary to take
along an escort when one went courting on the Tortilla.
The idea of Brazo and Longhorn tolerating any rival or
any company when courting struck him as ludicrous. "An'
which is goin' to win out, do you reckon?"

"Longhorn—he's bad; an' a better gun-man. Twenty-three for six. Got th' other tray?" anxiously grinned the Boss.

"Nothin' but an eight—that's two for th' go. My crib?"

The Boss nodded. "Ugly as blazes," he mused. "*I* wouldn't court her, not even in th' dark—huh! Fifteen two an' a pair. That's bad goin', very bad goin'," he sighed as he pegged.

"But you can't tell nothin' 'bout wimmen from their looks," remarked Jimmy, with the grave assurance of a man whose experience in that line covered years instead of weeks. "Now I knowed a right purty gal once. She was plumb sweet an' tender an' clingin', she was. An' she had high ideas, she did. She went an' told me she wouldn't have nothin' to do with no man what wasn't honest, an' all that. But when a feller I knowed rid in to her place one night she shore hid him under her bed for three days an' nights. He had got real popular with a certain posse because he was careless with a straight iron. Folks fairly yearned for to get a good look at him. They rid up to her place and she lied so sweet an' perfect they shore apologized for even botherin' her. Who'd 'a' thought to look under *her* bed, anyhow? Some day he'll go back an' natchurally run off with that li'l gal." He scanned his hand and reached for the pegs. "Got eight here," he grunted.

The Boss regarded him closely. "She stood off a posse with her eyes an' mouth, eh?"

"Didn't have to stand 'em off. They was plumb ashamed th' minute they saw her blushes. An' they was plumb sorry for her bein' even a li'l interested in a no-account brand-blotter like—him." He turned the crib over and spread it out with a sort of disgust. "Come purty near bein' some-thin' in that crib," he growled.

"An' did you know that feller?" the Boss asked carelessly.

Jimmy started a little. "Why, yes; he was once a pal of mine. But he got so he could blot a brand plumb clever.

Us cow-punchers shore like to gamble. We are plumb childish th' way we bust into trouble. I never seen one yet that was worth anythin' that wouldn't take 'most any kind of fool chance just for th' devilment of it."

The Boss ruffled his cards reflectively. "Yes; we are a careless breed. Sort of flighty an' reckless. Do you think that gal's still in love with you? Wimmin' is fickle," he laughed.

"*She* ain't," retorted Jimmy with spirit. "She'll wait all right—for him."

The Boss smiled cynically. "You can't hide it, Jimmy. Yo're th' man what got so popular with th' sheriff. Ain't you?"

Jimmy half arose, but the Boss waved him to be seated again. "Why, you ain't got nothin' to fear out here," he assured him. "We sorta like fellers that'll take a chance. I reckon we all have took th' short end one time or another. An' I got th' idea mebby yo're worth more'n fifty a month. Take any chances for a hundred?"

Jimmy relaxed and grinned cheerfully. "I reckon I'd do a whole lot for a hundred real dollars every month."

"Yo're on, fur's I'm concerned. I'll have to speak to th' boys about it, first. Well, I'm goin' to turn in. You ride Brazo's an' yore own range for th' next couple of days. Good night."

Jimmy arose and sauntered carelessly to the door, watched the Boss enter his own house, and then sat down on the wash bench and gazed contentedly across the moonlit range. "Gosh," he laughed as he went over his story of the beautiful girl with the high ideals. "I'm gettin' to be a sumptuous liar, I am. It comes so easy I gotta look out or I'll get th' habit. I'd do mor'n lie, too, to get my gun back, all right." He stretched ecstatically and then sat up straight. The Boss was coming toward him and something in his hand glittered in the soft moonlight as it swung back and forth. "Forget somethin'?" called Jimmy.

"You better stop watchin' th' moonlight," laughed the Boss as he drew near. "That's a bad sign—'specially while that gal's waitin' for you. Here's yore gun an' belt—I reckoned mebby you might need it."

Jimmy chuckled as he took the weapon. "I ain't so shore 'bout needin' it, but I was plumb lost without it. Kept feelin' for it all th' time an' it was gettin' on my nerves." He weighed it critically and spun the cylinder, carelessly feeling for the lead in the chambers as the cylinder stopped. Every one was loaded and a thrill of fierce joy surged over him. But he was suspicious—the offer was too quick and transparent. Slipping on the belt he let the gun slide into the blackened holster and grinned up at the Boss. "Much obliged. It feels right, now." He drew the Colt again and emptied the cartridges into his hand. "Them's th' only pills as will cure troubles a doctor can't touch," he observed, holding one up close to his face and shaking it at the smiling Boss in the way of emphasis. His quick ear caught the sound he strained to hear, the soft swish inside the shell. "Them's Law in this country," he soliloquized as he slid the tested shell in one particular chamber and filled all the others. "Yessir," he remarked as the cylinder slowly revolved until he had counted the right number of clicks and knew that the tested shell was in the right place. "Yessir, them's The Law." The soft moonlight suddenly kissed the leveled barrel and showed the determination that marked the youthful face behind it. "An' it shore works both ways, Boss," he said harshly. "Put up yore paws!"

As the Boss leaped forward the hammer fell and caused a faint, cap-like report. Then the stars streamed across Jimmy's vision and became blotted out by an inky-black curtain that suddenly enveloped him. The Boss picked up the gun and, tossing it on the bench, waited for the prostrate youth to regain his senses.

Jimmy stirred and looked around, his eyes losing their look of vacancy and slowly filling with murderous hatred as he saw the man above him and remembered what had occurred. "Sand *sounds* like powder, my youthful friend," the Boss was saying, "but it don't *work* like powder. I purty near swallowed yore gal story; but I sorta reckoned mebby I better make shore about you. Yo're clever, Jimmy; so clever that I dassn't take no chances with you. I'll just tie you up till th' boys come back—we both know what they'll say. I'd 'a' done it then only I like you; an' I wish you had been in earnest about joinin' us. Now get up."

Jimmy arose slowly and cautiously and then moved like a flash, only to look down the barrel of a Colt. His clenched hands fell to his side and he bowed his head; but the Boss was too wary to be caught by any pretenses of a broken spirit. "Turn 'round an' hol' up yore han's," he ordered. "I'll blow you apart if you even squirms."

Jimmy obeyed, seething with impotent fury, but the steady pressure of the Colt on his back told him how useless it was to resist. Life was good, even a few hours of it, for in those few hours perhaps a chance would come to him. The rope that had hung on the wall passed over his wrists and in a few moments he was helpless. "Now sit down," came the order and the prisoner obeyed sullenly. The Boss went in the bunkhouse and soon returned, picked up the captive and, carrying him to the bunk prepared for him, dumped him in it, tied a few more knots and, closing the door, securely propped it shut and strode toward his own quarters, swearing savagely under his breath.

An hour later, while a string of horsemen rode along the crooked, low-lying trail across the Tortilla, plain in the moonlight, a figure at the bunkhouse turned the corner, slipped to the door and carefully removed the props.

Waiting a moment it opened the door slowly and slipped into the black interior, and chuckled at the sarcastic challenge from the bunk. "Sneakin' back again, hey?" blazed

Jimmy, trying in vain to bridge on his head and heels and turn over to face the intruder. "Turn me loose an' gimme a gun—I oughta have a chance!"

"All right," said a quiet, strange voice. "That's what I'm here for; but don't talk so loud."

"Who're you?"

"My name's Cassidy. I'm from th' Bar-20, what owns them cows you been abusin'. Huh! he shore tied some knots! Wasn't takin' no more chances with you, all right!"

"G'wan! He never did take none."

"So I've observed. Get th' blood circulatin' an' I'll give you some war-medicine for that useless gun of yourn what ain't sand."

"Good for you! I'll sidle up agin' that shack an' fill him so full of lead he won't know what hit him!"

"Well, every man does things in his own way; but I've been thinkin' he oughta have a chance. He shore gave you some, Kid. Longhorn'd 'a' shot you quick tonight."

"Yes; an' I'm goin' to get him, too!"

"Now you ain't got no gratitude," sighed Cassidy. "You want to hog it all. I was figgerin' to clean out this place by myself, but now you cut in an' want to freeze me out. But, Kid, mebby Longhorn won't come back no more. My outfit's a-layin' for his li'l party. I sent 'em down word to expect a call on our north section; an' I reckon they got a purty good idea of th' way up here, in case they don't receive Longhorn an' his friends as per schedule."

"How long you been up here?" asked Jimmy in surprise, pausing in his operation of starting his blood to circulating.

"Long enough to know a lot about this layout. For instance, I know yo're honest. That's why I cut you loose tonight. You see, my friends might drop in here any minute an' if you was in bad company they might make a mistake. They acts some hasty, at times. I'm also offerin' you a good job if you wants it. We need another man."

"I'm yourn, all right. An' I reckon I will give th' Boss a chance. He'll be more surprised, that way."

Cassidy nodded in the dark. "Yes, I reckon so; he'll have time to wonder a li'l. Now you tell me how yo're goin' at this game."

But he didn't get a chance then, for his companion, listening intently, whistled softly and received an answer. In another moment the room was full of figures and the soft buzz of animated conversation held his interest. "All right," said a deep voice. "We'll keep on an' get that herd started back at daylight. If Longhorn shows up you can handle him; if you can't, there's yore friend Jimmy," and the soft laugh warmed Jimmy's heart. "Why, Buck," replied Jimmy's friend, "he's spoke for that job already." The foreman turned and paused as he stood in the door. "Don't forget; you ain't to wait for us. Take Jimmy, if you wants, an' head for Oleson's. I ain't shore that herd of hissn is good enough for us. We'll handle this li'l drive-herd easy. So-long."

Red Connors stuck his head through a small window: "Hey, if Longhorn shows up, give him my compliments. I shore bungled that shot."

" 'Tain't th' first," chuckled Cassidy. But Buck cut short the arguments and led the way to Jimmy's pasture.

At daylight the Boss rolled out of his bunk, started a fire and put on a kettle of water to get hot. Buckling on his gun he opened the door and started toward the bunk-house, where everything appeared to be as he had left it the night before.

"It's a cussed shame," he growled. "But I can't risk him bringin' a posse out here. *What* th' devil!" he shouted as he ducked. A bullet sang over his head, high above him, and he glanced at the bunkhouse with renewed interest.

Having notified the Boss of his intentions and of the change in the situation, Jimmy walked around the corner of the house and sent one dangerously close to strengthen the idea that sand was no longer sand. But the Boss had surmised this instantly and was greatly shocked by such miraculous happenings on his range. He nodded cheerfully at the nearing youth and as cheerfully raised his gun. "An' he gave me a chance, too! He could 'a' got me easy if he didn't warn me! Well, here goes, Kid," he muttered, firing.

Jimmy promptly replied and scored a hit. It was not much of a hit, but it carried reflection in its sting. The Boss's heart hardened as he flinched instinctively and he sent forth his shots with cool deliberation. Jimmy swayed and stopped, which sent the Boss forward on the jump. But the youth was only further proving his cleverness against a man whom he could not beat at so long a range. As the Boss stopped again to get the work over with, a flash of smoke spurted from Jimmy's hand and the rustler spun half way around, stumbled and fell. Jimmy paused in indecision, a little suspicious of the fall, but a noise behind him made him wheel around to look.

A horseman, having topped the little hill just behind the bunkhouse, was racing down the slope as fast as his worn-out horse could carry him, and in his upraised hand a Colt glittered as it swung down to become lost in a spurt of smoke. Longhorn, returning to warn his chief, felt savage elation at this opportunity to unload quite a cargo of accumulated grouches of various kinds and sizes, which collection he had picked up from the Bar-20 northward in a running fight of twenty miles. Only a lucky cross trail, that had led him off at a tangent and somehow escaped the eyes of his pursuers, had saved him from the fate of his companions.

Jimmy swung his gun on the newcomer, but it only clicked, and the vexed youth darted and dodged and ducked with a speed and agility very creditable as he jammed cartridges into the empty chambers. Jimmy's interest in the new conditions made him forget that he had a gun and he stared in rapt and delighted anticipation at the cloud of dust that swirled suddenly from behind the corral and raced toward the disgruntled Mr. Longhorn, shouting Red's message as it came.

Mr. Cassidy sat jauntily erect and guided his fresh, gingery mount by the pressure of cunning knees. The brim of his big sombrero, pinned back against the crown by the pressure of the wind, revealed the determination and optimism that struggled to show itself around his firmly set lips; his neckerchief flapped and cracked behind his head and the hairs of his snow-white goatskin chaps rippled like a thing of life and caused Jimmy, even in his fascinated interest, to covet them.

But Longhorn's soul held no reverence for goatskin and he cursed harder when Red's compliments struck his ear about the time one of Cassidy's struck his shoulder. He was firing hastily against a man who shot as though the devil had been his teacher. The man from the Bar-20 used two guns and they roared like the roll of a drum and flashed through the heavy, low-lying cloud of swirling smoke like the darting tongue of an angry snake.

Longhorn, enveloped in the acrid smoke of his own gun, which wrapped him like a gaseous shroud, knew that his end had come. He was being shot to pieces by a two-gun man, the like of whose skill he had never before seen or heard of. As the last note of the short, five second, cracking tattoo died away Mr. Cassidy slipped his empty guns in their holsters and turned his pony's head toward the fascinated spectator, whose mouth offered easy entry to smoke and dust. As Cassidy glanced carelessly back at the late rustler Jimmy shut his mouth, gulped, opened it to speak, shut it again and cleared his dry throat. Looking from Cassidy to Longhorn and back again, he opened his mouth once more. "You—you—what'd'ju pay for them chaps?" he blurted, idiotically.

CHAPTER IV

Jimmy Visits Sharpsville

BILL CASSIDY rode slowly into Sharpsville and dismounted in front of Carter's Emporium, nodding carelessly to the loungers hugging the shade of the store. "Howd'y," he said. "Seen anything of Jimmy Price—a kid, but about my height, with brown hair and a devilish disposition?"

Carter stretched and yawned, a signal for a salvo of yawns. "Nope, thank God. You needn't describe nothin' about that Price cub to none of us. *We* know him. He spent three days here about a year ago, an' th' town's been sorta restin' up ever since. You don't mean for to tell us he's comin' here again!" he exclaimed, sitting up with a jerk.

Bill laughed at the expression. "As long as you yearn for him so powerful hard, why I gotta tell you he's on his way, anyhow. I had to go east for a day's ride an' he headed this way. He's to meet me here."

Carter turned and looked at the others blankly. Old Dad Johnson nervously stroked his chin. "Well, then he'll git

here, all right," he prophesied pessimistically. "He usually
gets where he starts for; an' I'm plumb glad I'm goin' on
tomorrow."

"Ha, ha!" laughed George Bruce. "So'm I goin' on, by
Scott!"

Grunts and envious looks came from the group and
Carter squirmed uneasily. "That's just like you fellers, runnin' away an' leavin' me to face it. An' it was you fellers
what played most of th' tricks on him last time he was
here. Huh! now I gotta pay for 'em," he growled.

Bill glanced over the gloomy circle and laughed heartily. Two faces out of seven were bright, Dad's particularly
so. "Well, he seems to be quite a favorite around here,"
he grinned.

Carter snorted. "Huh! Seems to be nothin'."

"He ain't exactly a favorite," muttered Dawson. "He's
a—a—an event; that's what he is!"

Carter nodded. "Yep; that's what he is, 'though you just
can't help likin' th' cub, he's that cheerful in his devilment."

Charley Logan stretched and yawned. "Didn't hear
nothin' about no Injuns, did you? A feller rid through here
yesterday an' said they was out again."

Bill nodded. "Yes; I did. An' there's a lot of rumors goin'
around. They've been over in th' Crazy Butte country an'
I heard they raided through th' Little Mountain Valley last
week. Anyhow, th' Seventh is out after em', in four sections."

"Th' Seventh is *a* regiment," asserted George Bruce.
"Leastawise it was when I was in it. It is th' best in th'
Service."

Dad snorted. "Listen to him! It was when *he* was in it!
Lordy, Lordy, Lordy!" he chuckled."

"There hain't no cavalry slick enough to ketch
Apaches," declared Hank, dogmatically. "Troops has too
many fixin's an' sech. You gotta travel light an' live with-

out eatin' an' drinkin' to ketch them Injuns; an' then you never hardly sometimes see 'em, at that."

"Lemme tell you, Mosshead, th' Seventh can lick all th' Injuns ever spawned!" asserted Bruce with heat. "It wiped out Black Kettle's camp, in' th' dead of winter, too!"

"That was Custer as did that," snorted Carter.

"Well, he was leadin' th' Seventh, same as he is now!"

Charley Logan shook his head. "We are talking about ketchin' 'em, not fightin' 'em. An' no cavalry in th' hull country can ketch 'Paches in *this* country—it's too rough. 'Paches are only scared of punchers."

"Shore," asserted Carter. "Apaches laugh at troops, less'n it's a pitched battle, when they don't. Cavalry chases 'em so fur an' no farther; punchers chase 'em inter hell, out of it an' back again."

"They shore is 'lusive," cogitated Lefty Dawson, carefully deluging a fly ten feet away and shifting his cud for another shot. "An' I, for one, admits I ain't hankerin' for to chase 'em close."

"Wish we could get that cub Jimmy to chase some," exclaimed Carter. "Afore he gits here," he explained, thoughtfully.

"Oh, he's all right, Carter," spoke up Lefty. "We was all of us young and playful onct."

"But we all warn't he-devils workin' day *an'* night tryin' to make our betters miserable!"

"Oh, he's a good kid," remarked Dad. "I sorta hates to miss him. Anyhow, we got th' best of him, last time."

Bill finished rolling a cigarette, lit it and slowly addressed them. "Well, all I got to say is that he suits me right plumb down to th' ground. Now, just lemme tell you somethin' about Jimmy," and he gave them the story of Jimmy's part in the happenings on Tortilla Range, to the great delight of his audience.

"By Scott, it's just like him!" chuckled George Bruce.

"That's shore Jimmy, all right," laughed Lefty.

"What did *I* tell you?" beamed Dad. "He's a heller, he is. He's all right!"

"Then why don't you stay an' see him?" demanded Carter.

"I gotta go on, or I would. Yessir, I would!"

"Reckon them Injuns won't git so fur north as here," suggested Carter hopefully, and harking back to the subject which lay heaviest on his mind. "They've only been here twict in ten years."

"Which was twice too often," asserted Lefty.

"Th' last time they was here," remarked Dad, reminiscently, "they didn't stop long; though where they went to I dunno. We gave 'em more'n they could handle. That was th' time I just bought that new Sharps rifle, an' what I done with that gun was turrible." He paused to gather the facts in the right order before he told the story, and when he looked around again he flushed and swore. The audience had silently faded away to escape the moth-eaten story they knew by heart. The fact that Dad usually improved it and his part in it, each time he told it, did not lure them. "Cussed ingrates!" he swore, turning to Bill. "They're plumb jealous!"

"They act like it, anyhow," agreed Bill soberly. "I'd like to hear it, but I'm too thirsty. Come in an' have one with me?" The story was indefinitely postponed.

An accordion wheezed down the street and a mouth-organ tried desperately to join in from the saloon next door, but, owing to a great difference in memory, did not harmonize. A roar of laughter from Dawson's, and the loud clink of glasses told where Dad's would-have-been audience then was. Carter walked around his counter and seated himself in his favorite place against the door jamb. Bill, having eluded Dad, sat on a keg of edibles and smoked in silence and content, occasionally slapping at the flies which buzzed persistently around his head. Knocking the ashes from the cigarette he leaned back lazily and looked at Carter. "Wonder where he is?" he muttered.

"Huh?" grunted the proprietor, glancing around. "Oh, you worryin' about that yearlin'? Well, you needn't! Nothin' never sidetracks Jimmy."

A fusillade of shots made Bill stand up, and Carter leaped to his feet and dashed toward the counter. But he paused and looked around foolishly. "That's his yell," he explained. "Didn't I tell you? He's arrove, same as usual."

The drumming of hoofs came rapidly nearer and heads popped out of windows and doors, each head flanked by a rifle barrel. Above a swirling cloud of dust glinted a spurting Colt and thrust through the smudge was a hand waving a strange collection of articles.

"Hullo, Kid!" shouted Dawson. "What you got? See any Injuns?"

"It's a G-string an' a medicine-bag, by all that's holy!" cried Dad from the harness shop. "Where'd you git 'em, Jimmy?"

Jimmy drew rein and slid to a stand, pricking his nettlesome "Calico" until it pranced to suit him. Waving the Apache breech-cloth, the medicine-bag and a stocking-shaped moccasin in one hand, he proudly held up an old, dirty, battered Winchester repeater in the other and whooped a war-cry.

"Blame my hide!" shouted Dad, running out into the street. "It *is* a G-string! He's gone an' got one of 'em! He's gone an' got a 'Pache! Good boy, Kid! An' how'd you do it?"

Carter plodded through the dust with Bill close behind. "*Where'd* you do it?" demanded the proprietor eagerly. To Carter location meant more than method. He was plainly nervous. When he reached the crowd he, in turn, examined the trophies. They were genuine, and on the G-string was a splotch of crimson, muddy with dust.

"What's in the war-bag, Kid?" demanded Lefty, preparing to see for himself. Jimmy snatched it from his hands. "You never mind what's in it, Freckle-face!" he snapped. "That's my bag, *now*. Want to spoil my luck?"

"How'd you do it?" demanded Dad breathlessly.

"*Where'd* you do it?" snapped Carter. He glanced hurriedly around the horizon and repeated the question with vehemence. "Where'd you get him?"

"In th' groin, first. Then through th'—"

"I don't mean where, I mean *where*—near here?" interrupted Carter.

"Oh, fifteen mile east," answered Jimmy. "He was crawlin' down on a bunch of cattle. He saw me just as I saw him. But he missed an' I didn't," he gloated proudly. "I met a Pawnee scout just afterward an' he near got shot before he signaled. He says hell's a-poppin'. Th' 'Paches are raidin' all over th' country, down—"

"I knowed it!" shouted Carter. "Yessir, I knowed it! I felt it all along! Where you finds one you finds a bunch!"

"We'll give 'em blazes, like th' last time!" cried Dad, hurrying away to the harness shop where he had left his rifle.

"I've been needin' some excitement for a long time," laughed Dawson. "I shore hope they come."

Carter paused long enough to retort over his shoulder: "An' I hopes you drop dead! You never did have no sense! Not nohow!"

Bill smiled at the sudden awakening and watched the scrambling for weapons. "Why, there's enough men here to wipe out a tribe. I reckon we'll stay an' see th' fun. Anyhow, it'll be a whole lot safer here than fightin' by ourselves out in th' open somewhere. What you say?"

"You couldn't drag me away from this town right now with a cayuse," Jimmy replied, gravely hanging the medicine-bag around his neck and then stuffing the gory G-string in the folds of the slicker he carried strapped behind the cantle of the saddle. "We'll see it out right here.

But I do wish that 'Pache owned a better gun than this thing. It's most fallin' apart an' ain't worth nothin'."

Bill took it and examined the rifling and the breech-block. He laughed as he handed it back. "You oughta be glad it wasn't a better gun, Kid. I don't reckon he could put two in the same place at two hundred paces with this thing. I ain't even anxious to shoot it off on a bet."

Jimmy gasped suddenly and grinned until the safety of his ears was threatened. "Would you look at Carter?" he chuckled, pointing. Bill turned and saw the proprietor of Carter's Emporium carrying water into his store, and with a speed that would lead one to infer that he was doing it on a wager. Emerging again he saw the punchers looking at him and, dropping the buckets, he wiped his face on his sleeve and shook his head. "I'm fillin' everything," he called. "I reckon we better stand 'em off from my store— th' walls are thicker."

Bill smiled at the excuse and looked down the street at the adobe buildings. "What about th' 'dobes, Carter?" he asked. The walls of some of them were more than two feet thick.

Carter scowled, scratched his head and made a gesture of impatience. "They ain't big enough to hold us all," he replied, with triumph. "This here store is th' best place. An', besides, it's all stocked with water an' grub, an' everything."

Jimmy nodded. "Yo're right, Carter; it's th' best place." To Bill he said in an aside. "He's plumb anxious to protect that shack, now ain't he?"

Lefty Dawson came sauntering up. "Wonder if Carter'll let us hold out in his store?"

"He'll pay you to," laughed Bill.

"It's loop-holed. Been so since th' last raid," explained Lefty. "An' it's chock full of grub," he grinned.

They heard Dad's voice around the corner. "Just like last time," he was saying. "We oughta put four men in

Dick's 'dobe acrost th' street. Then we'd have a strategy position. You see—oh, hullo," he said as he rounded the corner ahead of George Bruce. "Who's goin' on picket duty?" he demanded.

Under the blazing sun a yellow dog wandered aimlessly down the deserted street, his main interest in life centered on his skin, which he frequently sat down to chew. During the brief respites he lounged in the doors of deserted buildings, frequently exploring the quiet interiors for food. Emerging from the "hotel" he looked across the street at the Emporium and barked tentatively at the man sitting on its flat roof. Wriggling apologetically, he slowly gained the middle of the street and then sat down to investigate a sharp attack. A can sailed out of the open door and a flurry of yellow streaked around the corner of the "hotel" and vanished.

In the Emporium grave men played poker for nails, Bill Cassidy having corralled all the available cash long before this, and conversed in low tones. The walls, reinforced breast high by boxes, barrels and bags, were divided into regular intervals by the open loopholes, each opening further indicated by a leaning rifle or two and generous piles of cartridges. Two tubs and half a dozen buckets filled with water stood in the center of the room, carefully covered over with boards and wrapping paper. Clouds of tobacco smoke lay in filmy stratums in the heated air and drifted up the resin-streaked sides of the building. The shimmering, gray sand stretched away in a glare of sunlight and seemed to writhe under the heated air, while droning flies flitted lazily through the windows and held caucuses on the sugar barrel. A slight, grating sound overhead caused several of the more able or energetic men to glance up lazily, grateful they were not in Hank's place. It was hot enough under the roof, and they stretched ecstatically as they thought of Hank. Three days' vigil and anxiety had become trying even to the most solid.

John Carter fretfully damned solitaire and pushed the cards away to pick up pencil and paper and figure thoughtfully. This seemed to furnish him with even less amusement, for he scowled and turned to watch the poker game. "Huh," he sniffed, "playin' poker for nails! An' you don't even own th' nails," he grinned facetiously, and glanced around to see if his point was taken. He suddenly stiffened when he noticed the man who sat on his counter and labored patiently and zealously with a pocket knife. "Hey, you!" he exclaimed excitedly, his wrath quickly aroused. "Ain't you never had no bringin' up? If yo're so plumb sot on whittlin', you tackle that sugar barrel!"

Jimmy looked the barrel over critically and then regarded the peeved proprietor, shaking his head sorrowfully. "This here is a better medjum for the ex-position of my art," he replied gravely. "An' as for bringin' up, lemme observe to these gents here assembled that you ain't never had no artistic trainin'. Yore skimpy soul is dwarfed an' narrowed by false weights and dented measures. You can look a sunset in th' face an' not see it for countin' yore profits." Carter glanced instinctively at the figures as Jimmy continued. "An' you can't see no beauty in a daisy's grace—which last is from a book. I'm here carvin' th' very image of my cayuse an' givin' you a work of art, free an' gratis. I'm timid an' sensitive, I am; an' I'll feel hurt if—"

"Stop that noise," snorted a man in the corner, turning over to try again. "Sensitive an' timid? Yes; as a mule! Shut up an' lemme get a little sleep."

"A-men," sighed a poker-player. "An' let him sleep—he's a cussed nuisance when he's awake."

"Two mules," amended the dealer. "Which is worse than one," he added thoughtfully.

"We oughta put four men in that 'dobe—" began Dad persistently.

"An' will you shut up about that 'dobe an' yore four men?" snapped Lefty. "Can't you say nothin' less'n it's about that mud hut?"

Jimmy smiled maddeningly at the irritated crowd. "As I was sayin' before you all interrupted me, I'll feel hurt—"

"You *will*; an' quick!" snapped Carter. "You quit gougin' that counter!"

Bill craned his neck to examine the carving, and forthwith held out a derisively pointing forefinger.

"Cayuse?" he inquired sarcastically. "Looks more like th' map of th' United States, with some almost necessary parts missin'. Your geography musta been different from mine."

The artist smiled brightly. "Here's a man with imagination, th' emancipator of thought. It's crude an' untrained, but it's there. Imagination is a hopeful sign, for it is only given to human bein's. From this we surmise an' must conclude that Bill is human."

"Will somebody be liar enough to say th' same of you?" politely inquired the dealer.

"Will you fools shut up?" demanded the man who would sleep. He had been on guard half the night.

"But you oughta label it, Jimmy," said Bill. "You've got California bulgin' too high up, an' Florida sticks out th' wrong way. Th' Great Lakes is *all* wrong—looks like a kidney slippin' off of Canada. An' where's Texas?"

"Huh! It'd have to be a cow to show Texas," grinned Dad Johnson, who, it appeared, also had an imagination and wanted people to know it.

"You cuttin' in on this teet-a-teet?" demanded Jimmy, dodging the compliments of the sleepy individual.

"As a map it is no good," decided Bill decisively.

"It is no map," retorted Jimmy. "I know where California bulges an' how Florida sticks out. What you call California is th' south end of th' cayuse, above which I'm goin' to put th' tail—"

"Not if I'm man enough, you ain't!" interposed Carter, with no regard for politeness.

"—where I'm goin' to put th' tail," repeated Jimmy. "Florida is one front laig raised off th' ground—"

"Trick cayuse, by Scott!" grunted George Bruce. "No wonder it looks like a map."

"Th' Great Lakes is th' saddle, an' Maine is where th' mane goes—*Ouch!*"

"Mangy pun," grinned Bill.

"Kentucky ought to be under th' saddle," laughed Dad, smacking his lips. "Pass th' bottle, John."

"You take too much an' we'll all be Ill-o'-noise," said Charley Logan alertly.

"Them Injuns can't come too soon to suit *me*," growled Fred Thomas. "Who started this, anyhow?"

The sleepy man arose on one elbow, his eyes glinting. "After th' fight, you ask *me* th' same thing! Th' answer will be ME!" he snapped. "I'm goin' to clean house in about two minutes, an' fire you all out in th' street!"

Jimmy smiled down at him. "Well, you needn't be so sweepin' an' extensive in yore cleanin' operations," he retorted. "All you gotta do is go outside an' roll in th' dust like a chicken."

The crowd roared its appreciation and the sleepy individual turned over again, growling sweeping opinions.

"But if them Injuns are comin' I shore wish they'd hurry up an' do it," asserted Dad. "I ought to 'a' been home three days ago."

"Wish to God you was!" came from the floor.

Bill tossed away his half-smoked cigarette, Carter promptly plunging into the sugar barrel after it. "They ain't comin'," Bill asserted. "Every time some drunk Injun gets in a fight or beats his squaw th' rumor starts. An' by th' time it gets to us it says that all th' Apaches are out follerin' old Geronimo on th' war trail. He can be more places at once than anybody *I* ever heard of. I'm ridin' on tomorrow morning, 'Paches or no 'Paches."

"Good!" exclaimed Jimmy, glancing at Carter. "I'll have this here carving all done by then."

There was a sudden scrambling and thumping overhead and hot exclamations zephyred down to them. Carter dashed to the door, while the others reached for rifles and began to take up positions.

"See 'em, Hank?" cried Carter anxiously.

"See what?" came a growl from above.

"Injuns, of course, you damned fool!"

"Naw," snorted Hank. "There ain't no Injuns out at all, not after Jimmy got that one."

"Then what's th' matter?"

"My dawg's lickin' yore dawg. *Sic* him, Pete! Hi, there! Don't you run!"

"My dawg still gettin' licked?" grinned Carter.

"I'll swap you," offered Hank promptly. "Mine can lick yourn, anyhow."

"In a race, mebby."

"Hell!" growled Hank, cautiously separating himself from a patch of hot resin that had exuded generously from a pine knot. "I'm purty nigh cooked an' I'm comin' down, Injuns or *no* Injuns. If they was comin' this way they'd 'a' been here long afore this."

"But that Pawnee told Price they was out," objected Carter. "Cassidy heard th' same thing, too. An' didn't Jimmy get one!" he finished triumphantly.

"Th' Pawnee was drunk!" retorted Hank, collecting splinters as he slipped a little down the roof. "Great Mavericks! This here is awful!" He grabbed a protruding nail and checked himself. "Price might 'a' shot a 'Pache, or he might not. I don't take him serious no more. An' that feller Cassidy can't help what scared folks tells him. Sufferin' *toads*, what a roof!"

Carter turned and look back in the store. "Jimmy, you shore they are out? An' *will* you quit cuttin' that counter!"

Jimmy slid off the counter and closed the knife. "That's what th' Pawnee said. When I told you fellers about it, you was so plumb anxious to fight, an' eager to interrupt an' ask fool questions that I shore hated to spoil it all. What that scout says was that th' 'Paches was out raidin' down Colby way, an' was headin' south when last re—"

"Colby!" yelled Lefty Dawson, as the others stared foolishly. *"Colby!* Why, that's three hundred miles south of here! An' you let us make fools of ourselves for *three* days! I'll bust you open!" and he arose to carry out his threat. "Where'd you git them trophies?" shouted Dad angrily. "Them was genuine!" Jimmy slipped through the door as Dawson leaped and he fled at top speed to the corral, mounted in one bound and dashed off a short distance. "Why, I got them trophies in a poker game from that same Pawnee scout, you Mosshead! He couldn't play th' game no better'n you fellers. An' th' blood is snake's blood, fresh put on. You *will* drive me out of town, hey?" he jeered, and, wheeling, forthwith rode for his life. Back in the store Bill knocked aside the rifle barrel that Carter shoved through a loop hole. "A joke's a joke, Carter," he said sternly. "You don't aim to hit him, but you might," and Carter, surprised at the strength of the twist, grinned, muttered something and went to the door without his rifle, which Bill suddenly recognized. It was the weapon that had made up Jimmy's "trophies"!

"Blame his hide!" spluttered Lefty, not knowing whether to shoot or laugh. A queer noise behind him made him turn, a movement imitated by the rest. They saw Bill rolling over and over on the floor in an agony of mirth. One by one the enraged garrison caught the infection and one by one lay down on the floor and wept. Lefty, propping himself against the sugar barrel, swayed to and fro, sense-lessly gasping. "They *allus* are raidin' down Colby way! Blame my hide, *oh*, blame my hide! Ha-ha-ha! Ha-ha-ha! They *allus* are raidin' down *Colby* way!"

"Three days, an' Hank *on* the roof!" gurgled George Bruce. "*Three* days, by Scott!"

"Hank on th' roof," sobbed Carter, "settin' on splinters an hot rosim! Whee-hee-hee! Three-hee-hee days hatchin' pine knots an' rosim!"

"Gimme a drink! Gimme a drink!" whispered Dad, dou-bled up in a corner. "Gimme a ho-ho-ho!" he roared in a fresh paroxysm of mirth. "Lefty an' George settin' up nights watchin' th' shadders! Ho-ho-ho!"

"An' Carter boardin' us *free*!" yelled Baldy Martin. "Oh, my God! He'll never get over it!"

"Yessir!" squeaked Dad. "*Free*; an' scared we'd let 'em burn his store. 'Better stand 'em off in my place,' he says. 'It's full of grub,' he says. He-he-he!"

"An' did you see Hank squattin' on th' roof like a horned toad waitin' for his dinner?" shouted Dickinson. "I'm goin' to die! I'm goin' to die!" he sobbed.

"No sich luck!" snorted Hank belligerently. "I'll skin him alive! Yessir; *alive*!"

Carter paused in his calculations of his loss in food and tobacco. "Better let him alone, Hank," he warned ear-nestly. "Anyhow, we pestered him nigh to death las' time, an' he's shore come back at us. Better let him alone!"

Up the street Jimmy stood beside his horse and thumped and scratched the yellow dog until its rolling eyes bespoke a bliss unutterable and its tail could not wag because of sheer ecstasy.

"Purp," he said gravely, "never play jokes on a pore unfortunate an' git careless. Don't never forget it. Last time I was here they abused me shameful. Now that th' storm has busted an' this is gettin' calm-like, you an' me'll go back an' get a good look at th' asylum," he suggested, vaulting into the saddle and starting toward the store. No invitation was needed because the dog had adopted him on the spot. And the next morning, when Jimmy and Bill, loaded with poker-gained wealth, rode out of town and headed south, the dog trotted along in the shadow made by Jimmy's horse and glanced up from time to time in hopeful expectancy and great affection.

A distant, flat pistol shot made them turn around in the saddle and look back. A group of the leading citizens of Sharpsville stood in front of the Emporium and waved hats in one last, and glad farewell. Now that Jimmy had left town, they altered their sudden plans and decided to continue to populate the town of Sharpsville.

CHAPTER V

The Luck of Fools

"DID YOU ever see a dog like Asylum?" demanded Jimmy, looking fondly at the mongrel as they rode slowly the second day after leaving Sharpsville.

Bill shook his head emphatically. "Never, nowheres."

Jimmy turned reproachfully. "Lookit how he's follered us."

"Follered *you*," hastily corrected Bill. "He ought to. You feed an' scratch him, an' he'll go anywhere for that. But he's big," he conceded.

"Mostly wolf-hound," guessed Jimmy, proudly.

"He looks like a wolf—God help it—at th' end of a hard winter."

"Well, he ain't yourn!"

"An' won't be, not if I can help it."

"He ain't no good, is he?" sneered Jimmy.

"I wouldn't say that, Kid," grunted Bill. "You know there's good *Injuns*; but he looks purty healthy right now. Why didn't you call him Hank? They look—Good God!"

he exclaimed as he glanced through an opening in the hills. The ring of ashes that had been a corral still smoldered, and smoke arose fitfully from the caved-in roof of the adobe bunkhouse, whose beams, weakened by fire, had fallen under their heavy load.

"Injuns!" whispered Jimmy. "Not gone long, neither. Mebby they ain't all—ain't all—" he faltered, thinking of what might lie under the roof. Bill, nodding, rode hurriedly to the ruins, wheeled sharply and returned, shaking his head slowly. There was no need to explain Apache methods to his companion, and he spoke of the Indians instead. "They split. About a dozen in th' big party an' about eight in th' other. It looks sorta serious, Kid."

Jimmy nodded. "I reckon so. An' they're usually where nobody wants 'em, anyhow. Wouldn't Sharpsville be disgusted if they went north? But let's get out of here, 'less you got some plan to bag a couple."

"I like you more all th' time," Bill smiled. "But I ain't got no plan, except to move."

"Now, if they ain't funny," muttered Jimmy. "If they only knowed what they was runnin' into!"

Bill turned in surprise. "I reckon I'm easy, but I'll bite: what are they runnin' into?"

"I don't mean th' Injuns; I mean that wagon," replied Jimmy, nodding to a canvas-covered "schooner" on the opposite hill. "Come here, 'Sylum!" he thundered. Bill wheeled, and smothered a curse when he saw the woman. "Fools!" he snarled. "Don't let *her* know," and he was galloping toward the newcomers.

"They shore is innercent," soliloquized Jimmy, following. "Just like a baby chasin' a rattler for to play with it."

Bill drew rein at the wagon and removed his sombrero. "Howd'y," he said. "Where you headin' for?" he asked pleasantly.

Tom French shifted the reins. "Sharpsville. And where in—thunder—is it?"

His brother stuck his head out through the opening in the canvas. "Yes; where?"

"You see, we are lost," explained the woman, glancing from Bill to Jimmy, whose spectacular sliding stop was purely for her benefit, though she knew it not. "We left Logan four days ago and have been wandering about ever since."

"Well, you ain't a-goin' to wander no more, ma'am," smiled Bill. "We're goin' to Logan an' we'll take you as far as th' Logan-Sharpsville trail," he said, wondering where it was. "You must 'a' crossed it without knowin' it."

"Then, thank goodness, everything is all right. We are very fortunate in having met you gentlemen and we will be very grateful to you," she smiled.

"You bet!" exclaimed Tom. "But where *is* Sharpsville?" he persisted.

"Sixty miles north," replied Jimmy, making a great effort to stop with the reins what he was causing with his shielded spur. His horse could cavort beautifully under persuasion. "Logan, ma'am," he said, indifferent to the antics of his horse, "is about thirty miles east. You must 'a' sashayed some to get only this far in four days," he grinned.

"And we would be 'sashaying' yet, if I hadn't found this trail," grunted Tom. There was a sudden disturbance behind his shoulder and the canvas was opened wider. "*You* found it!" snorted George. "You mean, *I* found it. Leave it to Mollie if I didn't! And I told you that you were going wrong. Didn't I?" he demanded.

"Hush, George," chided his sister.

"But *didn't* I? Didn't I say we should have followed that moth-eaten road running—er—north?"

"Did you?" shouted Tom, turning savagely. "You told me so many fool things I couldn't pick out those having a flicker of intelligence hovering around their outer edges. *You* drove two days out of the four, didn't you?"

"Tom!" pleaded Mollie, earnestly.

"Oh, let him rave, Sis," rejoined George, and he turned to the punchers. "Friends, I beg thee to take charge of this itinerant asylum and its charming nurse, for the good of our being and the salvation of our souls. Amen."

Tom found a weak grin. "Yes, so be it. We place ourselves and guide under your orders, though I reserve the right to beat him to a pleasing pulp when he gets sober enough to feel it. At present he reclines ungracefully within."

"You mean you got a drunk guide, in there?" demanded Bill angrily.

"He feels the yearning right away," observed George. "We'll have to take turns thrashing Bacchus, I fear."

"How long's he been that way?" demanded Bill.

"I haven't known him long enough to answer that," responded Tom. "I doubt if he were ever really sober. He is a peripatetic distillery and I believe he lived on blotters even as a child. The first day—"

"—hour," inserted George.

"—he became anxious about the condition of the rear axle and examined it so frequently that by night he had slipped back into the Stone Age—he was ossified and petrified. He could neither see, eat nor talk. Strange creatures peopled his imagination. He shot at one before we could get his gun away from him, and it was our best skillet. How the devil he could hit it is more than I know. At this moment he may be fleeing from green tigers."

"Beg pardon," murmured George. "At this moment I have my foot on his large, unwashed face."

"Why, George! You'll hurt him!" gasped Mollie.

"No such luck. He's beyond feeling."

"But you will! It isn't right to—"

"Don't bother your head about him, Sis," interrupted Tom, savagely.

"Sure," grinned George. "Save your sympathy until he gets sober. He'll need some then."

"Now, George, there is no use of having an argument," she retorted, turning to face him. And as she turned Bill took quick advantage. One finger slipped around his scalp and ended in a jerky, lifting motion that was horribly suggestive. His other hand and arm swept back and around, the gesture taking in the hills; and at the same time he nodded emphatically toward the rear of the wagon, where Jimmy was slowly going. Across the faces of the brothers there flashed in quick succession mystification, apprehensive doubt, fear and again doubt. But a sudden backward jerk of Bill's head made them glance at the ruined 'dobe and the doubt melted into fear, and remained. George was the first to reply and he spoke to his sister. "As long as you fear for his facial beauty, Sis, I'll look for a better place for my foot," and he disappeared behind the drooping canvas. Jimmy's words were powerful, if terse, and George returned to the seat a very thoughtful man. He took instant advantage of his sister's conversation with Bill and whispered hurriedly into his brother's ear. A faint furrow showed momentarily on Tom's forehead, but swiftly disappeared, and he calmly filled his pipe as he replied. "Oh, he'll sober up," he said. "We poured the last of it out. And I have a great deal of confidence in these two gentlemen."

Bill smiled as he answered Mollie's question. "Yes, we did have a bad fire," he said. "It plumb burned us out, ma'am."

"But *how* did it happen?" she insisted.

"Yes, yes; how did it happen—I mean it happened like this, ma'am," he floundered. "You see, I—that is, *we—we* had some trouble, ma'am."

"So I surmised," she pleasantly replied. "I presume it was a fire, was it not?"

Bill squirmed at the sarcasm and hesitated, but he was

saved by Jimmy, who turned the corner of the wagon and swung into the breach with promptness and assurance. "We fired a Mexican yesterday," he explained. "An' last night th' Mexican slipped back an' fired us. He got away, this time, ma'am; but we're shore comin' back for him, all right."

"But isn't he far away by this time?" she asked in surprise.

"Mexicans, ma'am, are funny people. I could tell you lots of funny things about 'em, if I had time. This particular coyote is nervy an' graspin'. I reckon he was a heap disappointed when he found we got out alive, an' I reckon he's in these hills waitin' for us to go to Logan for supplies. When we do he'll round up th' cows an' run 'em off. Savvy? I means, understand?" he hurriedly explained.

"But why don't you hunt him now?"

Jimmy shook his head hopelessly. "You just don't understand Mexicans, ma'am," he asserted, and looked around. "Does she?" he demanded.

There was a chorus of negatives, and he continued. "You see, he's plannin' to steal our cows."

"That's what he's doin'," cheerfully assented Bill.

"I believe you said that before," smiled Mollie.

"Ha, ha!" laughed Bill. "He shore did!"

"Yes, I did!" snapped Jimmy, glaring at him.

"Then, for goodness' sake, are you going away and let him do it?" demanded Mollie.

Jimmy grinned easily, and drawled effectively. "We're aimin' to stop him, ma'am. You see," he half whispered, whereat Bill leaned forward eagerly to learn the facts. "He won't show hisself an' we can't track him in th' hills without gettin' picked off at long range. It would be us that'd have to do th' movin', an' that ain't healthy in rough country. So we starts to Logan, but circles back an' gets him when he's plumb wrapped up in them cows he's honin' for."

"That's it," asserted Bill, promptly and proudly. Jimmy was the smoothest liar he had ever listened to. "An' th' plan is all Jimmy's, too," he enthused, truthfully.

"Doubtless it is quite brilliant," she responded, "but I certainly wish *I* were that 'Mexican'!"

"Sis!" exploded George, "I'm surprised!"

"Very well; you may remain so, if you wish. But will someone tell me this: How can these gentlemen take us to Logan if they are going only part way and then returning after that dense, but lucky, 'Mexican'?"

"I should 'a' told you, ma'am," replied Jimmy, "that th' Logan-Sharpsville trail is about half way. We'll put you on it an' turn back."

The strain was telling on Bill and he raised his arm. "Sorry to cut off this interestin' conversation, but I reckon we better move. Jimmy, tie that wolf-hound to th' axle—it won't make *him* drunk—an' then go ahead an' pick a new trail to Logan. Keep north of th' other, an' stay down from sky-lines. I'll foller back a ways. Get a-goin'," and he was obeyed.

Jimmy rode a quarter of a mile in advance, unjustly escaping the remarks that Mollie was directing at him, her brothers, Bill, the dog and the situation in general. A backward glance as he left the wagon apprised him that the dangers of scouting were to be taken thankfully. He rode carelessly up the side of a hill and glanced over the top, ducked quickly and backed down with undignified haste. He fervently endorsed Bill's wisdom in taking a different route to Logan, for the Apaches certainly would strike the other trail and follow hard; and to have run into them would have been disastrous. He approached the wagon leisurely, swept off his sombrero and grinned. "Reckon you could hit any game?" he inquired. The brothers nodded glumly. "Well, get yore guns handy." There was really no need for the order. "There's lots of it, an' fresh meat'll come in good. Don't shoot till I says so," he warned, earnestly.

"O.K., Hawkeye," replied Tom coolly.

"We'll wait for the whites of their eyes, *à la Bunker Hill*," replied George, uneasily, "before we wipe out the game of this large section of God's accusing and forgotten wilderness. Any *big* game loose?"

Jimmy nodded emphatically. "You bet! I just saw a bunch of copperhead snakes that'd give you chills." The tones were very suggestive and George stroked his rifle nervously and felt little drops of cold water trickle from his armpits. Mollie instinctively drew her skirts tighter around her and placed her feet on the edge of the wagon box under the seat. "They can't climb into the wagon, can they?" she asked apprehensively.

"Oh, no, ma'am," reassured Jimmy. "Anyhow, th' dog will keep them away." He turned to the brothers. "I ain't shore about th' way, so I'm goin' to see Bill. Wait till I come back," and he was gone. Tom gripped the reins more firmly and waited. Nothing short of an earthquake would move that wagon until he had been told to drive on. George searched the surrounding country with anxious eyes while his sister gazed fascinatedly at the ground close to the wagon. She suddenly had remembered that the dog was tied.

Bill drummed past, waving his arm, and swept out of sight around a bend, the wagon lurching and rocking after him. Out of the little valley and across a rocky plateau, down into an arroyo and up its steep, further bank went the wagon at an angle that forced a scream from Mollie. The dog, having broken loose, ran with it, eyeing it suspiciously from time to time. Jeff Purdy, the oblivious guide, slid swiftly from the front of the wagon box and stopped suddenly with a thump against the tailboard. George, playing rear guard, managed to hold on and then with a sigh of relief sat upon the guide and jammed his feet against the corners of the box.

"So he—went back for—his friend to—find the way!" gasped Mollie in jerks. "What a pity—he did—it. I could— do better myself. I'm being jolted—into a thousand— pieces!" Her hair, loosening more with each jolt, uncoiled and streamed behind her in a glorious flame of gold. Suddenly the wagon stopped so quickly that she gasped in dismay and almost left the seat. Then she screamed and jumped for the dashboard. But it was only Mr. Purdy sliding back again.

Before them was the perpendicular wall of a mesa and another lay several hundred yards away. Bill, careful of where he walked, led the horses past a boulder until the seat was even with it. "Step on nothing but rock," he quietly ordered, and had lifted Mollie in his arms before she knew it. Despite her protests he swiftly carried her to the wall and then slowly up its scored face to a ledge that lay half way to the top. Back of the ledge was a horizontal fissure that was almost screened from the sight of anyone below. Gaining the cave, he lowered her gently to the floor and stood up. "Do not move," he ordered.

Her face was crimson, streaked with white lanes of anger and her eyes snapped. "What does this mean?" she demanded.

He looked at her a moment, considering. "Ma'am, I wasn't goin' to tell you till I had to. But it don't make no difference now. It's Injuns, close after us. Don't show yoreself."

She regarded him calmly. "I beg your pardon—if I had only known—is there great danger?"

He nodded. "If you show yoreself. There's allus danger with Injuns, ma'am."

She pushed the hair back from her face. "My brothers? Are they coming up?"

Her courage set him afire with rage for the Apaches,

but he replied calmly. "Yes. Mebby th' Injuns won't know yo're here, Ma'am. Me an' Jimmy'll try to lead 'em past. Just lay low an' don't make no noise."

Her eyes glowed suddenly as she realized what he would try to do. "But yourself, and Jimmy? Wouldn't it be better to stay up here?"

"Yo're a thoroughbred, ma'am," he replied in a low voice. "Me an' Jimmy has staked our lives more'n onct out of pure devilment, with nothin' to gain. I reckon we got a reason this time, th' best we ever had. I'm most proud, ma'am, to play my cards as I get them." He bent swiftly and touched her head, and was gone.

Meeting the brothers as they toiled up with supplies, he gave them a few terse orders and went on. Taking a handful of sand from behind a boulder and scattering it with judicious care, he climbed to the wagon seat and waited, glancing back at the faint line that marked the arroyo's rim. In a few minutes a figure popped over it and whirled toward him in a high-flung, swirling cloud of dust. Overtaking the lurching wagon, Jimmy shouted a query and kept on, his pony picking its way with the agility and certainty of a mountain cat. The wagon, lurching this way and that, first on the wheels of one side and then on those of the other, bouncing and jumping at such speed that it was a miracle it was not smashed to splinters, careened after the hard-riding horseman. A rifle bounced over the tailboard, followed swiftly by a box of cartridges and an ebony-backed mirror, which settled on its back and glared into the sky like an angry Cyclops.

Mr. Purdy, bruised from head to foot and rapidly getting sober, emitted language in jerks and grabbed at the tailboard as the wagon box dropped two feet, leaving him in the air. But it met him half way and jolted him almost to the canvas top. He slid against the side and then jammed against the tailboard again and reached for it in desperation. Another drop in the trail made him miss it, and as

the wagon arose again like a steel spring Mr. Purdy, wondering what caused all the earthquakes, arose on his hands
and knees in the dust and spat angrily after the careening
vehicle. He scrambled unsteadily to his feet and shook
eager fists after the four-wheeled jumping-jack, and gave
the Recording Angel great anguish of mind and writer's
cramp. Pausing as he caught sight of the objects on the
ground, he stared at them thoughtfully. He had seen many
things during the past few days and was not to be fooled
again. He looked at the sky, and back to the rifle. Then
he examined the mesa wall, and quickly looked back at
the weapon. It was still there and had not moved. He
closed his eyes and opened them suddenly and grunted.
"Huh, bet a ten spot it's real." He approached it cautiously, ready to pounce on it if it moved, but it did not
and he picked it up. Seeing the cartridges, he secured
them and then gasped with fear at the glaring mirror.
After a moment's thought he grabbed at it and put it in
his pocket just before a sudden, swirling cloud of dust
drove him, choking and gasping, to seek the shelter of the
boulders close to the wall. When he raised his head again
and looked out he caught sight of a sudden movement in
the open, and promptly ducked, and swore. Apaches!
Twelve of them!

He had seen strange things during the last few days,
and just because the rifle and other objects had turned out
to be real was no reason that he should absolutely trust
his eyes in this particular instance. There was a limit,
which in this case was Apaches in full war dress; so he
arose swaggeringly and fired at the last, and saw the third
from the last slide limply from his horse. As the rest paused
and half of them wheeled and started back he rubbed his
eyes in amazement, damned himself for a fool and
sprinted for the mesa wall, up which he climbed with the
frantic speed of fear. He was favored by the proverbial
luck of fools and squirmed over a wide ledge without be-

ing hit. There was but one way to get him and he knew he could pick them off as fast as they showed above the rim. He rolled over and a look of mystification crept across his face. Digging into his pockets to see what the bumps were, he produced the mirror and a flask. The former he placed carelessly against the wall and the latter he raised hastily to his lips. The mirror glared out over the plain, its rays constantly interrupted by Mr. Purdy's cautious movements as he settled himself more comfortably for defense.

A bullet screamed up the face of the wall and he flattened, intently watching the rim. Chancing to glance over the plain, he noticed that the wagon was still moving, but slowly, while far to the south two horsemen galloped back toward the mesa on a wide circle, six Apaches tearing to intercept them before they could gain cover. "I was shore wise to leave th' schooner," he grinned. "I allus know when to jump," he said, and then swung the rifle toward the rim as a faint sound reached his ears. Its smoke blotted out the piercing black eyes that looked for an instant over the edge and found eternity, and Mr. Purdy grinned when the sound of impact floated up from below. "They won't try that no more," he grunted, and forthwith dozed in a drunken stupor. A sober man might have been tempted to try a shot over the rim, and would have been dead before he could have pulled the trigger. Mr. Purdy was again favored by luck.

Leaving two braves to watch him, the other two searched for a better way up the wall.

The race over the plain was interesting but not deadly or very dangerous for Bill and Jimmy. Armed with Winchesters and wornout Spencer carbines and not able to get close to the two punchers, the Apaches did no harm, and suffered because of Mr. Cassidy's use of a new, long-range Sharps. "You allus want to keep Injuns on long range, Kid," Bill remarked as another fell from its horse. The shot was a lucky one, but just as effective. "They ain't worth a damn figurin' windage an' th' drift of a fast-movin' target, 'specially when it's goin' over ground like this. It's a white man's weapon, Jimmy. Them repeaters ain't no good for over five hundred; they don't use enough powder. An' I reckon them Spencers was wore out long ago. They ain't even shootin' close." He whirled past the projecting spur of the mesa and leaped from his horse, Jimmy following quickly. Three hundred yards down the canyon two Apaches showed themselves for a moment as they squirmed around a projection high up on the wall and not more than ten feet below the ledge. The expressions which they carried into eternity were those of great surprise. The two who kept Mr. Purdy treed on his ledge saw their friends fall, and squirmed swiftly toward their horses. It could only be cowpunchers entering the canyon at the other end and they preferred the company of their friends until they could determine numbers. When half way to the animals they changed their minds and crept toward the scene of action. Mr. Purdy, feeling for his flask, knocked it over the ledge and looked over after it in angry dismay. Then he shouted and pointed down. Bill and Jimmy stared for a moment, nodded emphatically, and separated hastily. Mr. Purdy ducked and hugged the ledge with renewed affection. Glancing around, he was almost blinded by the mirror and threw it angrily into the canyon, and then rubbed his eyes again. Far away on the plain was a moving blot which he believed to be horsemen. He fired his rifle into the air on a chance and turned again to the events taking place close at hand. "Other way, Hombre!" he warned, and Jimmy, obeying, came upon the Apache from the rear, and saved Bill's life. At hide and seek among rocks the Apache has no equal, but here they did not have a chance with Mr. Purdy calling the moves in a language they did not well understand. A bird's-eye view is a distinct asset and Mr. Purdy was play-

ing his novel game with delighted interest and a plainsman's instinct. Consumed with rage, the remaining Indian
whirled around and sent the guide reeling against the wall
and then down in a limp heap. But Bill paid the debt and
continued to worm among the rocks.

There was a sudden report to the westward and Jimmy
staggered and dived behind a boulder. The other four,
having discovered the trick that had been played upon
them on the other side of the mesa, were anxious to pay
for it. Bill hurriedly crawled to Jimmy's side as the youth
brushed the blood out of his eyes and picked up his rifle.
"It's th' others, Kid," said Bill. "An' they're gettin' close.
Don't move an inch, for this is their game." A roar above
him made him glance upward and swear angrily. "Now
they've gone an' done it! After all we've done to hide
'em!" Another shot from the ledge and a hot, answering
fire broke out from below. "My God!" said a voice, weakly.
Bill shook his head. "That was Tom," he muttered. "Come
on, Kid," he growled. "We got to drive 'em out, damn it!"
They were too interested in picking their way in the direction of the Apaches to glance at Mr. Purdy's elevated
perch or they would have seen him on his knees at the
very edge making frantic motions with his one good arm.
He was facing the east and the plain. Beaming with joy,
he waved his arm toward Bill and Jimmy, shouted instructions in a weak voice, that barely carried to the canyon
floor, and collapsed, his duty done.

Bill was surprised fifteen minutes later to hear strange
voices calling to him from the rear and he turned like a
flash, his Colt swinging first. "Well, I'm damned!" he ejaculated. Four punchers were crawling toward him. "Glad
to see you," he said, foolishly.

"I reckon so," came the smiling reply. "That lookin' glass
of yourn shore bothered us. We couldn't read it, but we
didn't have to. Where are they?"

"Plumb ahead, som'ers. Four of 'em," Bill replied.

"There's two tenderfeet up on that ledge, with their sister. We was gettin' plumb worried for 'em."

"Not them as hired Whiskey Jeff for to guide 'em?" asked Dickinson, the leader.

"Th' same. But how'n hell did Logan ever come to let 'em start?" demanded Bill, angrily.

"We didn't pay no attention to th' rumors that has been flyin' around for th' last two months. Nobody had seen no signs of 'em," answered the Logan man. "We didn't reckon there was no danger till last night, when we learned they hadn't showed up in Sharpsville, nor been seen anywheres near th' trail. Then we remembers Jeff's habits, an', while we debates it, we gets word that th' Injuns was seen north of Cook's ranch yesterday. We moves sudden. Here comes th' boys back—I reckon th' job's done. They're a fine crowd, a'right. You should 'a' seen 'em cut loose an' raise th' dust when we saw that lookin' glass a-winkin'. We couldn't read it none, but we didn't have to. We just cut loose."

"Lookin' glass!" exclaimed Bill, staring. "That's twice you've mentioned it. What glass? We didn't have no lookin' glass, nohow."

"Well, Whiskey Jeff had one, a'right. An' he shore keeps her a-talkin', too. Ain't it a cussed funny thing that a feller that's got a hard-boiled face like his'n would go an' tote a lookin' glass around with him? We never done reckoned he was that vain."

Bill shook his head and gave it up. He glanced above him at the ledge and started for it as Jimmy pushed up to him through the little crowd. "Hello, Kid," Bill smiled. "Come on up an' help me get her down," he invited. Jimmy shook his head and refused. "Ah, what's th' use? She'll only gimme hell for handin' her that blamed lie," he snapped. "An' you can do it alone—didn't you tote her up th' cussed wall?" It had been a long-range view, but Jimmy had seen it, just the same, and resented it.

Bill turned and looked at him. "Well, I'm cussed!" he muttered, and forthwith climbed the wall. A few minutes later he stuck his head over the rim of the ledge and looked down upon a good-natured crowd that lounged in the shadow of the wall and told each other all about it. Jimmy was the important center of interest and he was flushed with pride. It would take a great deal to make him cut short his hour of triumph and take him away from the admiring circle that hedged him in and listened intently to his words. "Yessir, by God," he was saying, "just then I looks over th' top of a li'l hill an' what I sees makes me duck a-plenty. There was a dozen of 'em, stringin' south. I knowed they'd shore hit that—"

"Hey, Kid," said a humorous voice from above. Jimmy glanced up, vexed at the interruption. "Well, what?" he growled. Bill grinned down at him in a manner that bid fair to destroy the dignity that Jimmy had striven so hard to build up. "She says all right for you. She's done let you down easy for that whoppin' big lie you went an' spun her. She wants to know ain't you comin' up so she can talk to you? How about it?"

"Go on, Kid," urged a low and friendly voice at his elbow.

"Betcha!" grinned another. "Wish it was me! I done seen her in Logan."

Jimmy loosed a throbbing phrase, but obeyed, whereat Bill withdrew his grinning face from the sight of the grinning faces below. "He's comin' ma'am; but he's shore plumb bashful." He looked down the canyon and laughed. "There they go to get Purdy off'n his perch. I'm natchurally goin' to lick anybody as tries to thrash that man," he muttered, glancing at George as he passed Jimmy on the ledge. George grinned and shook his head. "I'm going to give him the spree of his sinful, long life," he promised, thoughtfully.

Far to the west, silhouetted for a moment against the

crimson sunset, appeared a row of mounted figures. It looked long and searchingly at the mesa and slowly disappeared from view. Bill saw it and pointed it out to Lefty Dickinson. "There's th' other eight," he said, smiling cheerfully. "If it wasn't for Whiskey Jeff's lookin' glass that eight'd mean a whole lot to us. We've had the luck of fools!"

CHAPTER VI

Hopalong's Hop

HAVING SENT Jimmy to the Bar-20 with a message for Buck Peters and seen the tenderfeet start for Sharpsville on the right trail and under escort, Bill Cassidy set out for the Crazy M ranch, by the way of Clay Gulch. He was to report on the condition of some cattle that Buck had been offered cheap and he was anxious to get back to the ranch. It was in the early evening when he reached Clay Gulch and rode slowly down the dusty, shack-lined street in search of a hotel. The town and the street were hardly different from other towns and streets that he had seen all over the cow-country, but nevertheless he felt uneasy. The air seemed to be charged with danger, and it caused him to sit even more erect in the saddle and assume his habit of indifferent alertness. The first man he saw confirmed the feeling by staring at him insolently and sneering in a veiled way at the low-hung, tied-down holsters that graced Bill's thighs. The guns proclaimed the gunman as surely as it would have been proclaimed by a sign;

and it appeared that gun-men were not at that time held in high esteem by the citizens of Clay Gulch. Bill was growing fretful and peevish when the man, with a knowing shake of his head, turned away and entered the harness shop. "Trouble's brewin' somewheres around," muttered Bill, as he went on. He had singled out the first of two hotels when another citizen, turning the corner, stopped in his tracks and looked Bill over with a deliberate scrutiny that left but little to the imagination. He frowned and started away, but Bill spurred forward, determined to make him speak.

"*Might* I inquire if this is Clay Gulch?" he asked, in tones that made the other wince.

"You might," was the reply. "It is," added the citizen, "an' th' Crazy M lays fifteen mile west." Having complied with the requirements of common politeness the citizen of Clay Gulch turned and walked into the nearest saloon. Bill squinted after him and shook his head in indecision.

"He wasn't guessin', neither. He shore knowed where I wants to go. I reckon Oleson must 'a' said he was expectin' me." He would have been somewhat surprised had he known that Mr. Oleson, foreman of the Crazy M, had said nothing to anyone about the expected visitor, and that no one, not even on the ranch, knew of it. Mr. Oleson was blessed with taciturnity to a remarkable degree; and he had given up expecting to see anyone from Mr. Peters.

As Bill dismounted in front of the "Victoria" he noticed that two men further down the street had evidently changed their conversation and were examining him with frank interest and discussing him earnestly. As a matter of fact they had not changed the subject of their conversation, but had simply fitted him in the place of a certain unknown. Before he had arrived they discussed in the abstract; now they could talk in the concrete. One of them laughed and called softly over his shoulder, whereupon a third man appeared in the door, wiping his lips with the back of a hairy, grimy hand, and focused evil eyes upon the innocent stranger. He grunted contemptuously and, turning on his heel, went back to his liquid pleasures. Bill covertly felt of his clothes and stole a glance at his horse, but could see nothing wrong. He hesitated: should he saunter over for information or wait until the matter was brought to his attention? A sound inside the hotel made him choose the latter course, for his stomach threatened to become estranged and it simply howled for food. Pushing open the door he dropped his saddle in a corner and leaned against the bar.

"Have one with me to get acquainted?" he invited. "Then I'll eat, for I'm hungry. An' I'll use one of yore beds to-night, too."

The man behind the bar nodded cheerfully and poured out his drink. As he raised the liquor he noticed Bill's guns and carelessly let the glass return to the bar.

"Sorry, sir," he said coldly. "I'm hall out of grub, the fire's hout, *hand* the beds are taken. But mebby 'Awley, down the strite, can tyke care of you."

Bill was looking at him with an expression that said much and he slowly extended his arm and pointed to the untasted liquor.

"Allus finish what you start, English," he said slowly and clearly. "When a man goes to take a drink with me, and suddenly changes his mind, why I gets riled. I don't know what ails this town, an' I don't care; I don't give a cuss about yore grub an' your beds; but if you don't drink that liquor you poured out *to* drink, why I'll natchurally shove it down yore British throat so cussed hard it'll strain yore neck. Get to it!"

The proprietor glanced apprehensively from the glass to Bill, then on to the business-like guns and back to the glass, and the liquor disappeared at a gulp. "W'y," he explained, aggrieved. "There hain't no call for to get riled hup like that, strainger. I bloody well forgot it."

"Then don't you go an' 'bloody well' forget this: Th' next time I drops in here for grub an' a bed, you have 'em both, an' be plumb polite about it. Do you get me?" he demanded icily.

The proprietor stared at the angry puncher as he gathered up his saddle and rifle and started for the door. He turned to put away the bottle and the sound came near being unfortunate for him. Bill leaped sideways, turning while in the air and landed on his feet like a cat, his left hand gripping a heavy Colt that covered the short ribs of the frightened proprietor before that worthy could hardly realize the move.

"Oh, all right," growled Bill, appearing to be disappointed. "I reckoned mebby you was gamblin' on a shore thing. I feels impelled to offer you my sincere apology; you ain't th' kind as would even gamble *on* a shore thing. You'll see me again," he promised. The sound of his steps on the porch ended in a thud as he leaped to the ground and then he passed the window leading his horse and scowling darkly. The proprietor mopped his head and reached twice for the glass before he found it. "Gawd, what a bloody 'eathen," he grunted. " '*E* won't be as easy as the lawst was, blime 'im."

Mr. Hawley looked up and frowned, but there was something in the suspicious eyes that searched his face that made him cautious. Bill dropped his load on the floor and spoke sharply. "I want supper an' a bed. You ain't full up, an' you ain't out of grub. So I'm goin' to get 'em both right here. Yes?"

"You shore called th' turn, stranger," replied Mr. Hawley in his Sunday voice. "That's what I'm in business for. An' business is shore dull these days."

He wondered at the sudden smile that illuminated Bill's face and half guessed it; but he said nothing and went to work. When Bill pushed back from the table he was more at peace with the world and he treated, closely watching his companion. Mr. Hawley drank with a show of pleasure and forthwith brought out cigars. He seated himself beside his guest and sighed with relief.

"I'm plumb tired out," he offered. "An' I ain't done much. You look tired, too. Come a long way?"

"Logan," replied Bill. "Do *you* know where I'm goin'? An' why?" he asked.

Mr. Hawley looked surprised and almost answered the first part of the question correctly before he thought. "Well," he grinned, "if I could tell where strangers was goin', an' why, I wouldn't never ask 'em where they come from. An' I'd shore hunt up a li'l game of faro, you bet!"

Bill smiled. "Well, that might be a good idea. But, say, what ails this town, anyhow?"

"What ails it? Hum! Why, lack of money for one thing; scenery, for another; wimmin, for another. Oh, hell, I ain't got time to tell you what ails it. Why?"

"Is there anything th' matter with me?"

"I don't know you well enough for to answer that kerrect."

"Well, would you turn around an' stare at me, an' seem pained an' hurt? Do I look funny? Has anybody put a sign on my back?"

"You looks all right to me. What's th' matter?"

"Nothin', yet," reflected Bill slowly. "But there will be, mebby. You was mentionin' faro. Here's a turn you can call: somebody in this wart of a two-by-nothin' town is goin' to run plumb into a big surprise. There'll mebby be a loud noise an' some smoke where it starts from; an' a li'l round hole where it stops. When th' curious delegation now holdin' forth on th' street slips in here after I'm in bed, an' makes inquiries about me, you can tell 'em that. An' if Mr.—Mr. Victoria drops in casual, tell him I'm cleanin' my guns. Now then, show me where I'm goin' to sleep."

Mr. Hawley very carefully led the way into the hall and

turned into a room opposite the bar. "Here she is, stranger," he said, stepping back. But Bill was out in the hall listening. He looked into the room and felt oppressed.

"No she ain't," he answered, backing his intuition. "She is upstairs, where there is a li'l breeze. By th' Lord," he muttered under his breath. "This is some puzzle." He mounted the stairs shaking his head thoughtfully. "It shore is, it shore is."

The next morning when Bill whirled up to the Crazy M bunkhouse and dismounted before the door a puncher was emerging. He started to say something, noticed Bill's guns and went on without a word. Bill turned around and looked after him in amazement. "Well, what th' devil!" he growled. Before he could do anything, had he wished to, Mr. Oleson stepped quickly from the house, nodded and hurried toward the ranch house, motioning for Bill to follow. Entering the house, the foreman of the Crazy M waited impatiently for Bill to get inside, and then hurriedly closed the door.

"They've got onto it some way," he said, his taciturnity gone; "but that don't make no difference if you've got th' sand. I'll pay you one hundred an' fifty a month, furnish yore cayuses an' feed you. I'm losin' more 'n two hundred cows every month an' can't get a trace of th' thieves. Harris, Marshal of Clay Gulch, is stumped, too. *He* can't move without proof; *you* can. Th' first man to get is George Thomas, then his brother Art. By that time you'll know how things lay. George Thomas is keepin' out of Harris' way. He killed a man last week over in Tuxedo an' Harris wants to take him over there. He'll not help you, so don't ask him to." Before Bill could reply or recover from his astonishment Oleson continued and described several men. "Look out for ambushes. It'll be th' hardest game you ever went up ag'in, an' if you ain't got th' sand to go through with it, say so."

Bill shook his head. "I got th' sand to go through with

anythin' I starts, but I don't start here. I reckon you got
th' wrong man. I come up here to look over a herd for
Buck Peters; an' here you go shovin' wages like that at
me. When I tells Buck what I've been offered he'll fall
dead." He laughed. "Now I knows th' answer to a lot of
things."

"Here, here!" he exclaimed as Oleson began to rave.
"Don't you go an' get all het up like that. I reckon I can
keep my face shut. An' lemme observe in yore hat-like
ear that if th' rest of this gang is like th' samples I seen in
town, a good gun-man would shore be robbin' you to take
all that money for th' job. Fifty a month, for two months,
would be a-plenty."

Oleson's dismay was fading, and he accepted the situation with a grim smile. "You don't know them fellers," he
replied. "They're a bad lot, an' won't stop at nothin'."

"All right. Let's take a look at them cows. I want to get
home soon as I can."

Oleson shook his head. "I gave you up, an' when I got
a better offer I let 'em go. I'm sorry you had th' ride for
nothin', but I couldn't get word to you."

Bill led the way in silence back to the bunkhouse and
mounted his horse. "All right," he nodded. "I shore was
late. Well, I'll be goin'."

"That gun-man is late, too," said Oleson. "Mebby he
ain't comin'. You wan th' job at *my* figgers?"

"Nope. I got a better job, though it don't pay so much
money. It's steady, an' a hull lot cleaner. So-long," and
Bill loped away, closely watched by Shorty Allen from the
corral. And after an interval, Shorty mounted and swung
out of the other gate of the corral and rode along the
bottom of an arroyo until he felt it was safe to follow Bill's
trail. When Shorty turned back he was almost to town,
and he would not have been pleased had he known that
Bill knew of the trailing for the last ten miles. Bill had

doubled back and was within a hundred yards of Shorty when that person turned ranchward.

"Huh! I must be popular," grunted Bill. "I reckon I will stay in Clay Gulch til t'morrow mornin'; an' at the Victoria," he grinned. Then he laughed heartily. "Victoria! I got a better name for it than that, all right."

When he pulled up before the Victoria and looked in the proprietor scowled at him, which made Bill frown as he went on to Hawley's. Putting his horse in the corral he carried his saddle and rifle into the barroom and looked around. There was no one in sight, and he smiled. Putting the saddle and rifle back in one corner under the bar and covering them with gunny sacks he strolled to the Victoria and entered through the rear door. The proprietor reached for his gun but reconsidered in time and picked up a glass, which he polished with exaggerated care. There was something about the stranger that obtruded upon his peace of mind and confidence. He would let someone else try the stranger out.

Bill walked slowly forward, by force of will ironing out the humor in his face and assuming his sternest expression. "I want supper an' a bed, an' don't forget to be plumb polite," he rumbled, sitting down by the side of a small table in such a manner that it did not in the least interfere with the movement of his right hand. The observing proprietor observed and gave strict attention to the preparation of the meal. The gun-man, glancing around, slowly arose and walked carelessly to a chair that had blank wall behind it, and from where he could watch windows and doors.

When the meal was placed before him he glanced up. "Go over there an' sit down," he ordered, motioning to a chair that stood close to the rifle that leaned against the wall. "Loaded?" he demanded. The proprietor could only nod. "Then sling it acrost yore knees an' keep still. Well, start movin'."

The proprietor walked as though he were in a trance but when he seated himself and reached for the weapon a sudden flash of understanding illumined him and caused cold sweat to bead upon his wrinkled brow. He put the weapon down again, but the noise made Bill look up.

"Acrost yore knees," growled the puncher, and the proprietor hastily obeyed, but when it touched his legs he let loose of it as though it were hot. He felt a great awe steal through his fear, for here was a gun-man such as he had read about. This man gave him all the best of it just to tempt him to make a break. The rifle had been in his hands, and while it was there the gun-man was calmly eating with both hands on the table and had not even looked up until the noise of the gun made him!

"My Gawd, 'e must be a wizard with 'em. I 'opes I don't forget!" With the thought came a great itching of his knee-cap; then his foot itched so as to make him squirm and wear horrible expressions. Bill, chancing to glance up carelessly, caught sight of the expressions and growled, whereupon they became angelic. Fearing that he could no longer hold in the laughter that tortured him, Bill arose.

"Shoulder, *arms!*" he ordered, crisply. The gun went up with trained precision. "Been a sojer," thought Bill. "Carry, *arms*! About, *face*! To a bedroom, *march*!" He followed, holding his sides, and stopped before the room. "This th' best?" he demanded. "Well, it ain't good enough for *me*. About, *face*! Forward, *march*! Column, *left*! Ground, *arms*! Fall out." Tossing a coin on the floor as payment for the supper Bill turned sharply and went out without even a backward glance.

The proprietor wiped the perspiration from his face and walked unsteadily to the bar, where he poured out a generous drink and gulped it down. Peering out of the door to see if the coast was clear, he scurried across the street and told his troubles to the harness-maker.

Bill leaned weakly against Hawley's and laughed until

the tears rolled down his cheeks. Pushing weakly from the building he returned to the Victoria to play another joke on its proprietor. Finding it vacant he slipped upstairs and hunted for a room to suit him. The bed was the softest he had seen for a long time and it lured him into removing his boots and chaps and guns, after he had propped a chair against the door as a warning signal, and stretching out flat on his back, he prepared to enjoy solid comfort. It was not yet dark, and as he was not sleepy he lay there thinking over the events of the past twenty-four hours, often laughing so hard as to shake the bed. What a reputation he would have in the morning! The softness of the bed got in its work and he fell asleep, for how long he did not know; but when he awakened it was dark and he heard voices coming up from below. They came from the room he had refused to take. One expression banished all thoughts of sleep from his mind and he listened intently.

" 'Red-headed Irish gun-man.' Why, they means me! 'Make him hop into hell.' I don't reckon I'd do that for anybody, even my friends."

"I tried to give 'im this room, but 'e wouldn't tyke *it*," protested the proprietor, hurriedly. " 'E says the bloody room wasn't good enough for 'im, and 'e marches me out and makes off. Likely 'e's in '*Awley's*."

"No, he ain't," growled a strange voice. "You've gone an' bungled th' whole thing."

"But I s'y I didn't, you know. I tries to give 'im this werry room, George, but 'e wouldn't 'ave it. D'y think I wants 'im running haround this blooming town? 'E's worse nor the other, *hand* Gawd knows 'e was bad enough. 'E's a cold-*blooded* beggar, 'e *is*!"

"You missed yore chance," grunted the other. "Wish *I* had that gun you had."

"I was wishing to Gawd you *did*," retorted the proprietor. "It never looked so bloody big before, damn 'is '*ide*!"

"Well, his cayuse is in Hawley's corral," said the first

speaker. "If I ever finds Hawley kept him under cover I'll
blow his head off. Come on; we'll get Harris first. He ought
to be gettin' close to town if he got th' word I sent over
to Tuxedo. He won't let us call him. He's a man of his
word."

"He'll be here, all right. Fred an' Tom is watchin' his
shack, an' we better take th' other end of town—there's
no tellin' how he'll come in now," suggested Art Thomas.
"But I wish I knowed where that cussed gun-man is."

As they went out Bill, his chaps on and his boots in his
hand, crept down the stairs, and stopped as he neared the
hall door. The proprietor was coming back. The others
were outside, going to their stations and did not hear the
choking gasp that the proprietor made as a pair of strong
hands reached out and throttled him. When he came to
he was lying face down on a bed, gagged and bound by
a rope that cut into his flesh with every movement. Bill,
waiting a moment, slipped into the darkness and was
swallowed up. He was looking for Mr. Harris, and looking
eagerly.

The moon arose and bathed the dusty street and its
crude shacks in silver, cunningly and charitably hiding its
ugliness; and passed on as the skirmishing rays of the sun
burst into the sky in close and eternal pursuit. As the dawn
spread swiftly and long, thin shadows sprang across the
sandy street, there arose from the dissipated darkness
close to the wall of a building an armed man, weary and
slow from a tiresome vigil. Another emerged from behind
a pile of boards that faced the marshal's abode, while
down the street another crept over the edge of a dried-
out water course and swore softly as he stood up slowly
to flex away the stiffness of cramped limbs. Of vain spec-
ulation he was empty; he had exhausted all the whys and
hows long before and now only muttered discontentedly
as he reviewed the hours of fruitless waiting. And he was
uneasy; it was not like Harris to take a dare and swallow

his own threats without a struggle. He looked around apprehensively, shrugged his shoulders and stalked behind the shacks across from the two hotels.

Another figure crept from the protection of Hawley's corral like a slinking coyote, gun in hand and nervously alert. He was just in time to escape the challenge that would have been hurled at him by Hawley, himself, had that gentleman seen the skulker as he grouchily opened one shutter and scowled sleepily at the kindling eastern sky. Mr. Hawley was one of those who go to bed with regret and get up with remorse, and his temper was always easily disturbed before breakfast. The skulker, safe from the remorseful gentleman's eyes, and gun, kept close to the building as he walked and was again fortunate, for he had passed when Mr. Hawley strode heavily into his kitchen to curse the cold, rusty stove, a rite he faithfully performed each morning. Across the street George and Art Thomas walked to meet each other behind the row of shacks and stopped near the harness shop to hold a consultation. The subject was so interesting that for a few moments they were oblivious to all else.

A man softly stepped to the door of the Victoria and watched the two across the street with an expression on his face that showed his smiling contempt for them and their kind. He was a small man, so far as physical measurements go, but he was lithe, sinewy and compact. On his opened vest, hanging slovenly and blinking in the growing light as if to prepare itself for the blinding glare of midday, glinted a five-pointed star of nickel, a lowly badge that every rural community knows and holds in an awe far above the metal or design. Swinging low on his hip gleamed the ivory butt of a silver-plated Colt, the one weakness that his vanity seized upon. But under the silver and its engraving, above and before the cracked and stained ivory handles, lay the power of a great force; and under the casing of the marshal's small body lay a virile manhood, strong in courage and determination. Toby Harris watched, smilingly; he loved the dramatic and found keen enjoyment in the situation. Out of the corner of his eye he saw a carelessly dressed cowpuncher slouching indolently along close to the buildings on the other side of the street with the misleading sluggishness of a panther. The red hair, kissed by the slanting rays of the sun where it showed beneath the soiled sombrero, seemed to be a flaming warning; the half-closed eyes, squinting under the brim of the big hat, missed nothing as they darted from point to point.

The marshal stepped silently to the porch and then on to the ground, his back to the rear of the hotel, waiting to be discovered. He had been in sight perhaps a minute. The cow-puncher made a sudden, eye-baffling movement and smoke whirled about his hips. Fred, turning the corner behind the marshal, dropped his gun with a scream of rage and pain and crashed against the window in sudden sickness, his gunhand hanging by a tendon from his wrist. The marshal stepped quickly forward at the shot and for an instant gazed deeply into the eyes of the startled rustlers. Then his Colt leaped out and crashed a fraction of a second before the brothers fired. George Thomas reeled, caught sight of the puncher and fired by instinct. Bill, leaving Harris to watch the other side of the street, was watching the rear corner of the Victoria and was unprepared for the shot. He crumpled and dropped and then the marshal, enraged, ended the rustler's earthly career in a stream of flame and smoke. Tom, turning into the street further down, wheeled and dashed for his horse, and Art, having leaped behind the harness shop, turned and fled for his life. He had nearly reached his horse and was going at top speed with great leaps when the prostrate man in the street, raising on his elbow, emptied his gun after him, the five shots sounding almost as one. Art Thomas arose convulsively, steadied himself and managed to gain the saddle. Harris looked hastily down the street and saw a cloud of dust racing northward, and grunted. "Let them go—*they* won't never come back no more." Running to the cowpuncher he raised him after a hurried examination of the wounded thigh. "Hop along, Cassidy," he smiled in encouragement. "You'll be a better man with one good laig than th' whole gang was all put together."

The puncher smiled faintly as Hawley, running to them, helped him toward his hotel. "Th' bone is plumb smashed. I reckon I'll hop along through life. It'll be hop along, for me, all right. That's *my* name, all right. Huh! Hopalong Cassidy! But I didn't hop into hell, did I, Harris?" he grinned bravely.

And thus was born a nickname that found honor and fame in the cow-country—a name that stood for loyalty, courage and most amazing gun-play. I have Red's word for this, and the endorsement of those who knew him at the time. And from this on, up to the time he died, and after, we will forsake "Bill" and speak of him as Hopalong Cassidy, a cowpuncher who lived and worked in the days when the West was wild and rough and lawless; and who, like others, through the medium of the only court at hand, Judge Colt, enforced justice as he believed it should be enforced.

CHAPTER VII

"Dealing the Odd"

FARO-BANK is an expensive game when luck turns a cold shoulder on any player, and "going broke" is as easy as ruffling a deck. When a man finds he has two dollars left out of more than two months' pay and that it has taken him less than thirty minutes to get down to that mark, he cannot be censored much if he rails at that Will-o'-the-wisp, the Goddess of Luck. Put him a good ten days' ride from home, acquaintances and money and perhaps he will be justified in adding heat in plenty to his denunciation. He had played to win when he should have coppered, coppered when he should have played to win, he had backed both ends against the middle and played the high card as well—but only when his bets were small did the turn show him what he wanted to see. Perhaps the case-keeper had hoodooed him, for he never did have any luck at cards when a tow-headed man had a finger in the game.

Fuming impotently at his helplessness, a man limped across the main street in Colby, constrained and a little

awkward in his new store clothes and new, squeaking
boots that were clumsy with stiffness. The only things on
him that he could regard as old and tried friends were the
battered sombrero and the heavy, walnut-handled Colt's
.45 which rubbed comfortably with each movement of his
thigh. The weapon, to be sure, had a ready cash value—
but he could not afford to part with it. The horse belonged
to his ranch, and the saddle must not be sold; to part with
it would be to lose his mark of caste and become a walking man, which all good punchers despised.

"Ten days from home, knowin' nobody, two measly dollars in my pocket, an' luck dead agin me," he growled
with pugnacious pessimism. "Oh, I'm a wise old bird, I am!
A hell of a wise bird. Real smart an' cute an' shiny, a
cache of wisdom, a real, bonyfied Smart Aleck with a head
full of spavined brains. I copper th' deuce an' th' deuce
wins; I play th' King to win for ten dollars when I ought
to copper it. I lay two-bits and it comes right—ten dollars
an' I see my guess go *loco*. Reckon I better slip these here
twin bucks down in my kill-me-soon boots afore some
blind papoose takes 'em away from me. Wiser'n Solomon,
I am; I've got old Caesar climbin' a cactus for pleasure an'
joy. S-u-c-k-e-r is my middle name—an' I'm busted."

He almost stumbled over a little tray of a three-legged
table on the corner of the street and his face went hard
as he saw the layout. Three halves of English walnut shells
lay on the faded and soiled green cloth and a blackened,
shriveled pea was still rolling from the shaking he had
given the table. He stopped and regarded it gravely, jin-
gling his two dollars disconsolately. "Don't this town do
nothin' else besides gamble?" he muttered, looking
around.

"Howd'y, stranger!" cheerfully cried a man who hastened up. "Want to see me fool you?"

The puncher's anger was aroused to a thin, licking
flame; but it passed swiftly and a cold, calculating look

came into his eyes. He glanced around swiftly, trying to
locate the cappers, but they were not to be seen, which
worried him a little. He always liked to have possible danger where he could keep an eye on it. Perhaps they were
eating or drinking—the thought stirred him again to anger: two dollars would not feed him very long, nor quench
his thirst.

"Pick it out, stranger," invited the proprietor, idly shifting the shells. "It's easy if yo're right smart—but lots of
folks just can't do it; they can't seem to get th' hang of
it, somehow. That's why it's a bettin' proposition. Here it is,
right before yore eyes! One little pea, three little shells,
right here plumb in front of yore eyes! Th' little pea hides
under one of th' little shells, right in plain sight: But can
you tell which one? That's th' whole game, right there.
See how it's done?" and the three little shells moved
swiftly but clumsily and the little pea disappeared. "Now,
then; where would *you* say it was?" demanded the hopeful operator, genially.

The puncher gripped his two dollars firmly, shifted his
weight as much as possible on his sound leg, and scowled:
he knew where it was. "Do I look like a kid? Do you
reckon you have to coax like a fool to get me all primed
up to show how re-markably smart an' quick I am? You
don't; I know how smart I am. Say, you ain't, not by any
kinda miracle, a blind papoose, are you?" he demanded.

"What you mean?" asked the other, smiling as he waited
for the joke. It did not come, so he continued. "Don't take
no harm in my fool wind-jammin', stranger. It's in th'
game. It's a habit; I've said it so much I just can't help it
no more—I up an' says it at a funeral once; that is, part
of it—th' first part. That's dead right! But I reckon I'm
wastin' my time—unless you happen to feel coltish an'
hain't got nothin' to do for an age. I've been playin' in
hard luck th' last week or so—you see, I ain't as good as
I uster be. I ain't quite so quick, an' a little bit off my

quickness is a whole lot off my chances. But th' game's square—an' that's a good deal more'n you can say about most of 'em."

The puncher hesitated, a grin flickering about his thin lips and a calm joy warming him comfortably. He knew the operator. He knew that face, the peculiar, crescent-shaped scar over one brow, and the big, blue eyes that years of life had not entirely robbed of their baby-like innocence. The past, sorted thoroughly and quickly by his memory, shoved out that face before a crowd of others. Five years is not a long time to remember something unpleasant; he had reasons to remember that countenance. Knowing the face he also knew that the man had been, at one time, far from "square." The associations and means of livelihood during the past five years, judging from the man's present occupation, had not been the kind to correct any evil tendency. He laid a forefinger on the edge of the tray. "Start th' machinery—I'll risk a couple of dollars, anyhow. That ain't much to lose. I bet two dollars I can call it right," he said, watching closely.

He won, as he knew he would; and the result told him that the gambler had not reformed. The dexterous fingers shifting the shells were slower than others he had seen operate and when he had won again he stopped, as if to leave. "When I hit town a short time ago I didn't know I'd be so lucky. I went an' drawed two months' pay when I left th' ranch; I shore don't need it. Shuffle 'em again—it's yore money, anyhow," he laughed. "You should 'a' quit th' game before you got so slow."

"Goin' back to work purty soon?" queried the shell-man, wondering how much this "sucker" had left unspent.

"Not me! I've only just had a couple of drinks since I hit town—an' *I*'m due to celebrate."

The other's face gave no hint of his thoughts, which were that the fool before him had about a hundred dollars on his person. "Well, luck's with you today—you've called it right twice. I'll bet you a cool hundred that you can't call it th' third time. It's th' quickness of my hands agin yore eyes—an' you can't beat me three straight. Make it a hundred? I hate to play all day."

"I'll lay you my winnin's an' have some more of yore money," replied the puncher, feverishly. "Ain't scared, are you?"

"Don't know what it means to be scared," laughed the other. "But I ain't got no small change, nothin' but tens. Play a hundred an' let's have some real excitement."

"Nope; eight or nothin'."

He won again. "Now, sixteen even. Come on; I've got you beat."

"But what's th' use of stringin' 'long like that?" demanded the shell-man.

"Gimme a chance to get my hand in, won't you?" retorted the puncher.

"Well, all right," replied the gambler, and he lost the sixteen.

"Now thirty," suggested the puncher. "Next time all I've got, every red cent. Once more to practice—then every red," he repeated, shifting his feet nervously. "I'll clean you out an' have a real, genuine blow-out on yore money. Come on, I'm in a hurry."

"I'll fool you *this* time, by th' Lord!" swore the gambler, angrily. "You've got more luck than sense. An' I'll fool you next time, too. Yo're quicker'n most men I've run up agin, but I can beat you, shore as shootin'. Th' game's square, th' play fair—my hand agin yore eye. Ready? Then watch me!"

He swore luridly and shoved the money across the board to the winner, bewailing his slowness and getting angrier every moment. "Yo're th' cussedest man I ever bet agin! But I'll get you *this* time. You can't guess right all th' time, an' I know it."

"There she is; sixty-two bucks, three score an' two dollars; all I've got, every cent. Let's see you take it away from me!"

The gambler frowned and choked back a curse. He had risked sixty dollars to win two, and the fact that he had to let this fool play again with the fire hurt his pride. He had no fear for his money—he knew he could win at every throw—but to play that long for two dollars! And suppose the sucker had quit with the sixty!

"Do you get a dollar a month?" he demanded, sarcastically. "Well, I reckon you earn it, at that. Thought you had money, thought you drew down two months' pay an' hain't had nothin' more'n two drinks? Did you go an' lose it on th' way?"

"Oh, I drew it a month ago," replied the sucker, surprised. "I've only had two drinks in this town, which I hit 'bout an hour ago. But I shore lost a wad playin' faro-bank agin a towhead. Come on—lemme take sixty more of yore money, anyhow."

"Sixty-*two*!" snapped the proprietor, determined to have those two miserable dollars and break the sucker for revenge. "Every cent, you remember."

"*All* right; I don't care! I ain't no tin-horn," grumbled the other. "Think I care 'bout two dollars?" But he appeared to be very nervous, nevertheless.

"Well, put it on th' table."

"After you put yourn down."

"There it is. Now watch me close!" A gleam of joy flashed up in the angry man's eyes as he played with the shells. "Watch me close! Mebby it is, an' mebby it ain't— th' game's square, th' play's fair. It's my hand agin yore eye. Watch me close!"

"Oh, go ahead! I'm watchin', all right. Think I'd go to sleep now!"

The shifting hands stopped, the shells lay quiet, and the gambler gazed blankly down the unsympathetic barrel of a Colt.

"Now, Thomas, old thimble-rigger," crisply remarked the supposed sucker as he cautiously slid the money off the table, to be picked up later when conditions would be more favorable. "Th' little pea ain't under *no* shell. *Stop!* Step back one pace an' elevate them paws. Don't make no more funny motions with that hand, savvy? But you can drop th' pea if it hurts them two fingers. Now we'll see if I win; I allus like to be shore," and he cautiously turned over the shells, revealing nothing but the dirty green cloth. "I win; it ain't there—just like I thought."

"Who are you, an' how'd you know my name?" demanded the gambler, mentally cursing his two missing cappers. They were drinking once too often and things were going to happen in their vicinity, and very soon.

"Why, you took twenty-five dollars from me up in Alameda onct, when I couldn't afford to lose it," grinned the puncher. "I was something of a kid then. I remember you, all right. My foreman told me about yore bang-up fight agin th' Johnson brothers, who gave you that scar. I thought then that you were a great man—now I know you ain't. I wouldn't 'a' played at all if I hadn't knowed how crooked you was. Take yore layout an' yore crookedness, find th' pea an' yore cappers, an' clear out. An' if anybody asks you if you've seen Hopalong Cassidy you tell 'em I'm up here in Colby makin' some easy money beatin' crooked games. So-long, an' *don't* look back!"

Hopalong watched him go and then went to the nearest place where he could get something to eat. In due time, having disposed of a square meal, Hopalong called for a drink and a cigar, and sat quietly smoking for nearly half an hour, so lost in thought that his cigar went out repeatedly. As he reviewed his disastrous play at faro many small details came to him and now he found them interesting. The dealer was not a master at his trade and Hopalong had seen many better; in fact the man was not even second class, and this fact hurt his pride. He had played a careful game, and the great majority of his small bets had won—it was only when he risked twenty or thirty dollars that he lost. The only big bet that he had been at all lucky on was one where doubles showed on the turn and he had been split, losing half of his stake. But when he had played his last fifty dollars on the Jack, open, the final blow fell and he had left the table in disgust.

Why weren't there cue-cards, so the players could keep their own tally of the cards instead of having to depend on the cue-box kept by the case-keeper? This made him suspicious; a crooked dealer and case-keeper can trim a big bet at will, unless the players keep their own cases or are exceptionally wise; and even then a really good dealer will get away with his play nine times out of ten. While he seldom played a system, he had backed one that morning; but he was cured of that weakness now. If the game were square he figured he could get at least an even break; if crooked, nothing but a gun could beat it, and he had a very good gun. When he thought of the gun, he reviewed the arrangement of the room and estimated the weight of the rough, deal table on which rested the faro layout. He smiled and turned to the bartender. "Hey, barkeeper! Got any paper an' a pencil?"

After some rummaging the taciturn dispenser of liquid forget-it produced the articles in question and Hopalong, drawing some hurried lines, paid his bill, treated, kept the pencil and headed for the faro game across the street.

When he entered the room the table was deserted and he nodded to the dealer as he seated himself at the right of the case-keeper, who now took his place, and opposite the dealer and the lookout. He was not surprised to find no other players in the room, for the hour was wrong; later in the afternoon there would be many and at night the place would be crowded. This suited him perfectly and he settled himself to begin playing.

When the deck was shuffled and placed in the deal box

Hopalong put his ruled paper in front of him on the table, tallied once against the King for the soda card and started to play quarters and half dollars. He caught the fugitive look that passed between the men as they saw his cue-card but he gave no sign of having observed it. After that he never looked up from the cards while his bets were small. Two deals did not alter his money much and he knew that so far the game was straight. If it were not to remain straight the crookedness would not come more than once in a deal if the frame-up was "single-odd" and then not until the bet was large enough to practically break him. His high-card play ran in his favor and kept him gradually drawing ahead. He lost twice in calling the last turn and guessed it right once, at four to one, which made him win in that department of the game.

When the fifth deal began he was quite a little ahead and his play became bolder, some of the bets going as high as ten dollars. He broke even and then played heavier on the following deal. His first high bet, twenty dollars, was on the eight, open, only one eight having shown. Double eights showed on the next turn and he was split, losing half the stake.

It was about this time that the lookout discovered that Mr. Cassidy was getting a little excited and several times had nearly forgotten to keep his cases. This information was cautiously passed to the dealer and case-keeper and from then on they evinced a little more interest in the game. Finally the player, after studying his cue-card, placed fifty dollars on the Queen, open, and coppered the deuce, a case-card, and then put ten more on the high card. This came in the middle of the game and he was prepared for trouble as the turn was made, but fortune was kind to him and he raked in sixty dollars. He was mildly surprised that he had won, but explained it to himself by thinking that the stakes were not yet high enough. From then on he was keenly alert, for the crookedness would come soon if it ever did, but he strung small sums on the next dozen turns and waited for a new deal before plunging.

As the dealer shuffled the cards the door opened and closed noisily and a surprised and doubting voice exclaimed: "Ain't you Hopalong Cassidy? Cassidy, of th' Bar-20?"

Hopalong glanced up swiftly and back to the cards again: "Yes; what of it?"

"Oh, nothin'. I saw you onct an' I wondered if I was right."

"Ain't got time now; see you later, mebby. You might stick around outside so I can borrow some money if I go broke." The man who knew Mr. Cassidy silently faded, but did not stick around, thereby proving that the player knew human nature and also how to get rid of a pest.

When the dealer heard the name he glanced keenly at the owner of it, exchanged significant looks with the case-keeper and faltered for an instant as he shoved the cards together. He was not sure that he had shuffled them right, and an anxious look came into his eyes as he realized that the deal must go on. It was far from reassuring to set out to cheat a man so well known for expert short-gun work as the Bar-20 puncher and he wished he could be relieved. There was no other dealer around at that time of the day and he had to go through with it. He did not dare to shuffle again and chance losing the card beyond hope, and for the reason that the player was watching him like a hawk.

A ten lay face up on the deck and Hopalong, tallying against it on his sheet, began to play small sums. Luck was variable and remained so until the first twenty dollar bet, when he reached out excitedly and raked in his winnings, his coat sleeve at the same time brushing the cue-card off the table. But he had forgotten all about the tally sheet in his eagerness to win and played several more cards before he noticed it was missing and sought for it. Smothering a curse he glanced at the case-keeper's tally and went on with the play. He did not see the look of relief that showed momentarily on the faces of the dealer and his associates, but he guessed it.

He had no use for cue-cards when he felt like doing without them; he liked to see them in use by the players because it showed the game to be more or less straight, and it also saved him from over-heating his memory. When he had brushed his tally sheet off the table he knew what he was doing, and he knew every card that had been drawn out of the box. So far he had seen no signs of cheating and he wished to give the dealer a chance. There should now remain in the deal box three cards, a deuce, five and a four, with a Queen in sight as the last winner. He knew this to be true because he had given all his attention to memorizing the cards as they showed in the deal box, and had made his bets small so he would not have to bother about them. As he had lost three times on a four he now believed it was due to win.

Taking all his money he placed it on the four: "Two hundred and seventy on th' four to win," he remarked, crisply.

The dealer sniffed almost inaudibly and the case-keeper prepared to cover him on the cue-rack under cover of the excitement of the turn. If the four lay under the Queen, Cassidy lost; if not he either won or was in hock. The dealer was unusually grave as he grasped the deal box to make the turn and as the Queen slid off a five-spot showed.

The dealer's hand trembled as he slid the five off, showing a four, and a winner for Hopalong. He went white—he had bungled the shuffle in his indecision and now he didn't know what might develop. And in his agitation he exposed the hock card before he realized what he was doing, and showed another five. He had made the mistake of showing the "odd."

Hopalong, ready for trouble, was more prepared than the others and he was well under way before they started. His left hand swung hard against the case-keeper's jaw, his Colt roared at the drawing bartender, crumpling the trouble-hunter into a heap on the floor dazed from shock of a ball that "creased" his head. He had done this as he sprang to his feet and his left hand, dropping swiftly to the heavy table, threw it over onto the lookout and the dealer at the instant their hands found their guns. Caught off their balance they went down under it and before they could move sufficiently to do any damage, Hopalong vaulted the table and kicked their guns out of their hands. When they realized just what had happened a still-smoking Colt covered them. Many of Hopalong's most successful and spectacular plays had been less carefully thought out beforehand than this one and he laughed sneeringly as he looked at the men who had been so greedy as to try to clean him out the second time.

"Get up!" he snarled.

They crawled out of their trap and sullenly obeyed his hand, backing against the wall. The case-keeper was still unconscious and Hopalong, disarming him, dragged him to the wall with the others.

"I wondered where that deuce had crawled to," Mr. Cassidy remarked, grimly, "an' I was goin' to see, only it's plain now. I knowed you was clumsy, but my God! Any man as can't deal 'single-odd' ought to quit th' business, or play straight. So you had five fives agin me, eh? Instead of keepin' th' five under th' Queen, you bungled th' deuce in its place. When you went to pull off th' Queen an' five like they was one card, you had th' deuce under her. You see, I keep cases in my old red head an' I didn't have to believe what th' cue-rack was all fixed to show me. An' I was waitin', all ready for th' play that'd make me lose.

"As long as this deal was framed up, we'll say it was this mornin'. You cough up th' hundred an' ten I lost then, an' another hundred an' ten that I'd won if it wasn't crooked. An' don't forget that two-seventy I just pulled down, neither. Make it in double eagles an' don't be slow 'bout it. Money or lead—with *you* callin' th' turn." It was not a very large amount and it took only a moment to count it out. The eleven double eagles representing the morning's play seemed to slide from the dealer's hand with reluctance—but a man lives only once, and they slid without stopping.

The winner, taking the money, picked up the last money he had bet and, distributing it over his person to equalize the weight, gathered up the guns from the floor. Backing toward the door he noticed that the bartender moved and a keen glance at that unfortunate assured him that he would live.

When he reached the door he stopped a moment to ask a question, the tenseness of his expression relaxing into a broad, apologetic grin. "Would you mind tellin' me where I can find some more frame-ups? I shore can use th' money."

The mumbled replies mentioned a locality not to be found on any map of the surface of the globe, and grinning still more broadly, Mr. Cassidy side-stepped and disappeared to find his horse and go on his way rejoicing.

CHAPTER VIII

The Norther

JOHNNY KNEW I had a notebook crammed with the stories his friends had told me; but Johnny, being a wise youth, also knew that there was always room for one more. Perhaps that explains his sarcasm, for, as he calmly turned his back on his fuming friend, he winked at me and sauntered off, whistling cheerfully.

Red spread his feet apart, jammed his fists against his thighs and stared after the youngster. His expression was a study and his open mouth struggled for a retort, but in vain. After a moment he shook his head and slowly turned to me. "Hear th' fool? He's from *Idyho*, he is. It never gets cold nowhere else on earth. Ain't it terrible to be so ignorant?" He glanced at the bunkhouse, into which Johnny had gone for dry clothing. "So I ain't never seen no cold weather?" he mused thoughtfully. Snapping his fingers irritably, he wheeled toward the corral. "I'm goin' down to look at th' dam—there's been lots of water leanin' ag'in it th' last week. Throw th' leather on Saint, if you wants, an' come along. I'll tell you about some cold weather that had th' *Idyho* brand faded. *Cold* weather! Huh!"

As he swung past the bunkhouse we saw Johnny and Billy Jordan leaning in the doorway ragging each other, as cubs will. Johnny grinned at Red and executed a one-hand phrase of the sign language that is universally known, which Red returned with a chuckle. "Wish he'd been here th' time God took a hand in a big game on this ranch," he said. "I'm minus two toes on each foot in consequence thereof. They can't scare me none by preachin' a red-hot hell. No, sir; not any."

He was silent a moment. "Mebby it ain't so bad when a feller is used to it; but we ain't. An' it frequent hits us goin' over th' fence, with both feet off th' ground. Anyhow, that Norther wasn't no storm—it was th' attendant agitation caused by th' North Pole visitin' th' Gulf.

"Cowan had just put Buckskin on th' map by buildin' th' first shack. John Bartlett an' Shorty Jones, damn him, was startin' th' Double Arrow with two hundred head. When th' aforementioned agitation was over they had less'n one hundred. We lost a lot of cows, too; but our range is sheltered good, an' that rock wall down past Meeker's bunkhouse stopped our drifts, though lots of th' cows died there.

"We'd had a mild winter for two weeks, an' a lot of rain. We was chirpin' like li'l fool birds about winter bein' over. Ever notice how many times winter is over before it is? But Buck didn't think so; an' he shore can smell weather. We was also discussin' a certain campin' party Jimmy had discovered across th' river. Jimmy was at th' bunkhouse that shift an' he was a great hand for snoopin' around kickin' up trouble. He reports there's twelve in th' party an' they're camped back of Split Hill. Now, Split Hill is no place for a camp, even in th' summer; an' what got us was th' idea of campin' at all in th' winter. It riled Buck till he forgot to cross off three days on th' calendar, which we later discovered by help of th' almanac an' th' moon.

Buck sends Hoppy over to scout around Split Hill. You know Hoppy. He scouted for two days without bein' seen, an' without discoverin' any lawful an' sane reason why twelve hard-lookin' fellers should be campin' back of Split Hill in th' winter time. He also found they had come from th' south, an' he swore there wasn't no cow tracks leadin' toward them from our range. But there was lots of hoss tracks back and forth. An' when he reports that th' campers had left an' gone on north we all feel better. Then he adds they turned east below th' Double Arrow an' went back south again. That's different. It's plain to some of us they was lookin' us over for future use; learnin' our ways an' th' lay of th' land. There was seven of us at th' time, but we could 'a' licked 'em in a fair fight.

"In them days we only had two line houses. Number One was near Big Coulee, with Cowan's at th' far end of its fifteen miles of north line; th' west line was a twenty-five mile ride south to Lookout Peak. Number Two was where th' Jumpin' Bear empties into th' river, now part of Meeker's range. From it th' riders went west twenty-five miles to th' Peak an' north from it twenty-five miles along th' east line. There was a hundred thousan' acres in Conroy Valley an' thirty thousan' in th' Meeker triangle, which made up Section Two. At that time mebby ten thousan' cows was on this section—two-thirds of all of 'em. When we built Number Three on th' Peak this section was cut down to a reasonable size. Th' third headquarters then was th' bunkhouse, with only th' east line to ride. One part, th' shortest, ran north to Cowan's; th' other run about seventeen miles south to Li'l Timber, where th' line went on as part of Number Two's. We paired off an' had two weeks in each of 'em in them days.

"When we shifted at th' end of that week Jimmy Price an' Ace Fisher got Number One; Skinny an' Lanky was in Number Two; an' me an' Buck an' Hoppy took life easy in th' bunkhouse, with th' cook to feed us. Buck, he scouted all over th' ranch between th' lines an' worked harder than any of us, spendin' his nights in th' nearest house.

"One mornin', about a week after th' campers left, Buck looked out of th' bunkhouse door an' cautions me an' Hoppy to ride prepared for cold weather. I can see he's worried, an' to please him we straps a blanket an' a buffalo robe behind our saddles, cussin' th' size of 'em under our breath. I've got th' short ride that day, an' Buck says he'll wait for me to come back, after which we'll scout around Medicine Bend. He's still worried about them campers. In th' Valley th' cows are thicker'n th' other parts of th' range, an' it wouldn't take no time to get a big herd together. He's got a few things to mend, so he says he'll do th' work before I get back.

"Down on Section Two things is happenin' fast, like they mostly do out here. Twelve rustlers can do a lot if they have things planned, an' 'most any fair plan will work once. They only wanted one day—after that it would be a runnin' fight, with eight or nine of 'em layin' back to hold us off while th' others drove th' cows hard. Why, Slippery Trendley an' Tamale Jose was th' only ones that ever slid across our lines with that many men.

"Three rustlers slipped up to Number Two at night an' waited. When Skinny opened th' door in th' mornin' he was drove back with a hole in his shoulder. Then there was hell a-poppin' in that li'l mud shack. But it didn't do no good, for neither of 'em could get out alive until after dark. They learned that with sorrow, an' pain. An' they shore was het up about it. Ace Fisher, ridin' along th' west line from Number One, was dropped from ambush. Two more rustlers lay back of Medicine Bend lookin' for any of us that might ride down from the bunkhouse. An' they sent two more over to Li'l Timber to lay under that ledge of rock that sticks out of th' south side of th' bluff like a

porch roof. Either me or Hoppy would be ridin' that way.
They stacked th' deck clever; but Providence cut it square.

"Th' first miss-cue comes when a pert gray wolf lopes
past ahead of Hoppy when he's quite some distance above
Li'l Timber. This gray wolf was a whopper, an' Hoppy was
all set to get him. He wanted that sassy devil more'n he
wanted money just then, so he starts after it. Mr. Gray
Wolf leads him a long chase over th' middle of th' range
an' then suddenly disappears. Hoppy hunts around quite
a spell, an' then heads back for th' line. While he's huntin'
for th' wolf it gets cold, an' it keeps on gettin' colder fast.

"Me, I leaves later'n usual that mornin'. An' I don't get
to Cowan's until late. I'm there when I notices how cussed
cold it's got all of a sudden. Cowan looks at his thermom-
eter, which Jimmy later busts, an' says she has gone down
thirty degrees since daylight. He gives me a bottle of liquor Buck wanted, an' I ride west along th' north line,
hopin' to meet Jimmy or Ace for a short talk.

"All at once I notice somebody's pullin' a slate-covered
blanket over th' north sky, an' I drag *my* blanket out an'
wrap it around me. I'm gettin' blamed cold, an' also a li'l
worried. Shall I go back to Cowan's or head straight for
th' bunkhouse? Cowan's the nearest by three miles, but
what's three miles out here? It's got a lot colder than it
was when I was at Cowan's, an' while I'm debatin' about
it th' wind dies out. I look up an' see that th' slate-covered
blanket has traveled fast. It's 'most over my head, an' th'
light is gettin' poor. When I look down again I notice my
cayuses's ears movin' back an' forth, an' he starts pawin'
an' actin' restless. That settles it. I'm backin' instinct just
then, an' I head for home. I ain't cussin' that blanket none
now, an' I'm glad I got th' robe handy; an' that quart of
liquor ain't bulky no more.

"All at once th' bottom falls out of that lead sky, an'
flakes as big as quarters sift down so fast they hurts my
eyes, an' so thick I can't see twenty feet. In ten minutes

everythin' is white, an' in ten more I'm in a strange country. My hands an' feet ache with cold, an' I'm drawin' th' blanket closer, when there's a puff of wind so cold it cuts into my back like a knife. It passes quick, but it don't fool me. I know what's behind it. I reach for th' robe an' has it 'most unfastened when there's a roar an' I'm 'most unseated by th' wind before I can get set. I didn't know then that it's goin' to blow that hard for three days, an' it's just as well. It's full of ice—li'l slivers that are sharp as needles an' cut an' sting till they make th' skin raw. I let loose of th' robe an' tie my bandanna around my face, so my nose an' mouth is covered. My throat burns already almost to my lungs. Good Lord, but it *is* cold! My hands are stiff when I go back for th' robe, an' it's all I can do to keep it from blowin' away from me. It takes me a long time to get it over th' blanket, an' my hands are 'most froze when it's fastened. That was a good robe, but it didn't make much difference that day. Th' cold cuts through it an' into my back as if it wasn't there. My feet are gettin' worse all th' time, an' it ain't long before I ain't got none, for th' achin' stops at th' ankles. Purty soon only my knees ache, an' I know it won't be long till they won't ache no more.

"I'm squirmin' in my clothes tryin' to rub myself warm when I remember that flask of liquor. Th' cork was out far enough for my teeth to get at it, an' I drink a quarter of it quick. It's an awful load—any other time it would 'a' knocked me cold, for Cowan sold a lot worse stuff then than he does now. But it don't phase me, except for takin' most of th' linin' out of my mouth an' throat. It warms me a li'l, an' it makes my knees ache a li'l harder. But it don't last long—th' cold eats through me just as hard as ever a li'l later, an' then I begin to see things an' get sleepy. Cows an' cayuses float around in th' air, an' I'm countin' money, piles of it. I get warm an' drowsy an' find myself noddin'. That scares me a li'l, an' I fight hard ag'in it. If I go to sleep it's all over. It keeps gettin' worse, an' I finds my eyes shuttin' more an' more frequent, an' more an' more frequent thinkin' I don't care, anyhow. An' so I drifts along pullin' at th' bottle till it's empty. That should 'a' killed me, then an' there—but it don't even make me real drunk. Mebby I spilled some of it, my hands bein' nothin' but sticks. I can't see more'n five feet now, an' my eyes water, which freezes on 'em. I've given up all hope of hearin' any shootin'. So I close th' peekhole in th' blanket an' robe, drawin' 'em tight to keep out some of th' cold. I am sittin' up stiff in th' saddle, like a soldier, just from force of habit, and after a li'l while I don't know nothin' more. Pete says I was a corpse, froze stiff as a ramrod, an' he calls me ghost for a long time in fun. But Pete wasn't none too clear in his head about that time.

"Down at Li'l Timber, Hoppy managed to get under th' shelter of that projectin' ledge of rock on th' south side of th' bluff. Th' snow an' ice is whirlin' under it because of a sort of back draft, but th' wind don't hit so hard. He's fightin' that cayuse every foot, tryin' to get to th' cave at th' west end, an' disputin' th' right of way with th' cows that are packed under it. There's firewood under that ledge an' there's food on th' hoof, an' snow water for drink; so if he can make th' cave he's safe. He's more worried about his supply of smokin' tobacco than anythin' else, so far as he's concerned.

"All at once he runs onto four men huddled half-froze in a bunch right ahead of him. He knows in a flash who they are, an' he draws fumblingly, an' holds th' gun in his two hands, they are so cold. One clean hit an' five clean misses in twenty feet! They're gropin' for their guns when a sudden gust of wind whirls down from th' top of th' hill, pilin' snow an' ice on 'em till they can't see nor breathe. An' a couple of old trees come down to make things nicer. Hoppy is blinded, an' when he gets so he can see again there's one rustler's arm stickin' up out of th' snow, but no signs of th' other three. They blundered out into th' open tryin' to get **away from** th' stuff comin' down on 'em, an' that means they won't be back no more.

"Hoppy manages to get to th' cave, tie his cayuse to a fallen tree, an' gather enough firewood for a good blaze, which he puts in front of th' cave. It takes him a long time to use up his matches one by one, an' then he pulls th' lead out of a cartridge with his teeth, shakes th' powder loose in it an' along th' barrel. Usin' his cigarette papers for tinder he gets th' fire started an' goin' good an' is feelin' some cheerful when he remembers th' three rustlers driftin' south. They was bound to hit a big arroyo that would lead 'em almost ag'in' Number Two's door. With th' wind drivin' 'em straight for it, Hoppy thinks it might mean trouble for Lanky or Skinny. He didn't think about 'em only havin' wool-lined slickers on, or he'd 'a' knowed they couldn't live till they got halfway. They left their blankets in camp so they could work fast.

"People have called us clannish, an' said we was a 'lovin' bunch' because we stick together so tight. We've faced so much together that us of th' old bunch has got th' same blood in our veins. We ain't eight men—we're one man in eight different kinds of bodies. God help anybody that tries to make us less! It's one thing to stand up an' swap shots with a gunman; but it's another to turn yore back on a cave an' a fire like that an' go out into what is purty nigh shore death on a long chance of helpin' a couple of friends that was able to take care of themselves. That's one of th' things that explains why we made Shorty Jones an' his eleven men pay with their lives for takin' Jimmy's life. Twelve for one! That fight at Buckskin ain't generally understood, even by our friends. An' Hoppy crowns his courage twice in that one storm. Ain't he an old son-of-a-gun?

"He leaves that fire an' forces his cayuse to take him out in th' storm again, finds that th' arroyo is level full of snow, but has both banks swept bare. He passes them three rustlers in th' next ten minutes—they won't do no

more cow-liftin'. Then he tries to turn back, but that's foolish. So he drifts on, gettin' a li'l loco by now. He's purty
near asleep when he thinks he hears a shot. He fights his
cayuse again, but can't stop it, so he falls off an' lets it
drift, an' crawls an' fights his way back to where that shot
was fired from. God only knows how he does it, but he
falls over a cow an' sees Lanky huggin' its belly for th' li'l
warmth in th' carcass. An' he ought to 'a' found him, after
leavin' his cayuse an' turnin' back on foot in that hell
storm! Th' drifts was beginnin' to make then—when th'
storm was over I saw drifts thirty feet high in th' open;
an' in th' valley there was some that run 'most to th' top
of th' bluffs, an' they're near sixty feet high.

"Well, Lanky is as crazy as him, an' won't let go of that
cow, an' they have a fight, which is good for both of 'em.
Finally Lanky gets some sense in his head an' realizes
what Hoppy is tryin' to do for him, an' they go staggerin'
down wind, first one fallin' an' then th' other. But they
keep fightin' like th' game boys they are, neither givin' a
cuss for himself, but shore obstinate that he's goin' to get
th' other out of it. That's *our* spirit; an' we're proud of it,
by God! Hoppy wraps th' robe around Lanky, an' so they
stagger on, neither one knowin' very much by that time.
Th' Lord must 'a' pitied that pair, an' admired th' stuff He'd
put in 'em, for they bump into th' line house kerslam, an'
drop, all done an' exhausted.

"Meanwhile Skinny's hoppin' around inside, prayin' an'
cussin' by streaks, every five minutes openin' th' door
an' firin' off his Colt. He has tied th' two ropes together, an'
frequent he ties one end to th' door, th' other to hisself,
an' goes out pokin' around in th' snow, hopin' to stumble
over his pardner. He's plumb forgot his bad shoulder long
ago. Purty soon he opens th' door again to shoot off th'
gun, an' in streaks somethin' between his laigs. He slams
th' door as he jumps aside, an' then looks scared at Lanky's sombrero! Mebby he's slow hoppin' outside an' dig-

gin' them out of th' drift that's near covered 'em! Now, don't think bad of Skinny. He dassn't leave th' house to search any distance, even if he could 'a' seen anythin'. His best play is to stick there an' shoot off his gun—Lanky might drift past if he was not there to signal. Skinny thought more of Lanky any time than he did of hisself, th' emaciated match!

"It don't take long to kick in a lot of snow with that wind blowin' an' he rubs them two till he's got tears in his eyes. Then he fills 'em with hot stew an' whisky, rolls 'em up together an' leaves 'em in th' same bunk. It ain't warm enough in that house, even with th' fire goin', to make 'em lose no arms or laigs.

"It seems that Lanky, watchin' his chance as soon as th' snow fell heavy enough to cover his movements, slipped out of th' house an' started to circle out around them festive rustlers that held him an' his friend prisoners. He made Skinny stay behind to hold th' house an' keep a gun poppin'. Lanky has worked up behind where th' rustlers was layin' when th' Norther strikes full force. It near blows him over, an', not havin' on nothin' but an old army overcoat that was wore out, th' cold gets him quick. He can't see, an' he can't hear Skinny's shots no more! He does th' best he can an' tries to fight back along his trail, but in no time there ain't no tracks to follow. Then he loses his head an' starts wanderin' until a cow blunders down on him. He shoots th' cow an' hugs its belly to keep warm an' then he don't really remember nothin' 'till he wakes up in th' bunk alongside of Hoppy, both gettin' over an awful drunk. Skinny kept feedin' liquor to 'em till it was gone, an' he had a plenty when he began.

"Jimmy Price was at Number One when th' blow started, an' Buck was in th' bunkhouse, an' it was three weeks before they could get out an' around, on account of th' snow fallin' so steady an' hard they couldn't see nothin'.

"Well, getting back to me explains how Pete Wilson came to th' Bar-20. He is migratin' south, just havin' had th' pleasure of learnin' that his wife sloped with a better-lookin' man. He was scared she might get tired of th' other feller an' sift back, so he sells out his li'l store, loads a waggin with blankets, grub, an' firewood, an' starts south, winter or no winter. He moves fast for a new range, where he can make a new beginnin' an' start life fresh, with five years of burnin' matrimonial experience as his valuablest asset. Pete says he reckoned mebby he wouldn't have so many harness sores if he run single th' rest of his life; heretofore he'd been so busy applyin' salve that he didn't have time to find out just what was th' trouble with th' double harness. Lots of men feel that way, but they ain't got Pete's unlovely outspoken habit of thought. We used to reckon mebby he wasn't as smart as th' rest of us, him bein' slow an' blunderin' in his retorts. We've played that with coppers lots of times since, though. While he ain't what you'd call quick at retortin', his retorts usually is heard by th' whole county. It ain't every collar-galled husband that's got th' gumption or smartness to jump th' minute th' hat is lifted. Pete had.

"He's drivin' across our range, an' when th' wind dies out sudden an' th' snow sifts down, he's just smart enough to get out his beddin' an' wrap it around him till he looks like a bale of cotton. An' even at that he's near froze an' lookin' for a place to make a stand when he feels a bump. It's me, fallin' off my cayuse, against his front wheel. He emerges from his beddin', lifts me into th' waggin, puts most of his blankets around me, an' stops. Knowin' he can't save th' cayuses, he shoots 'em. That means grub for us, anyhow, if we run short of th' good stuff. Nobody but Pete could 'a' got th' canvas off that waggin in such a gale, but he did it. He busts th' arches an' slats off th' top of th' waggin an' uses 'em for firewood. Th' canvas he drapes over th' box, lettin' it hang down on both sides to th' ground. An' in about five minutes th' whole thing was covered over with snow. Pete's the strongest man we ever saw, an' we've seen some good ones. Wrastlin' that canvas with stiff hands was a whole lot more than what he done to Big Sandy up there on Thunder Mesa.

"Pete says I was dead when he grabbed me, an' smellin' disgraceful of liquor. But th' first thing I know is lookin' up in th' gloom at a ceilin' that's right close to my head, an' at a sorta rafter. That rafter gives me a shock. It don't even touch th' ceilin', but runs along 'most a foot below it. I close my eyes an' do a lot of thinkin'. I remember freezin' to death, but that's all. An' just then I hears a faint voice say: 'He shore was dead.' I don't know Pete then, or that he talked to hisself sometimes. An' I reckon I was a li'l off in my head, at that. I begin to wonder if he means me, an' purty soon I'm shore of it. An' don't I sympathize with myself? I'm dead an' gone somewhere; but no preacher I ever heard ever described no place like this. Then I smell smoke an' burnin' meat—which gives me a clew to th' range I'm on. Mebby I'm shelved in th' ice box, waitin' my turn, or somethin'. I knew I'd led a sinful life. But there wasn't no use of rubbin' it in—it's awful to be dead an' know it.

"Th' next time I opens my eyes I can't see nothin'; but I can feel somethin' layin' alongside of me. It's breathin' slow an' regular, an it bothers me till I get th' idea all of a sudden. It's another dead one, cut out of th' herd an' shoved in my corral to wait for subsequent events. I felt sorry for him, an' lay there tryin' to figger it out, an' I'm still figgerin' when it starts to get light. Th' other feller grunts an' sits up, bumpin' his head solid against that fool rafter. No dead man that was shoved in a herd consigned to heaven ever used such language, which makes me all the shorer of where I am. But if hell's hot we've still got a long way to go.

"He sits there rubbin' his head an' cussin' steadily, an'

I'm so moved by it that I compliments him. He jumps an' bumps his head again, an' looks at me close. 'Damned if you ain't a husky corpse,' he says. That settles it. I ain't crazy, like I was hopin', but I'm dead. 'You an' me is on th' ragged edge of hell,' he adds.

" 'But who tipped *you* off?' I asks. 'They just shoved me in here an' didn't tell me nothin' at all.'

" 'Crazy as th' devil,' he grunts, lookin' at me harder.

" 'Yo're a liar,' I replies. 'I may be dead, but damned if I'm crazy!'

" 'An' I don't blame you, either,' he mused, sorrowful. 'Now you keep quiet till I gets somethin' to eat,' an' he crawls into a li'l round hole at th' other end of th' room.

"Purty soon I smell smoke again, an' after a long time he comes back with some hot coffee an' burned meat. I grab for th' grub, an' while I'm eatin' I demands to know where I am.

"He laughs, real cheerful, an' tells me. I'm under his waggin, surrounded by canvas an' any God's quantity of snow. Th' drift over us is fifteen foot high, th' wind had died down, an' it's still snowin' so hard he can't see twenty feet. It is also away down below freezin'.

"We stayed under that drift 'most three weeks, livin' on raw meat after our firewood gave out. We didn't suffer none from th' cold, though, under all that snow an' with all th' blankets we had. When it stopped snowin' we discovered a drift shamefully high about a mile northeast of us, an' from th' smoke comin' out of it I knew it was th' bunkhouse.

"Well, to cut it short, it was. An' mebby Buck wasn't glad to see me! He was worried 'most sick an' as soon as we could, we got cayuses and started out to look for th' others, scared stiff at what we expected to find."

He paused and was silent a moment. "But only Ace was missin'," he added. "We found him an' th' rustlers later, when th' snow went off."

He paused again and shook his head. "It shore was a miracle that we didn't go with 'em, all of us, except Buck. Pete was so plumb disgusted with travelin' in th' winter, an' had lost his cayuses, that when Buck offers him Ace's bunk he stays. An' he ain't never left us since. Huh! Cold? That cub don't know nothin'—mebby he will when he grows up, but I dunno, at that. *Idyho!*"

CHAPTER IX

The Drive

THE NORTHER was a thing of the past, but it left its mark on Buck Peters, whose grimness of face told what the winter had been to him. His daily rides over the range, the reports of his men since that deadly storm had done a great deal to lift the sagging weight that rested on his shoulders; but he would not be sure until the round-up supplied facts and figures.

That the losses had not been greater he gave full credit to the valley with its arroyos, rock walls, draws, heavily grassed range and groves of timber; for the valley, checking the great southward drift by its steep ridges of rock, sheltered the herds in timber and arroyos and fed them on the rich profusion of its grasses, which, by some trick of the rushing winds, had been whirled clean of snow.

But over the cow-country, north, east, south and west, where vast ranges were unprotected against the whistling blasts from the north, the losses had been stupendous, appalling, stunning. Outfits had been driven on and on before the furious winds, sleepy and apathetic, drifting steadily southward in the white, stinging shroud to a drowsy death. Whole herds, blindly moving before the wind, left their weaker units in constantly growing numbers to mark the trail, and at last lay down to a sleep eternal. And astonishing and incredible were the distances traveled by some of those herds.

Following the Norther came another menace and one which easily might surpass the worst efforts of the blizzard. Warm winds blew steadily, a hot sun glared down on the snow-covered plain and then came torrents of rain which continued for days, turning the range into a huge expanse of water and mud and swelling the watercourses with turgid floods that swirled and roared above their banks. Should this be quickly followed by cold, even the splendid valley would avail nothing. Ice, forming over the grasses, would prove as deadly as a pestilence; the cattle, already weakened by the hardships of the Norther, and not having the instinct to break through the glassy sheet and feed on the grass underneath, would search in vain for food, and starve to death. The week that followed the cessation of the rains started gray hairs on the foreman's head; but a warm, constant sun and warm winds dried off the water before the return of freezing weather. The herds were saved.

Relieved, Buck reviewed the situation. The previous summer had seen such great northern drives to the railroad shipping points in Kansas that prices fell until the cattlemen refused to sell. Rather than drive home again, the great herds were wintered on the Kansas ranges, ready to be hurled on the market when Spring came with better prices. Many ranches, mortgaged heavily to buy cattle, had been on the verge of bankruptcy, hoping feverishly for better prices the following year. Buck had taken advantage of the situation to stock his ranch at a cost far less than he had dared to dream. Then came the Norther and in the three weeks of devastating cold and high winds the Kansas ranges were swept clean of cattle, and even the ranges in the South were badly crippled. Knowing this, Buck also knew that the following Spring would show record high prices. If he had the cattle he could clean up a fortune for his ranch; and if his herd was the first big one to reach the railroad at Sandy Creek it would practically mean a bonus on every cow.

Under the long siege of uncertainty his impatience smashed through and possessed him as a fever and he ordered the calf round-up three weeks earlier than it ever had been held on the ranch. There was no need of urging his men to the task—they, like himself, sprang to the call like springs freed from a restraining weight, and the work went on in a fever of haste. And he took his place on the firing line and worked even harder than his outfit of fanatics.

One day shortly after the work began a stranger rode up to him and nodded cheerfully. "Li'l early, ain't you?" Buck grunted in reply and sent Skinny off at top speed to close a threatened gap in the lengthy driving line. "Goin' to git 'em on th' trail early this year?" persisted the stranger. Buck, swayed by some swift intuition, changed his reply. "Oh, I dunno; I'm mainly anxious to see just what that storm did. An' I hate th' calf burnin' so much I allus like to get it over quick." He shouted angrily at the cook and waved his arms frantically to banish the chuck wagon. "He can make more trouble with that waggin than anybody I ever saw," he snorted. "Get out of there, you fool!" he yelled, dashing off to see his words obeyed. The cook, grinning cheerfully at his foreman's language and heat, forthwith chose a spot that was not destined to be the center of the cut-out herd. And when Buck again thought of the stranger he saw a black dot moving toward the eastern skyline.

The crowded days rolled on, measured full from dawn

to dark, each one of them a panting, straining, trying ordeal. Worn out, the horses were turned back into the temporary corral or to graze under the eyes of the horse wranglers, and fresh ones took up their work; and woe unto the wranglers if the supply fell below the demand. For the tired men there was no relief, only a shifting in the kind of work they did, and they drove themselves with grave determination, their iron wills overruling their aching bodies. First came the big herds in the valley; then, sweeping north, they combed the range to the northern line in one grand, mad fury of effort that lasted day after day until the tally man joyously threw away his chewed pencil and gladly surrendered the last sheet to the foreman. The first half of the game was over. Gone as if it were a nightmare was the confusion of noise and dust and cows that hid a remarkable certainty of method. But as if to prove it not a dream, four thousand cows were held in three herds on the great range, in charge of the extra men.

Buck, leading the regular outfit from the north line and toward the bunkhouse, added the figures of the last tally sheet to the totals he had in a little book, and smiled with content. Behind him, cheerful as fools, their bodies racking with weariness, their faces drawn and gaunt, knowing that their labors were not half over, rode the outfit, exchanging chaff and banter in an effort to fool themselves into the delusion that they were fresh and "chipper." Nearing the bunkhouse they cheered lustily as they caught sight of the hectic cook laboring profanely with two balking pintos that had backed his wagon half over the edge of a barranca and then refused to pull it back again. Cookie's reply, though not a cheer, was loud and pregnant with feeling. To think that he had driven those two animals for the last two weeks from one end of the ranch to the other without a mishap, and then have them balance him and his wagon on the crumbling edge of a twenty-foot drop when not a half mile from the bunkhouse, thus threatening the loss of the wagon and all it contained and the mangling of his sacred person! And to make it worse, here came a crowed of whooping idiots to feast upon his discomfiture.

The outfit, slowing so as not to frighten the devilish pintos and start them backing again, drew near; and suddenly the air became filled with darting ropes, one of which settled affectionately around Cookie's apoplectic neck. In no time the strangling, furious dough-king was beyond the menace of the crumbling bank, flat on his back in the wagon, where he had managed to throw himself to escape the whistling hoofs that quickly turned the dashboard into matchwood. When he managed to get the rope from his neck he arose, unsteady with rage, and choked as he tried to speak before the grinning and advising outfit. Before he could get command over his tongue the happy bunch wheeled and sped on its way, shrieking with mirth unholy. They had saved him from probable death, for Cookie was too obstinate to have jumped from the wagon; but they not only forfeited all right to thanks and gratitude, but deserved horrible deaths for the conversation they had so audibly carried on while they worked out the cook's problem. And their departing words and gestures made homicide justifiable and a duty. It was in this frame of mind that Cookie watched them go.

Buck, emerging from the bunkhouse in time to see the rescue, leaned against the door and laughed as he had not laughed for one heartbreaking winter. Drying his eyes on the back of his hand, he looked at the bouncing, happy crowd tearing southward with an energy of arms and legs and lungs that seemed a miracle after the strain of the round-up. Just then a strange voice made him wheel like a flash, and he saw Billy Williams sitting solemnly on his horse near the corner of the house.

"Hullo, Williams," Buck grunted, with no welcoming warmth in his voice. "What th' devil brings *you* up here?"

"I want a job," replied Billy. The two, while never enemies nor interested in any mutual disagreements, had never been friends. They never denied a nodding acquaintance, nor boasted of it. "That Norther shore raised hell. There's ten men for every job, where I came from."

The foreman, with that quick decision that was his in his earlier days, replied crisply. "It's your'n. Fifty a month, to start."

"Keno. Lemme chuck my war-bag through that door an' I'm ready," smiled Billy. He believed he would like this man when he knew him better. "I thought th' Diamond Bar, over east a hundred mile, had weathered th' storm lucky. You got 'em beat. They're movin' heaven an' earth to get a herd on the trail, but they didn't have no job for *me*," he laughed, flushing slightly. "Sam Crawford owns it," he explained naïvely.

Buck laughed outright. "I reckon you didn't have much show with Sam, after that li'l trick you worked on him in Fenton. So Sam is in this country? How are they fixed?"

"They aims to shove three thousan' east right soon. It's fancy prices for th' first herd that gets to Sandy Creek," he offered. "I heard they're havin' lots of wet weather along th' Comanchee; mebby Sam'll have trouble a-plenty gettin' his herd acrost. Cows is plumb aggervatin' when it comes to crossin' rivers," he grinned.

Buck nodded. "See that V openin' on th' sky line?" he asked, pointing westward. "Ride for it till you see th' herd. Help 'em with it. We'll pick it up t'morrow." He turned on his heel and entered the house, grave with a new worry. He had not known that there was a ranch where Billy had said the Diamond Bar was located; and a hundred miles handicap meant much in a race to Sandy Creek. Crawford was sure to drive as fast as he dared. He was glad that Billy had mentioned it, and the wet weather along the

Comanchee—Billy already had earned his first month's pay.

All that day and the next the consolidation of the three herds and the preparation for the drive went on. Sweeping up from the valley the two thousand three- and four-year-olds met and joined the thousand that waited between Little Timber and Three Rocks; and by nightfall the three herds were one by the addition of the thousand head from the Big Coulee. Four thousand head of the best cattle on the ranch spent the night within gunshot of the bunkhouse and corrals on Snake Creek.

Buck, returning from the big herd, smiled as he passed the chuck-wagon and heard Cookie's snores, and went on, growing serious all too quickly. At the bunkhouse he held a short consultation with his regular outfit and then returned to the herd again while his drive crew turned eagerly to their bunks. Breakfast was eaten by candle light and when the eastern sky faded into a silver gray Skinny Thompson vaulted into the saddle and loped eastward without a backward glance. The sounds of his going scarcely had died out before Hopalong, relieved of the responsibilities of trail boss, shouldered others as weighty and rode into the northeast with Lanky at his side. Behind him, under charge of Red, the herd started on its long and weary journey to Sandy Creek, every man of the outfit so imbued with the spirit of the race that even with its hundred miles' advantage the Diamond Bar could not afford to waste an hour if it hoped to win.

Out of the side of a verdant hill, whispering and purling, flowed a small stream and shyly sought the crystal depths of a rock-bound pool before gaining courage enough to flow gently over the smooth granite lip and scurry down the gentle slope of the arroyo. To one side of it towered a splinter of rock, slender and gray, washed clean by the recent rains. To the south of it lay a baffling streak a little lighter than the surrounding grass lands. It was, perhaps, a quarter of a mile wide and ended only at the horizon. This faint band was the Dunton trail, not used enough to show the strong characteristics of the depressed bands found in other parts of the cow-country. If followed it would lead one to Dunton's Ford on the Comanchee, forty miles above West Bend, where the Diamond Bar aimed to cross the river.

The shadow of the pinnacle drew closer to its base and had crossed the pool when Skinny Thompson rode slowly up the near bank of the ravine, his eyes fixed smilingly on the splinter of rock. He let his mount nuzzle and play with the pool for a moment before stripping off the saddle and turning the animal loose to graze. Taking his rifle in the hope of seeing game, he went up to the top of the hill, glanced westward and then turned and gazed steadily into the northeast, sweeping slowly over an arc of thirty degrees. He stood so for several minutes and then grunted with satisfaction and returned to the pool. He had caught sight of a black dot far away on the edge of the skyline that split into two parts and showed a sidewise drift. Evidently his friends would be on time. Of the herd he had seen no sign, which was what he had expected.

When at last he heard hoofbeats he arose lazily and stretched, chiding himself for falling asleep, and met his friends as they turned into sight around the bend of the hill. "Reckoned you might 'a' got lost," he grinned sleepily.

"G'wan!" snorted Lanky.

"What'd you find?" eagerly demanded Hopalong.

"Three thousan' head on th' West Bend trail five days ahead of us," replied Skinny. "Ol' Sam is drivin' hard." He paused a moment. "Acts like he knows we're after him. Anyhow, I saw that feller that visited us on th' third day of th' round-up. So I reckon Sam knows."

Lanky grinned. "He won't drive so hard later. I'd like

to see him when *he* sees th' Comanchee! Bet it's a lake south of Dunton's 'cordin' to what he found. But it ain't goin' to bother us a whole lot."

Hopalong nodded, dismounted and drew a crude map in the sand of the trail. Skinny watched it, grave and thoughtful until, all at once, he understood. His sudden burst of laughter startled his companions and they exchanged foolish grins. It appeared that from Dunton's Ford north, in a distance of forty miles, the Comanchee was practically born. So many feeders, none of them formidable, poured into it that in that distance it attained the dignity of a river. Hopalong's plan was to drive off at a tangent running a little north from the regular trail and thus cross numerous small streams in preference to going on straight and facing the swollen Comanchee at Dunton's Ford. As the regular trail turned northward when not far from Sandy Creek they were not losing time. Laughing gaily they mounted and started west for the herd which toiled toward them many miles away. Thanks to the forethought that had prompted their scouting expedition the new trail was picked out in advance and there would be no indecision on the drive.

Eighty miles to the south lay the fresh trail of the Diamond Bar herd, and five days' drive eastward on it, facing the water-covered lowlands at West Bend, Sam Crawford held his herd, certain that the river would fall rapidly in the next two days. It was the regular ford, and the best on the river. The water did fall, just enough to lure him to stay; but, having given orders at dark on the second night for an attempt at crossing at daylight the next morning, he was amazed when dawn showed him the river was back to its first level.

Sam was American born, but affected things English and delighted in spelling "labor" and like words with a "u." He hated hair chaps and maintained that the gun-play of the West was mythical and existed only in the minds of effete Easterners. Knowing that, it was startling to hear him tell of Plummer, Hickock, Roberts, Thompson and a host of other gunmen who had splotched the West with blood. Not only did every man of that section pack a gun, but Crawford, himself, packed one, thus proving himself either a malicious liar or an imbecile. He acted as though the West belonged to him and that he was the arbiter of its destiny and its chosen historian—which made him troublesome on the great, free ranges. Only that his pretensions and his crabbed, irascible, childish temper made him ludicrous he might have been taken seriously, to his sorrow. Failing miserably at law, he fled from such a precarious livelihood, beset with a haunting fear that he had lost his grip, to an inherited ranch. This fear that pursued him turned him into a carping critic of those who excelled him in most things, except in fits of lying about the West as it existed at that time.

When he found that the river was over the lowlands again he became furious and, carried away by rage, shouted down the wiser counsel of his clear-headed night boss and ordered the herd into the water. Here and there desperate, wide-eyed steers wheeled and dashed back through the cordon of riders, their numbers constantly growing as the panic spread. The cattle in the front ranks, forced into the swirling stream by the pressure from the rear, swam with the current and clambered out below, adding to the confusion. Steers fought throughout the press and suddenly, out of the right wing of the herd, a dozen crazed animals dashed out in a bunch for the safety of the higher ground; and after them came the herd, an irresistible avalanche of maddened beef. It was not before dark that they were rounded up into a nervous, panicky herd once more. The next morning they were started north along the river, to try again at Dunton's Ford, which they reached in three days, and where another attempt at crossing the river proved in vain.

Meanwhile the Bar-20 herd pushed on steadily with no confusion. It crossed the West Run one noon and the upper waters of the Little Comanchee just before dark on the same day. Next came East Run, Pawnee Creek and Ten Mile Creek, none of them larger than the stream the cattle were accustomed to back on the ranch. Another day's drive brought them to the west branch of the Comanchee itself, the largest of all the rivers they would meet. Here they were handled cautiously and "nudged" across with such care that a day was spent in the work. The following afternoon the east branch held them up until the next day and then, with a clear trail, they were sent along on the last part of the long journey.

When Sam Crawford, forced to keep on driving north along the Little Comanchee, saw that wide, fresh trail, he barely escaped apoplexy and added the finishing touches to the sullenness of his outfit. Seeing the herd across, he gave orders for top speed and drove as he never had driven before; and when the last river had been left behind he put the night boss in charge of the cattle and rode on ahead to locate his rivals of the drive. Three days later, when he returned to his herd, he was in a towering fury and talked constantly of his rights and an appeal to law, and so nagged his men that mutiny stalked in his shadow.

When the Bar-20 herd was passing to the south of the little village of Depau, Hopalong turned back along the trail to find the Diamond Bar herd. So hard had Sam pushed on that he was only two days' drive behind Red and his outfit when Hopalong rode smilingly into the Diamond Bar camp. He was talking pleasantly of shop to some of the Diamond Bar punchers when Sam dashed up and began upbraiding him and threatening dire punishment. Hopalong, maintaining a grave countenance, took the lacing meekly and humbly as he winked at the grinning punchers. Finally, after exasperating Sam to a point but one degree removed from explosion, he bowed cyni-

cally, said "so-long" to the friendly outfit and loped away
toward his friends. Sam, choking with rage, berated his
punchers for not having thrown out the insulting visitor
and commanded more speed, which was impossible. Re-
porting to Red the proximity of their rivals, Hopalong fell
in line and helped drive the herd a little faster. The cattle
were in such condition from the easy traveling of the last
week that they could easily stand the pace if Crawford's
herd could. So the race went on, Red keeping the same
distance ahead day after day.

Then came the night when Sandy Creek lay but two
days' drive away. A storm had threatened since morning
and the first lightning of the drive was seen. The cattle
were mildly restless when Hopalong rode in at midnight
and he was cheerfully optimistic. He was also very much
awake, and after trying in vain to get to sleep he finally
arose and rode back along the trail toward the stragglers,
which Jimmy and Lanky were holding a mile away. Red
had pushed on to the last minute of daylight and Lanky
had decided to hold the stragglers instead of driving them
up to the main herd so they would start even with it the
following morning. It was made up of the cattle that had
found the drive too much for them and was smaller than
the outfit had dared to hope for.

Hopalong had just begun to look around for the herd
when it passed him with sudden uproar. Shouting to a
horseman who rode furiously past, he swung around and
raced after him, desperately anxious to get in front of the
stampede to try to check it before it struck the main herd
and made the disaster complete. For the next hour he was
in a riot of maddened cattle and shaved death many times
by the breadth of a hand. He could hear Jimmy and Lanky
shouting in the black void, now close and now far away.
Then the turmoil gradually ceased and the remnant of the
herd paused, undecided whether to stop or go on. He flung
himself at it and by driving cleverly managed to start a

number of cows to milling, which soon had the rest following suit. The stampede was over. A cursing blot emerged from the darkness and hailed. It was Lanky, coldly ferocious. He had not heard Jimmy for a long time and feared that the boy might be lying out or the black plain, trampled into a shapeless mass of flesh. One stumble in front of the charging herd would have been sufficient.

Daylight disclosed the missing Jimmy hobbling toward the breakfast fire at the cook wagon. He was bruised and bleeding and covered with dirt, his clothes ripped and covered with mud; and every bone and muscle in his body was alive with pain.

The Diamond Bar's second squad had ridden in to breakfast when a horseman was seen approaching at a leisurely lope. Sam, cursing hotly, instinctively fumbled at the gun he wore at his thigh in defiance to his belief concerning the wearing of guns. He blinked anxiously as the puncher stopped at the wagon and smiled a heavy-eyed salutation. The night boss emerged from the shelter of the wagon and grinned a sheepish welcome. "Well, Cassidy, you fellers got th' trail somehow. We was some surprised when we hit yore trail. How you makin' it?"

"All right, up to last night," replied Hopalong, shaking hands with the night boss. "Got a match, Barnes?" he asked, holding up an unlighted cigarette. They talked of things connected with the drive and Hopalong cautiously swung the conversation around to mishaps, mentioning several catastrophes of past years. After telling of a certain stampede he had once seen, he turned to Barnes and asked a blunt question. "What would you do to anybody as stampeded yore stragglers within a mile of th' main herd on a stormy night?" The answer was throaty and rumbling. "Why, shoot him, I reckon." The others intruded their ideas and Crawford squirmed, his hand seeking his gun under the pretense of tightening his belt.

Hopalong arose and went to his horse, where a large bundle of canvas was strapped behind the saddle. He loosened it and unrolled it on the ground. "Ever see this afore, boys?" he asked, stepping back. Barnes leaped to his feet with an ejaculation of surprise and stared at the canvas. "Where'd you git it?" he demanded. "That's our old wagon cover!"

Hopalong, ignoring Crawford, looked around the little group and smiled grimly. "Well, last night our stragglers was stampeded. Lanky told me he saw somethin' gray blow past him in th' darkness, an' then th' herd started. We managed to turn it from th' trail an' so it din't set off our main herd. Jimmy was near killed—well, you know what it is to ride afore stampeded cows. I found this cover blowed agin' a li'l clump of trees, an' when I sees yore mark, I reckoned I ought to bring it back." He dug into his pocket and brought out a heavy clasp knife. "I just happened to see this not far from where th' herd started from, so I reckoned I'd return it, too." He held it out to Barnes, who took it with an oath and wheeled like a flash to face his employer.

Crawford was backing toward the wagon, his hand resting on the butt of his gun, and a whiteness of face told of the fear that gripped him. "I'll take my time, right now," growled Barnes. "Damned if I works another day for a low-lived coyote that'd do a thing like that!" The punchers behind him joined in and demanded their wages. Hopalong, still smiling, waved his hand and spoke. "Don't leave him with all these cows on his hands, out here on th' range. If you quits him, wait till you get to Sandy Creek. He ain't no man, he ain't; he's a nasty li'l brat of a kid that couldn't never grow up into a man. So, that bein' true, he ain't goin' to get handled like a man. I'm goin' to lick him, 'stead of shootin' him like he was a man. You know," he smiled, glancing around the little circle, "us cowpunchers don't never carry guns. We don't swear, nor wear chaps,

even if all of us has got 'em on right now. We say 'please'
an' 'thank you' an' never get mad. Not never wearin' a
gun I can't shoot him; but, by God, I can lick him th' worst
he's ever been licked, an' I'm goin' to do it right now."
He wheeled to start after the still-backing cowman, and
leaped sideways as a cloud of smoke swirled around his
hips. Crawford screamed with fear and pain as his Colt
tore loose from his fingers and dropped near the wheel of
the wagon. Terror gripped him and made him incapable
of flight. Who was this man, *what* was he, when he could
draw and fire with such speed and remarkable accuracy?
Crawford's gun had been half raised before the other had
seen it. And before his legs could perform one of their
most cherished functions the limping cowpuncher was on
him, doing his best to make good his promise. The other
half of the Diamond Bar drive crew, attracted by the com-
motion at the chuck wagon, rode in with ready guns, saw
their friends making no attempt at interference, asked a
few terse questions and, putting up their guns, forthwith
joined the circle of interested and pleased spectators to
root for the limping red-head.

Red, back at the Bar-20 wagon, inquired of Cookie the
whereabouts of Hopalong. Cookie, still smarting under
Jimmy's galling fire of language, grunted ignorance and a
wish. Red looked at him, scowling. "You can talk to th'
Kid like that, mebby; but you get a civil tongue in yore
head when any of us grown-ups ask questions." He turned
on his heel, looked searchingly around the plain and
mounting, returned to the herd, perplexed and vexed. As
he left the camp, Jimmy hobbled around the wagon and
stared after him. "Kid!" he snorted. "Grown-ups!" he
sneered. "Huh!" He turned and regarded Cookie evilly.
"Yo're gonna get a good lickin' when I get so I can move
better," he promised. Cookie lifted the red flannel dish-rag
out of the pan and regarded it thoughtfully. "You bet-

ter wait," he agreed pleasantly. "You can't run now. I'm honin' for to drape this mop all over yore wall-eyed face; but I can wait." He sighed and went back to work. "Wish Red would shove you in with th' rest of th' cripples back yonder, an' get you off'n my frazzled nerves."

Jimmy shook his head sorrowfully and limped around the wagon again, where he resumed his sun bath. He dozed off and was surprised to be called for dinner. As he arose, grunting and growling, he chanced to look westward, and his shout apprised his friends of the return of the missing red-head.

Hopalong dismounted at the wagon and grinned cheerfully, despite the suspicious marks on his face. Giving an account of events as they occurred at the Diamond Bar chuck wagon, he wound up with: "Needn't push on so hard, Red. Crawford's herd is due to stay right where it is an' graze peaceful for a week. I heard Barnes give th' order before I left. How's things been out here while I was away?"

Red glared at him, ready to tell his opinion of reckless fools that went up against a gun-packing crowd alone when his friends had never been known to refuse to back up one of their outfit. The words hung on his lips as he waited for a chance to launch them. But when that chance came he had been disarmed by the cheerfulness of his happy friend. "Hoppy," he said, trying to be severe, "yo're nothing' but a crazy, damned fool. But what did they say when you started for huffy Sam like that?"

CHAPTER X

The Hold-up

THE HERD delivered at Sandy Creek had traveled only half way, for the remaining part of the journey would be on the railroad. The work of loading the cars was fast, furious fun to anyone who could find humor enough in his make-up to regard it so. Then came a long, wearying ride for the five men picked from the drive outfit to attend to the cattle on the way to the cattle pens of the city. Their work at last done, they "saw the sights" and were now returning to Sandy Creek.

The baggage smoking-car reeked with strong tobacco, the clouds of smoke shifting with the air currents, and dimly through the haze could be seen several men. Three of these were playing cards near the baggage-room door, while two more lounged in a seat half way down the aisle and on the other side of the car. Across from the card-players, reading a magazine, was a fat man, and near the water cooler was a dyspeptic-looking individual who was grumbling about the country through which he was passing.

The first five, as their wearing apparel proclaimed, were not of the kind usually found on trains, not the drummer, the tourist, or the farmer. Their heads were covered with heavy sombreros, their coats were of thick, black woolens, and their shirts were also of wool. Around the throat of each was a large handkerchief, knotted at the back; their trousers were protected by "chaps," of which three were of goatskin. The boots were tight-fitting, narrow, and with high heels, and to them were strapped heavy spurs. Around the waist, hanging loosely from one hip, each wore a wide belt containing fifty cartridges in the loops, and supporting a huge Colt's revolver, which rested against the thigh.

They were happy and were trying to sing but, owing to different tastes, there was noticeable a lack of harmony. "Oh Susanna" never did go well with "Annie Laurie," and as for "Dixie," it was hopelessly at odds with the other two. But they were happy, exuberantly so, for they had enjoyed their relaxation in the city and now were returning to the station where their horses were waiting to carry them over the two hundred miles which lay between their ranch and the nearest railroad-station.

For a change the city had been pleasant, but after they had spent several days there it lost its charm and would not have been acceptable to them even as a place in which to die. They had spent their money, smoked "top-notcher" cigars, seen the "shows" and feasted each as his fancy dictated, and as behooved cowpunchers with money in their pockets. Now they were glad that every hour reduced the time of their stay in the smoky, jolting, rocking train, for they did not like trains, and this train was particularly bad. So they passed the hours as best they might and waited impatiently for the stop at Sandy Creek, where they had left their horses. Their trip to the "fence country" was now a memory, and they chafed to be again in the saddle on the open, wind-swept range, where miles were insignificant and the silence soothing.

The fat man, despairing of reading, watched the card-players and smiled in good humor as he listened to their conversation, while the dyspeptic, nervously twisting his newspaper, wished that he were at his destination. The baggage-room door opened and the conductor looked down on the card-players and grinned. Skinny moved over in the seat to make room for the genial conductor.

"Sit down, Simms, an' take a hand," he invited. Laughter arose continually and the fat man joined in it, leaning forward more closely to watch the play.

Lanky tossed his cards face down on the board and grinned at the onlooker.

"Billy shore bluffs more on a varigated flush than any man I ever saw."

"Call him once in a while and he'll get cured of it," laughed the fat man, bracing himself as the train swung around a sharp turn.

"He's too smart," growled Billy Williams. "He tried than an' found I didn't have no varigated flushes. Come on, Lanky, if yo're playing cards, put up."

Farther down the car, their feet resting easily on the seat in front of them, Hopalong and Red puffed slowly at their large, black cigars and spoke infrequently, both idly watching the plain flit by in wearying sameness, and both tired and lazy from doing nothing but ride.

"Blast th' cars, anyhow," grunted Hopalong, but he received no reply, for his companion was too disgusted to say anything.

A startling, sudden increase in the roar of the train and a gust of hot, sulphurous smoke caused Hopalong to look up at the brakeman, who came down the swaying aisle as the door slammed shut.

"Phew!" he exclaimed genially. "Why in thunder don't you fellows smoke up?"

Hopalong blew a heavy ring, stretched energetically and grinned: "Much farther to Sandy Creek?"

"Oh, you don't get off for three hours yet," laughed the brakeman.

"That's shore a long time to ride this bronc train," moodily complained Red as the singing began again. "She shore pitches a-plenty," he added.

The train-hand smiled and seated himself on the arm of the front seat:

"Oh, it might be worse."

"Not this side of hades," replied Red with decision, watching his friend, who was slapping the cushions to see the dust fly out: "Hey, let up on that, will you! There's dust a-plenty without no help from you!"

The brakeman glanced at the card-players and then at Hopalong.

"Do your friends always sing like that?" he inquired.

"Mostly, but sometimes it's worse."

"On the level?"

"Shore enough; they're singing 'Dixie,' now. It's their best song."

"That ain't 'Dixie!' "

"Yes it is: that is, most of it."

"Well, then, what's the rest of it?"

"Oh, them's variations of their own," remarked Red, yawning and stretching. "Just wait till they start something sentimental; you'll shore weep."

"I hope they stick to the variations. Say, you must be a pretty nifty gang on the shoot, ain't you?"

"Oh, some," answered Hopalong.

"I wish you fellers had been aboard with us one day about a month ago. We was the wrong end of a hold-up, and we got cleaned out proper, too."

"An' how many of 'em did you get?" asked Hopalong quickly, sitting bolt upright.

The fat man suddenly lost his interest in the card-game and turned an eager ear to the brakeman, while the dyspeptic stopped punching holes in his time-card and listened. The card-players glanced up and then returned to their game, but they, too, were listening.

The brakeman was surprised: "How many did we get! Gosh! we didn't get none! They was six to our five."

"How many cards did you draw, you Piute?" asked Lanky.

"None of yore business; I ain't dealing, an' I wouldn't tell you if I was," retorted Billy.

"Well, I can ask, can't I?"

"Yes—you can, an' did."

"You didn't get none?" cried Hopalong, doubting his ears.

"I should say not!"

"An' they owned th' whole train?"

"They did."

Red laughed. "Th' cleaning-up must have been sumptuous an' elevating."

"Every time I holds threes he allus has better," growled Lanky to Simms.

"On th' level, we couldn't do a thing," the brakeman ran on. "There's a water tank a little farther on, and they must 'a' climbed aboard there when we stopped to connect. When we got into the gulch the train slowed down and stopped and I started to get up to go out and see what was the matter; but I saw *that* when I looked down a gun-barrel. The man at the throttle end of it told me to put up my hands, but they were up as high then as I could get 'em without climbin' on the top of the seat."

"Can't you listen and play at th' same time?" Lanky asked Billy.

"I wasn't countin' on takin' the gun away from him,"

the brakeman continued, "for I was too busy watchin' for the slug to come out of the hole. Pretty soon somebody on the outside whistled and then another feller come in the car; he was the one that did the cleanin' up. All this time there had been a lot of shootin' outside, but now it got worse. Then I heard another whistle and the engine puffed up the track, and about five minutes later there was a big explosion, and then our two robbers backed out of the car among the rocks shootin' back regardless. They busted a lot of windows."

"An' you didn't git none," grumbled Hopalong, regretfully.

"When we got to the express-car, what had been pulled around the turn," continued the brakeman, not heeding the interruption, "we found a wreck. And we found the engineer and fireman standin' over the express-messenger, too scared to know he wouldn't come back no more. The car had been blowed up with dynamite, and his fighting soul went with it. He never knowed he was licked."

"An' nobody tried to help him!" Hopalong exclaimed, wrathfully now.

"Nobody wanted to die with him," replied the brakeman.

"Well," cried the fat man, suddenly reaching for his valise, "I'd like to see anybody try to hold me up!" Saying which he brought forth a small revolver.

"You'd be praying out of your bald spot about that time," muttered the brakeman.

Hopalong and Red turned, perceived the weapon, and then exchanged winks.

"That's a fine shootin'-iron, stranger," gravely remarked Hopalong.

"You bet it is!" purred the owner, proudly. "I paid six dollars for that gun."

Lanky smothered a laugh and his friend grinned

broadly: "I reckon that'd kill a man—if you stuck it in his ear."

"Pshaw!" snorted the dyspeptic, scornfully. "You wouldn't have time to get it out of that grip. Think a train-robber is going to let you unpack? Why don't you carry it in your hip-pocket, where you can get at it quickly?"

There were smiles at the stranger's belief in the hip-pocket fallacy but no one commented upon it.

"Wasn't there no passengers aboard when you was stuck up?" Lanky asked the conductor.

"Yes, but you can't count passengers in on a deal like that."

Hopalong looked around aggressively: "We're passengers, ain't we?"

"You certainly are."

"Well, if any misguided maverick gets it into his fool head to stick *us* up, you see what happens. Don't you know th' fellers outside have all th' worst o' th' deal?"

"They have not!" cried the brakeman.

"They've got all the best of it," asserted the conductor emphatically. "I've been inside, and I know."

"Best nothing!" cried Hopalong. "They are on th' ground, watching a danger-line over a hundred yards long, full of windows and doors. Then they brace th' door of a car full of people. While they climb up the steps they can't see inside, an' then they go an' stick their heads in plain sight. It's an even break who sees th' other first, with th' men inside training their guns on th' glass in th' door!"

"Darned if you ain't right!" enthusiastically cried the fat man.

Hopalong laughed: "It all depends on th' men inside. If they ain't used to handling guns, 'course they won't try to fight. We've been in so many gun-festivals that we wouldn't stop to think. If any coin-collector went an' stuck his ugly face against th' glass in that door he'd turn a backflip off'n th' platform before he knowed he was hit. Is there any chance for a stick-up to-day, d'y think?''

"Can't tell," replied the brakeman. "But this is about the time we have the section-camps' pay on board," he said, going into the baggage end of the car.

Simms leaned over close to Skinny. "It's on this train now, and I'm worried to death about it. I wish we were at Sandy Creek."

"Don't you go worryin' none, then," the puncher replied. "It'll get to Sandy Creek all right."

Hopalong looked out of the window again and saw that there was a gradual change in the nature of the scenery, for the plain was becoming more broken each succeeding mile. Small woods occasionally hurtled past and banks of cuts flashed by like mottled yellow curtains, shutting off the view. Scrub timber stretched away on both sides, a billow sea of green, and miniature valleys lay under the increasing number of trestles twisting and winding toward a high horizon.

Hopalong yawned again: "Well, it's none o' our funeral. If they let us alone I don't reckon we'll take a hand, not even to bust up this monotony."

Red laughed derisively: "Oh, no! Why, you couldn't sit still nohow with a fight going on, an' you know it. An' if it's a stick-up! Wow!"

"Who gave you any say in this?" demanded his friend. "Anyhow, you ain't no angel o' peace, not nohow!"

"Mebby they'll plug yore new sombrero," laughed Red.

Hopalong felt of the article in question: "If any two-laigged wolf plugs my war-bonnet he'll be some sorry, an' so'll his folks," he asserted, rising and going down the aisle for a drink.

Red turned to the brakeman, who had just returned: "Say," he whispered, "get off at th' next stop, shoot off a gun, an' yell, just for fun. Go ahead, it'll be better'n a circus."

"Nix on the circus, says I," hastily replied the other. "I ain't looking for no excitement, an' I ain't paid to amuse th' passengers. I hope we don't even run over a track-torpedo this side of Sandy Creek."

Hopalong returned, and as he came even with them the train slowed.

"What are we stopping for?" he asked, his hand going to his holster.

"To take on water; the tank's right ahead."

"What have you got?" asked Billy, ruffling his cards.

"None of yore business," replied Lanky. "You call when you gets curious."

"Oh, th' devil!" yawned Hopalong, leaning back lazily. "I shore wish I was on my cayuse pounding leather on th' home trail."

"Me, too," grumbled Red, staring out of the window. "Well, we're moving again. It won't be long now before we gets out of this."

The card-game continued, the low-spoken terms being interspersed with casual comment; Hopalong exchanged infrequent remarks with Red, while the brakeman and conductor stared out of the same window. There was noticeable an air of anxiety, and the fat man tried to read his magazine with his thoughts far from the printed page. He read and re-read a single paragraph several times without gaining the slightest knowledge of what it meant, while the dyspeptic passenger fidgeted more and more in his seat, like one sitting on hot coals, anxious and alert.

"We're there now," suddenly remarked the conductor, as the bank of a cut blanked out the view. "It was right here where it happened; the turn's farther on."

"How many cards did you draw, Skinny?" asked Lanky.

"Three; drawin' to a straight flush," laughed the dealer.

"Here's the turn! We're through all right," exclaimed the brakeman.

Suddenly there was a rumbling bump, a screeching of

air-brakes and the grinding and rattle of couplings and
pins as the train slowed down and stopped with a suddenness that snapped the passengers forward and back. The
conductor and brakeman leaped to their feet, where the
latter stood quietly during a moment of indecision.

A shot was heard and the conductor's hand, raised
quickly to the whistle-rope sent blast after blast shrieking
over the land. A babel of shouting burst from the other
coaches and, as the whistle shrieked without pause, a shot
was heard close at hand and the conductor reeled suddenly and sank into a seat, limp and silent.

At the first jerk of the train the card-players threw the
board from across their knees, scattering the cards over
the floor, and crouching, gained the center of the aisle,
intently peering through the windows, their Colts ready
for instant use. Hopalong and Red were also in the aisle,
and when the conductor had reeled Hopalong's Colt exploded and the man outside threw up his arms and pitched
forward.

"Good boy, Hopalong!" cried Skinny, who was fighting
mad.

Hopalong wheeled and crouched, watching the door,
and it was not long before a masked face appeared on the
farther side of the glass. Hopalong fired and a splotch of
red stained the white mask as the robber fell against the
door and slid to the platform.

"Hear that shooting?" cried the brakeman. "They're at
the messenger. They'll blow him up!"

"Come on, fellers!" cried Hopalong, leaping toward the
door, closely followed by his friends.

They stepped over the obstruction on the platform and
jumped to the ground on the side of the car farthest from
the robbers.

"Shoot under the cars for legs," whispered Skinny.
"That'll bring 'em down where we can get 'em."

"Which is a good idea," replied Red, dropping quickly and looking under the car.

"Somebody's going to be surprised, all right," exulted Hopalong.

The firing on the other side of the train was heavy, being for the purpose of terrifying the passengers and to forestall concerted resistance. The robbers could not distinguish between the many reports and did not know they were being opposed, or that two of their number were dead.

A whinny reached Hopalong's ears and he located it in a small grove ahead of him: "Well, we know where th' cayuses are in case they make a break."

A white and scared face peered out of the cab-window and Hopalong stopped his finger just in time, for the inquisitive man wore the cap of fireman.

"You idiot!" muttered the gunman, angrily. "Get back!" he ordered.

A pair of legs ran swiftly along the other side of the car and Red and Skinny fired instantly. The legs bent, their owner falling forward behind the rear truck, where he was screened from sight.

"They had it their own way before!" gritted Skinny. "Now we'll see if they can stand th' iron!"

By this time Hopalong and Red were crawling under the express-car and were so preoccupied that they did not notice the faint blue streak of smoke immediately over their heads. Then Red glanced up to see what it was that sizzed, saw the glowing end of a three-inch fuse, and blanched. It was death not to dare and his hand shot up and back, and the dynamite cartridge sailed far behind him to the edge of the embankment, where it hung on a bush.

"Good!" panted Hopalong. "We'll pay 'em for that!"

"They're worse'n rustlers!"

They could hear the messenger running about over their

heads, dragging and up-ending heavy objects against the doors of the car, and Hopalong laughed grimly:

"Luck's with this messenger, all right."

"It ought to be—he's a fighter."

"Where are they? Have they tumbled to our game?"

"They're waiting for the explosion, you chump."

"Stay where you are then. Wait till they come out to see what's th' matter with it."

Red snorted: "Wait nothing!"

"All right, then; I'm with you. Get out of my way."

"I've been in situations some peculiar, but this beats 'em all," Red chuckled, crawling forward.

The robber by the car truck revived enough to realize that something was radically wrong, and shouted a warning as he raised himself on his elbow to fire at Skinny but the alert puncher shot first.

As Hopalong and Red emerged from beneath the car and rose to their feet there was a terrific explosion and they were knocked to the ground, while a sudden, heavy shower of stones and earth rained down over everything. The two punchers were not hurt and they arose to their feet in time to see the engineer and fireman roll out of the cab and crawl along the track on their hands and knees, dazed and weakened by the concussion.

Suddenly, from one of the day-coaches, a masked man looked out, saw the two punchers, and cried:

"It's all up! Save yourselves!"

As Hopalong and Red looked around, still dazed, he fired at them, the bullet singing past Hopalong's ear. Red smothered a curse and reeled as his friend grasped him. A wound over his right eye was bleeding profusely and Hopalong's face cleared of its look of anxiety when he realized that it was not serious.

"They creased you! Blamed near got you for keeps!" he cried, wiping away the blood with his sleeve.

Red, slightly stunned, opened his eyes and looked about confusedly. "Who done that! Where is he?"

"Don't know, but I'll shore find out," Hopalong replied. "Can you stand alone?"

Red pushed himself free and leaned against the car for support: "Course I can! Git that cuss!"

When Skinny heard the robber shout the warning he wheeled and ran back, intently watching the windows and doors of the car for trouble.

"We'll finish yore tally right here!" he muttered.

When he reached the smoker he turned and went toward the rear, where he found Lanky and Billy lying under the platform. Billy was looking back and guarding their rear, while his companion watched the clump of trees where the second herd of horses was known to be. Just as they were joined by their foreman, they saw two men run across the track, fifty yards distant, and into the grove, both going so rapidly as to give no chance for a shot at them.

"There they are!" shouted Skinny, opening fire on the grove.

At that instant Hopalong turned the rear platform and saw the brakeman leap out of the door with a Winchester in his hands. The puncher sprang up the steps, wrenched the rifle from its owner, and, tossing it to Skinny, cried: "Here, this is better!"

"Too late," grunted the puncher, looking up, but Hopalong had become lost to sight among the rocks along the right of way. "If I only had this a minute ago!" he grumbled.

The men in the grove, now in the saddle, turned and opened fire on the group by the train, driving them back to shelter. Skinny, taking advantage of the cover afforded, ran toward the grove, ordering his friends to spread out and surround it; but it was too late, for at that minute galloping was heard and it grew rapidly fainter.

Red appeared at the end of the train: "Where's th' rest of the coyotes?"

"Two of 'em got away," Lanky replied.

"Ya-ho!" shouted Hopalong from the grove. "Don't none of you fools shoot! I'm coming out. They plumb got away!"

"They near got *you*, Red," Skinny cried.

"Nears don't count," Red laughed.

"Did you ever notice Hopalong when he's fighting mad?" asked Lanky, grinning at the man who was leaving the woods. "He allus wears his sombrero hanging on one ear. Look at it now!"

"Who touched off that cannon some time back?" asked Billy.

"I did. It was an anti-gravity cartridge what I found sizzling on a rod under th' floor of th' express car," replied Red.

"Why didn't you pinch out th' fuse 'stead of blowing everything up?" Lanky asked.

"I reckon I was some hasty," grinned Red.

"It blowed me under th' car an' my lid through a windy," cried Billy. "An' Skinny, he went up in th' air like a shore-'nough grasshopper."

Hopalong joined them, grinning broadly: "Hey, reckon ridin' in th' cars ain't so bad after all, is it?"

"Holy smoke!" cried Skinny. "What's that a-popping?"

Hopalong, Colt in hand, leaped to the side of the train and looked along it, the others close behind him, and saw the fat man with his head and arm out of the window, blazing away into the air, which increased the panic in the coaches. Hopalong grinned and fired into the ground, and the fat man nearly dislocated parts of his anatomy by his hasty disappearance.

"Reckon he plumb forgot all about his fine, six-dollar gun till just now," Skinny laughed.

"Oh, he's making good," Red replied. "He said he'd take a hand if anything busted loose. It's a good thing he didn't come to life while me an' Hoppy was under his windy looking for laigs."

"Reckon some of us better go in th' cars an' quiet th' stampede," Skinny remarked, mounting the steps, followed by Hopalong. "They're shore *loco*."

The uproar in the coach ceased abruptly when the two punchers stepped through the door, the inmates shrinking into their seats, frightened into silence. Skinny and his companion did not make a reassuring sight, for they were grimy with burned powder and dust, and Hopalong's sleeve was stained with Red's blood.

"Oh, my jewels, my pretty jewels," sobbed a woman, staring at Skinny and wringing her hands.

"Ma'am, we shore don't want yore jewelry," replied Skinny, earnestly. "Ca'm yoreself; we don't want nothin'."

"*I* don't want that!" growled Hopalong, pushing a wallet from him. "How many times do you want us to tell you we don't want nothin'? We ain't robbers; we licked th' robbers."

Suddenly he stooped and, grasping a pair of legs which protruded into the aisle obstructing the passage, straightened up and backed toward Red, who had just entered the car, dragging into sight a portly gentleman, who kicked and struggled and squealed, as he grabbed at the stanchions of seats to stay his progress. Red stepped aside between two seats and let his friend pass, and then leaned over and grasped the portly gentleman's coat-collar. He tugged energetically and lifted the frightened man clear of the aisle and deposited him across the back of a seat, face down, where he hung balanced, yelling and kicking.

"Shut yore face, you cave-hunter!" cried Red in disgust. "Stop that infernal noise! You fat fellers make all yore noise after th' fighting is all over!"

The man on the seat, suddenly realizing what a sight he made, rolled off his perch and sat up, now more angry than frightened. He glared at Red's grinning face and sputtered:

"It's an outrage! It's an outrage! I'll have you hung for this day's work, young man!"

"That's right," grinned Hopalong. "He shore deserves it. I told him more'n once that he'd get strung up some day."

"Yes, and you, too!"

"Please don't," begged Hopalong. "I don't want t' die!"

Tense as the past quarter of an hour had been a titter ran along the car and, fuming impotently, the portly gentleman fled into the smoker.

"I'll bet he had a six-dollar gun, too," laughed Red.

"I'll bet he's calling hisself names right about now," Hopalong replied. Then he turned to reply to a woman: "Yes, ma'am, we did. But they wasn't real badmen."

At this a young woman, who was about as pretty as any young woman could be, arose and ran to Hopalong and, impulsively throwing her arms around his neck, cried: "You brave man! You hero! You dear!"

"Skinny! Red! Help!" cried the frightened and embarrassed puncher, struggling to get free.

She kissed him on the cheek, which flamed even more red as he made frantic efforts to keep his head back.

"Ma'am!" he cried, desperately. "Leggo, ma'am! Leggo!"

"Oh! Ho! Ho!" roared Red, weak from his mirth and, not looking to see what he was doing, he dropped into a seat beside another woman. He was on his feet instantly; fearing that he would have to go through the ordeal his friend was going through, he fled down the aisle, closely followed by Hopalong, who by this time had managed to break away. Skinny backed off suspiciously and kept close watch on Hopalong's admirer.

Just then the brakeman entered the car, grinning, and Skinny asked about the condition of the conductor.

"Oh, he's all right now," the brakeman replied. "They

shot him through the arm, but he's repaired and out boss-in' the job of clearin' the rocks off the track. He's a little shaky yet, but he'll come around all right."

"That's good. I'm shore glad to hear it."

"Won't you wear this pin as a small token of my grati-tude?" asked a voice at Skinny's shoulder.

He wheeled and raised his sombrero, a flush stealing over his face:

"Thank you, ma'am, but I don't want no pay. We was plumb glad to do it."

"But this is not pay! It's just a trifling token of my ap-preciation of your courage, just something to remind you of it. I shall feel hurt if you refuse."

Her quick fingers had pinned it to his shirt while she spoke and he thanked her as well as his embarrassment would permit. Then there was a rush toward him and, having visions of a shirt looking like a jeweler's window, he turned and fled from the car, crying: "Pin 'em on th' brakeman!"

He found the outfit working at a pile of rocks on the track, under the supervision of the conductor, and Hopa-long looked up apprehensively at Skinny's approach.

"Lord!" he ejaculated, grinning sheepishly, "I was some scairt you was a woman."

Red dropped the rock he was carrying and laughed de-risively.

"Oh, yo're a brave man, you are! Scared to death by a purty female girl! If I'd 'a' been you I wouldn't 'a' run, not a step!"

Hopalong looked at him witheringly: "Oh, no! You wouldn't 'a' run! You'd dropped dead in your tracks, you would!"

"You was both of you a whole lot scared," Skinny laughed. Then, turning to the conductor: "How do you feel, Simms?"

"Oh, I'm all right: but it took the starch out of me for awhile."

"Well, I don't wonder, not a bit."

"You fellows certainly don't waste any time getting busy," Simms laughed.

"That's the secret of gun-fightin'," replied Skinny.

"Well, you're a fine crowd all right. Any time you want to go any place when you're broke, climb aboard my train and I'll see't you get there."

"Much obliged."

Simms turned to the express-car: "Hey, Jackson! You can open up now if you want to."

But the express-messenger was suspicious, fearing that the conductor was talking with a gun at his head: "You go to hell!" he called back.

"Honest!" laughed Simms. "Some cowboy friends o' mine licked the gang. Didn't you hear that dynamite go off? If they hadn't fished it out from under your feet you'd be communing with the angels 'bout now."

For a moment there was no response, and then Jackson could be heard dragging things away from the door. When he was told of the cartridge and Red had been pointed out to him as the man who had saved his life, he leaped to the ground and ran to where that puncher was engaged in carrying the ever-silenced robbers to the baggage-car. He shook hands with Red, who laughed deprecatingly, and then turned and assisted him.

Hopalong came up and grinned: "Say, there's some cayuses in that grove up th' track; shall I go up an' get 'em?"

"Shore! I'll go an' get 'em with you," replied Skinny.

In the grove they found seven horses picketed, two of them being pack-animals, and they led them forth and reached the train as the others came up.

"Well, here's five saddled cayuses, an' two others," Skinny grinned.

"Then we can ride th' rest of th' way in th' saddle instead of in that blamed train," Red eagerly suggested.

"That's just what we can do," replied Skinny. "Leather beats car-seats any time. How far are we from Sandy Creek, Simms?"

"About twenty miles."

"An' we can ride along th' track, too," suggested Hopalong.

"We shore can," laughed Skinny, shaking hands with the train-crew: "We're some glad we rode with you this trip: we've had a fine time."

"And we're glad you did," Simms replied, "for that ain't no joke, either."

Hopalong and the others had mounted and were busy waving their sombreros and bowing to the heads and handkerchiefs which were decorating the car-windows.

"All aboard!" shouted the conductor, and cheers and good wishes rang out and were replied to by bows and waving of sombreros. Then Hopalong jerked his gun loose and emptied it into the air, his companions doing likewise. Suddenly five reports rang out from the smoker and they cheered the fat man as he waved at them. They sat quietly and watched the train until the last handkerchief became lost to sight around a curve, but the screeching whistle could be heard for a long time.

"Gee!" laughed Hopalong as they rode on after the train, "won't th' fellers home on th' ranch be a whole lot sore when they hears about the good time what they missed!"

CHAPTER XI

Sammy Finds a Friend

THE LONG train ride and the excitement were over and the outfit, homeward bound, loped along the trail, noisily discussing their exciting and humorous experiences and laughingly commented upon Hopalong's decision to follow them later. They could not understand why he should be interested in a town like Sandy Creek after a week spent in the city.

Back in the little cow-town their friend was standing in the office of the hotel, gazing abstractedly out of the window. His eyes caught and focused on a woman who was walking slowly along the other side of the square and finally paused before McCall's "Palace," a combination saloon, dance and gambling hall. He smiled cynically as his memory ran back over those other women he had seen in cow-towns and wondered how it was that the men of the ranges could rise to a chivalry that was famed. At that distance she was strikingly pretty. Her complexion was an alluring blend of color that the gold of her hair crowned like a burst of sunshine. He noticed that her eyebrows were too prominent, too black and heavy to be Nature's contribution. And there was about her a certain forwardness, a dash that bespoke no bashful Miss; and her clothes, though well-fitting, somehow did not please his untrained eye. A sudden impulse seized him and he strode to the door and crossed the dusty square, avoiding the piles of rusted cans, broken bottles and other rubbish that littered it.

She had become interested in a dingy window but turned to greet him with a resplendent smile as he stepped to the wooden walk. He noted with displeasure that the white teeth displayed two shining panels of gold that drew his eyes irresistibly; and then and there he hated gold teeth.

"Hello," she laughed. "I'm glad to see somebody that's alive in this town. Ain't it awful?"

He instinctively removed his sombrero and was conscious that his habitual bashfulness in the presence of members of her sex was somehow lacking. "Why, I don't see nothin' extra dead about it," he replied. "Most of these towns are this way in daylight. Th' moths ain't out yet. You should 'a' been here last night!"

"Yes? But you're out; an' you look like you might be able to fly," she replied.

"Yes; I suppose so," he laughed.

"I see you wear *two* of 'em," she said, glancing at his guns. "Ain't one of them things enough?"

"One usually is, mostly," he assented. "But I'm pig-headed, so I wears two."

"Ain't it awful hard to use two of 'em at once?" she asked, her tone flattering. "Then you're one of them two-gun men I've heard about, ain't you?"

"An' seen?" he smiled.

"Yes, I've seen a couple. Where you goin' so early?"

"Just lookin' th' town over," he answered, glancing over

her shoulder at a cub of a cow-puncher who had opened the door of the "Retreat," but stopped in his tracks when he saw the couple in front of McCall's. There was a look of surprised interest on the cub's face, and it swiftly changed to one of envious interest. Hopalong's glance did not linger, but swept carelessly along the row of shacks and back to his companion's face without betraying his discovery.

"Well; you can look it over in about ten seconds, from th' outside," she rejoined. "An' it's so dusty out here. My throat is awful dry already."

He hadn't noticed any dust in the air, but he nodded. "Yes; thirsty?"

"Well, it ain't polite or ladylike to say yes," she demurred, "but I really am."

He held open the door of the "Palace" and preceded her to the dance hall, where she rippled the keys of the old piano as she swept past it. The order given and served, he sipped at his glass and carried on his share of a light conversation until, suddenly, he arose and made his apologies. "I got to attend to somethin'," he regretted as he picked up his sombrero and turned. "See you later."

"Why!" she exclaimed. "I was just beginnin' to get acquainted!"

"A moth without money ain't no good," he smiled. "I'm goin' out to find th' money. When I'm in good company I like to spend. See you later?" He bowed as she nodded, and departed.

Emerging from McCall's he glanced at the "Retreat" and sauntered toward it. When he entered he found the cub resting his elbows on the pine bar, arguing with the bartender about the cigars sold in the establishment. The cub glanced up and appealed to the newcomer. "Ain't they?" he demanded.

Hopalong nodded. "I reckon so. But what is it about?"

"These cigars," explained the cub, ruefully. "I was just sayin' there ain't a good one in town."

"You lose," replied Hopalong. "Are you shore you knows a good cigar when you smokes it?"

"I know it so well that I ain't found one since I left Kansas City. You said I lose. Do *you* know one well enough to be a judge?"

Hopalong reached to his vest pocket, extracted a cigar and handed it to the cub, who took it hesitatingly. "Why, I'm much obliged. I—I didn't mean that—you know."

Hopalong nodded and rearranged the cigar's twin-brothers in his pocket. He would be relieved when they were smoked, for they made him nervous with their frailty. The cub lighted the cigar and an unaffected grin of delight wreathed his features as the smoke issued from his nostrils. "Who sells 'em?" he demanded, excitedly.

"Corson an' Lukins, up th' hill from th' depot," answered Hopalong. "Like it?"

"Like it! Why, stranger, I used to spend most of my week's pocket money for these." He paused and stared at the smiling puncher. "Did you say Corson an' Lukins?" he demanded incredulously. "Well, I'll be hanged! When was you there?"

"Last week. Here, bartender; liquor for all hands."

The cub touched the glass to his lips and waved his hand at a table. Seated across from the stranger with the heaven-sent cigars he ordered the second round, and when he went to pay for it he drew out a big roll of bills and peeled off the one on the outside.

Hopalong frowned. "Sonny," he said in a low voice, "it ain't none of my affair, but you oughta put that wad away an' forget you have it when out in public. You shouldn't tempt yore feller men like that."

The cub laughed: "Oh, I had my eye teeth cut long ago. Play a little game?"

Hopalong was amused. "Didn't I just tell you not to tempt yore feller men?"

The cub grinned. "I reckon it'll fade quick, anyhow; but it took me six months' hard work to get it together. It'll last about six days, I suppose."

"Six hours, if you plays every man that comes along," corrected Hopalong.

"Well, mebby," admitted the cub. "Say: that was one fine girl you was talkin' to, all right," he grinned.

Hopalong studied him a moment. "Not meanin' no offense, what's yore name?"

"Sammy Porter; why?"

"Well, Sammy," remarked Hopalong as he arose. "I reckon we'll meet again before I leave. You was remarkin' she was a fine girl. I admit it; she was. So long," and he started for the door.

Sammy flushed. "Why, I—I didn't mean nothin'!" he exclaimed. "I just happened to think about her—that's all! You know, I saw you talkin' to her. Of course, you saw her first," he explained.

Hopalong turned and smiled kindly. "You didn't say nothin' to offend me. I was just startin' when you spoke. But as long as you mentioned it I'll say that my interest in th' lady was only brief. Her interest in me was th' same. Beyond lettin' you know that I'll add that I don't generally discuss wimmin. I'll see you later," and, nodding cheerily, he went out and closed the door behind him.

Hopalong leaned lazily against the hotel, out of reach of the spring wind, which was still sharp, and basked in the warmth of the timid sun. He regarded the little cow-town cynically but smilingly and found no particular fault with it. Existing because the railroad construction work of the season before had chanced to stop on the eastern bank of the deceptive creek, and because of the nearness of three drive trails, one of them important, the town had

sprung up, mushroom-like, almost in a night. Facing on
the square were two general stores, the railroad station
and buildings, two restaurants, a dozen saloons where
gambling either was the main attraction or an ambitious
side-line, McCall's place and a barber shop with a dingy,
bullet-peppered red-and-white pole set close to the door.
Between the barber shop and McCall's was a narrow
space, and the windows of the two buildings, while not
opposite, opened on the little strip of ground separating
them.

Rubbing a hand across his chin he regarded the barber
shop thoughtfully and finally pushed away from the sun-
warmed wall of the hotel and started lazily toward the
red-and-white pole. As he did so the tin-panny notes of a
piano redoubled and a woman's voice shrilly arose to a
high note, flatted, broke and swiftly dropped an octave.
He squirmed and looked speculatively along the westward
trail, wondering how far away his outfit was and why he
had not gone with them. Another soaring note that did
not flat and a crashing chord from the piano were followed by a burst of uproarious, reckless laughter. Hopalong frowned, snapped his fingers in sudden decision and
stepped briskly toward the barber shop as the piano began anew.

Entering quietly and closing the door softly, he glanced
appraisingly through the windows and made known his
wants in a low voice. "I want a shave, haircut, shampoo,
an' anythin' else you can think of. I'm tired an' don't want
to talk. Take yore own time an' do a good job; an' if I'm
asleep when yo're through, don't wake me till somebody
else wants th' chair. Savvy? All right—start in."

In McCall's a stolid bartender listened to the snatches
of conversation that filtered under the door to the dance
hall alongside and on his face there at times flickered the
suggestion of a cynical smile. A heavy, dark complex-
ioned man entered from the street and glanced at the

closed door of the dance hall. The bartender nodded and held up a staying hand, after which he shoved a drink across the bar. The heavy-set man carefully wiped a few drops of spilled liquor from his white, tapering hands and seated himself with a sigh of relief, and became busy with his thoughts until the time should come when he would be needed.

On the other side of that door a little comedy was being enacted. The musician, a woman, toyed with the keys of the warped and scratched piano, the dim light from the shaded windows mercifully hiding the paint and the hardness of her face and helping the jewelry, with which her hands were covered, keep its tawdry secret.

"I don't see what makes you so touchy," grumbled Sammy in a pout. "I ain't goin' to hurt you if I touch yore arm." He was flushed and there was a suspicious unsteadiness in his voice.

She laughed. "Why, I thought you wanted to talk?"

"I did," he admitted, sullenly; "but there's a limit to most wants. Oh, well: go ahead an' play. That last piece was all right; but give us a gallop or a mazurka—anything lively. Better yet, a caprice: it's in keepin' with yore temperament. If you was to try to interpert mine you'd have to dig it out of Verdi an' toll a funeral bell."

"Say; who told you so much about music?" she demanded.

"Th' man that makes harmonicas," he grinned. He arose and took a step toward her, but she retreated swiftly, smiling. "Now behave yourself, for a little while, at least. What's th' matter with you, anyhow? What makes you so silly?"

"You, of course. I don't see no purty wimmin out on th' range, an' you went to my head th' minute I laid eyes on you. *I* ain't in no hurry to leave this town, now nohow."

"I'm afraid you're going to be awful when you grow up. But you're a nice boy to say such pretty things. Here," she said, filling his glass and handing it to him, "let's drink another toast—you know such nice ones."

"Yes; an' if I don't run out of 'em purty soon I'll have to hunt a solid, immovable corner somewheres; an' there ain't nothin' solid or immovable about *this* room at present," he growled. "What you allus drinkin' to somethin' for? Well, here's a toast—I don't know any more fancy ones. Here's to—*you!*"

"That's nicer than—oh, pshaw!" she exclaimed, pouting. "An' you wouldn't drink a full glass to *that* one. You must think I'm nice, when you renig like that! Don't tell me any more pretty things—an' stop right where you are! Think you can hang onto me after that? Well, that's better; why didn't you do it th' first time? You can be a nice boy when you want to."

He flushed angrily. "Will you stop callin' me a boy?" he demanded unsteadily. "I ain't no kid! I do a man's work, earn a man's pay, an' I spend it like a man."

"An' drink a boy's drink," she teased. "You'll grow up some day." She reached forward and filled his glass again, for an instant letting her cheek touch his. Swiftly evading him she laughed and patted him on the head. "Here, *man*," she taunted, "drink this if you dare!"

He frowned at her but gulped down the liquor. "There, like a fool!" he grumbled, bitterly. "You tryin' to get me drunk?" he demanded suddenly in a heavy voice.

She threw back her head and regarded him coldly. "It will do me no good. Why should I? I merely wanted to see if you would take a dare, if you were a man. You are either not sober now, or you are insultingly impolite. I don't care to waste any more words or time with you," and she turned haughtily toward the door.

He had leaned against the piano, but now he lurched forward and cried out. "I'm sorry if I hurt yore feelin's that way—I shore didn't mean to. Ain't we goin' to make up?" he asked, anxiously.

"Do you mean that?" she demanded, pausing and looking around.

"You know I do, Annie. Le's make up—come on; le's make up."

"Well; I'll try you, an' see."

"Play some more. You play beautiful," he assured her with heavy gravity.

"I'm tired of—but, say: Can you play poker?" she asked, eagerly.

"Why, shore; who can't?"

"Well, I can't, for one. I want to learn, so I can win my money back from Jim. He taught me, but all I had time to learn was how to lose."

Sammy regarded her in puzzled surprise and gradually the idea became plain. "Did he teach you, an' win money from you? Did he *keep* it?" he finally blurted, his face flushed a deeper red from anger.

She nodded. "Why, yes; why?"

He looked around for his sombrero, muttering savagely.

"Where you goin'?" she asked in surprise.

"To get it back. He ain't goin' to keep it, th' coyote!"

"Why, he won't give it back to you if he wouldn't to me. Anyhow, he won it."

"*Won* it!" he snapped. "He stole it, that's how much he won it. He'll give it back or get shot."

"Now look here," she said, quickly. "You ain't goin' gunnin' for no friend of mine. If you want to get that money for me, an' I certainly can use it about now, you got to try some other way. Say! Why don't you win it from him?" she exulted. "That's th' way—get it back th' way it went."

He weighed her words and a grin slowly crept across his face. "Why, I reckon you called it, that time, Annie. That's th' way I'll try first, anyhow, Li'l Girl. Where is this good friend of yourn that steals yore money? Where is this feller?"

As if in answer to his inquiry the heavy-set man strolled in, humming cheerily. And as he did so the sleepy occupant of the barber's chair slowly awoke, rubbed his eyes, stretched luxuriously and, paying his bill, loafed out and lazily sauntered down the street, swearing softly.

"Why, here he is now," laughed the woman. "You must 'a' heard us talkin' about you, Jim. I'm goin' to get my money back—this is Mr. Porter, Jim, who's goin' to do it."

The gambler smiled and held out his hand. "Howd'y, Mr. Porter," he said.

Sammy glared at him: "Put yore paw down," he said, thickly. "I ain't shakin' han's with no dogs or tin-horns."

The gambler recoiled and flushed, fighting hard to repress his anger. "What you mean?" he growled, furiously.

"What I said. If you want revenge sit down there an' play, if you've got th' nerve to play with a man. I never let no coyote steal a woman's money, an' I'm goin' to get Annie her twenty. Savvy?"

The gambler's reply was a snarl. "Play!" he sneered. "I'll play, all right. It'll take more'n a sassy kid to get that money back, too. I'm goin' to take yore last red cent. You can't talk to me like that an' get it over. An' don't let me hear you call her 'Annie' no more, neither. Yo're too cussed familiar!"

Her hand on Sammy's arm stopped the draw and he let the gun drop back into the holster. *"No!"* she whispered. "Make a fool of him, Sammy! Beat him at his own game."

Sammy nodded and scowled blackly. "I call th' names as suits me," he retorted. "When I see you on th' street I'm goin' to call you some that I'm savin' up now because a lady's present. They're hefty, too."

At first he won, but always small amounts. Becoming reckless, he plunged heavily on a fair hand and lost. He plunged again on a better hand and lost. Then he steadied as much as his befuddled brain would permit and played

a careful game, winning a small pot. Another small winning destroyed his caution and he plunged again, losing
heavily. Steadying himself once more he began a new
deal with excess caution and was bluffed out of the pot,
the gambler sneeringly showing his cards as he threw
them down. Sammy glanced around to say something
to the woman, but found she had gone. "Aw, never mind
her!" growled his opponent. "She'll be back—she can't stay
away from a kid like you."

The woman was passing through the barroom and,
winking at the bartender, opened the door and stepped
to the street. She smiled as she caught sight of the limping
stranger coming toward her. He might have found money,
but she was certain he had found something else and in
generous quantities. He removed his sombrero with an
exaggerated sweep of his hand and hastened to meet her,
walking with the conscious erectness of a man whose feet
are the last part of him to succumb. "Hullo, Sugar," he
grinned. "I found some, a'right. Now we'll have some music. Come 'long."

"There ain't no hurry," she answered. "We'll take a little walk first."

"No, we won't. We'll have some music an' somethin' to
drink. If you won't make th' music, I will; or shoot up th'
machine. Come 'long, Sugar," he leered, pushing open the
door with a resounding slam. He nodded to the bartender
and apologized. "No harm meant, Friend. It sorta slipped;
jus' slipped, tha's all. Th' young lady an' me is goin' to
have some music. What? All right for you, Sugar! Then I'll
make it myself," and he paraded stiffly toward the inner
door.

The bartender leaned suddenly forward. "Keep out of
there! You'll bust that pianner!"

The puncher stopped with a jerk, swung ponderously
on his heel and leveled a forefinger at the dispenser of
drinks. "I won't," he said. "An' if I do, I'll pay for it. Come

on, Sugar—le's play th' old thing, jus' for spite." Grasping her arm he gently but firmly escorted her into the dance hall and seated her at the piano. As he straightened up he noticed the card players and, bowing low to her, turned and addressed them.

"Gents," he announced, bowing again, "we are goin' to have a li'l music an' we hopes you won't objec'. Not that we gives a damn, but we jus' hopes you won't." He laughed loudly at his joke and leaned against the piano. "Let 'er go," he cried, beating time. "Allaman lef' an' ladies change! Swing yore partner's gal—I mean, swing some other gal: but what's th' diff'rence? All join han's an' hop to th' middle—nope! It's all han's roun' an' swing 'em again. But it don't make no diff'rence, does it, Lulu?" He whooped loudly and marched across the room, executed a few fancy steps and marched back again. As he passed the card table Sammy threw down his hand and arose with a curse. The marcher stopped, fiddled a bit with his feet until obtaining his balance, and then regarded the youth quizzically. "S'matter, Sonny?" he inquired.

Sammy scowled, slowly recognized the owner of the imported cigars and shook his head. "Big han's, but not big enough; an' I lost my pile." Staggering to the piano he plumped down on a chair near it and watched the rippling fingers of the player in drunken interest.

The hilarious cowpuncher, leaning backward perilously, recovered his poise for a moment and then lurched forward into the chair the youth had just left. "Come on, pardner," he grinned across at the gambler. "Le's gamble. I been honin' for a game, an' here she is." He picked up the cards, shuffled them clumsily and pushed them out for the cut. The gambler hesitated, considered and then turned over a jack. He lost the deal and shoved out a quarter without interest.

The puncher leaned over, looked at it closely and grinned. "Two bits? That ain't poker; that's—that's dominoes!" he blurted, angrily, with the quick change of mood of a man in his cups.

"I ain't anxious to play," replied the gambler. "I'll kill a li'l time at a two-bit game, though. Otherwise I'll quit."

"A'right," replied the dealer. "I didn't expec' nothin' else from a tin-horn, no how. I want two cards after you get yourn." The gambler called on the second raise and smiled to himself when he saw that his opponent had drawn to a pair and an ace. He won on his own deal and on the one following.

The puncher increased the ante on the fourth deal and looked up inquiringly, a grin on his face. "Le's move out th' infant class," he suggested.

The gambler regarded him sharply. "Well, th' other *was* sorta tender," he admitted, nodding.

The puncher pulled out a handful of gold coins and clumsily tried to stack them, which he succeeded in doing after three attempts. He was so busy that he did not notice the look in the other's eyes. Picking up his hand he winked at it and discarded one. "Goin' to raise th' ante a few," he chuckled. "I got a feelin' I'm goin' t' be lucky." When the card was dealt to him he let it lay and bet heavily. The gambler saw it and raised in turn, and the puncher, frowning in indecision, nodded his head wisely and met it, calling as he did so. His four fives were just two spots shy to win and he grumbled loudly at his luck. "Huh," he finished, "she's a jack pot, eh?" He slid a double eagle out to the center of the table and laughed recklessly. The deals went around rapidly, each one calling for a ten-dollar sweetener and when the seventh hand was dealt the puncher picked his cards and laughed. "She's open," he cried, "for fifty," and shoved out the money with one hand while he dug up a reserve pile from his pocket with the other.

The gambler saw the opener and raised it fifty, smiling at his opponent's expression. The puncher grunted his surprise, studied his hand, glanced at the pot and shrugging his shoulders, saw the raise. He drew two cards and chuckled as he slid them into his hand; but before the dealer could make his own draw the puncher's chuckle died out and he stared over the gambler's shoulder. With an oath he jerked out his gun and fired. The gambler leaped to his feet and whirled around to look behind. Then he angrily faced the frowning puncher. "What you think yo're doin'?" he demanded, his hand resting inside his coat, the thumb hooked over the edge of the vest.

The puncher waved his hand apologetically. "I never have no luck when I sees a cat," he explained. "A black cat is worse; but a yaller one's bad enough. I'll bet that yaller devil won't come back in a hurry—judgin' by th' way it started. I won't miss him, if he does."

The gambler, still frowning, glanced at the deck suspiciously and saw that it lay as he had dropped it. The bartender, grinning at them from the door, cracked a joke and went back to the bar. Sammy, after a wild look around, settled back in his chair and soothed the pianist a little before going back to sleep.

Drawing two cards the gambler shoved them in his hand without a change in his expression—but he was greatly puzzled. It was seldom that he bungled and he was not certain that he had. The discard contained the right number of cards and his opponent's face gave no hint to the thoughts behind it. He hesitated before he saw the bet— ten dollars was not much, for the size of the pot justified more. He slowly saw it, willing to lose the ten in order to see his opponent's cards. There was something he wished to know, and he wanted to know it as soon as he could. "I call that," he said. The puncher's expression of tenseness relaxed into one of great relief and he hurriedly dropped his cards. Three kings, an eight, and a deuce was his offering. The gambler laid down a pair of queens, a ten, an eight and a four, waved his hand and smiled. "It's just as well I didn't draw another queen," he observed, calmly. "I might 'a' raised once for luck."

The puncher raked in the pot and turned around in his chair. "I cleaned up that time," he exulted to the woman. She had stopped playing and was stroking Sammy's forehead. Smiling at the exuberant winner she nodded. "You should have let the cat stay—I think it really brought you luck." He shook his head emphatically. "*No*, ma'am! It was chasin' it away as did that. That's what did it, a'right."

The gambler glanced quickly at the two top cards on the deck and was picking up those scattered on the table when his opponent turned around again. How that queen and ten had got two cards too deep puzzled him greatly—he was willing to wager even money that he would not look away again until the game was finished, not if all the cats in the world were being slaughtered. One hundred and ninety dollars was too much money to pay for being caught off his guard, as he was tempted to believe he had been. He did not know how much liquor the other had consumed, but he seemed to be sobering rapidly.

The next few deals did not amount to much. Then a jackpot came around and was pushed hard. The puncher was dealing and as he picked up the deck after the cut he grinned and winked. "Th' skirmishin' now bein' over, th' battle begins. If that cat stays away long enough mebby I'll make a killin'."

"All right; but don't make no more gun-plays," warned the gambler, coldly. "I allus get excited when I smells gun powder an' I do reckless things sometimes," he added, significantly.

"Then I shore hopes you keep ca'm," laughed the puncher, loud enough to be heard over the noise of the piano, which was now going again.

The pot was sweetened three times and then the gambler dealt his opponent openers. The puncher looked anxiously through the door, grinning coltishly. He slowly pushed out twenty dollars. "There's th' key," he grunted. "A'right; see that an' raise you back. Good for you! I'm stayin' an' boostin' same as ever. Fine! See it again, an' add this. I'm playin' with yore money, so I c'n afford to be reckless. All right; I'm satisfied, too. Gimme one li'l card. I shore am glad I don't need th' king of hearts—that was shore on th' bottom when th' deal *begun*."

The gambler, having drawn, cursed and reached swiftly toward his vest pocket; but he stopped suddenly and contemplated the Colt that peeked over the edge of the table. It looked squarely at his short ribs and was backed by a sober, angry man who gazed steadily into his eyes. "Drop that hand," said the puncher in a whisper just loud enough to be heard by the other over the noise of the piano. "I never did like them shoulder holsters—I carry my irons where everybody can see 'em." Leaning forward swiftly he reached out his left hand and cautiously turned over the other's cards. The fourth one was the king of hearts. "Don't move," he whispered, not wishing to have the bartender take a hand from behind. "An' don't talk," he warned as he leaned farther forward and shoved his Colt against the other's vest and with his left hand extracted a short-barreled gun from the sheath under the gambler's armpit. Sinking back in his chair he listened a moment and, raking in the pot, stowed it away with the other winnings in his pockets.

The gambler stirred, but stopped as the Colt leaped like a flash of light to the edge of the table. "Tin-horn," said the puncher, softly, "you ain't slick enough. I didn't stop you when you wanted that queen an' ten because I wanted you to go on with th' crookedness. Yaller cats is more unlucky to you than they are to me. But when I saw that last play I lost my temper; an' I stopped you. Now if you'll cheat with me, you'll cheat with a drunk boy. So, havin' cheated him, you really stole his money away from him. That bein' so, you will dig up six months' wages at about fifty per month. I'd shoot you just as quick as I'd shoot a snake; so don't get no fool notions in yore head. Dig it right up."

The gambler studied the man across from him, but after a moment he silently placed some money on the table. "It was only two forty," he observed, holding to three double eagles. The puncher nodded: "I'll take yore word for that. Now, in th' beginnin' I only wanted to get th' boy his money; but when you started cheatin' against me I changed my mind. I played fair. Now here's your short-five," he said as he slid the gun across the table. "Mebby you might want to use it sometime," he smiled. "Now you vamoose; an' if I see you in town after th' next train leaves, I'll *make* you use that shoulder holster. An' tell yore friends that Hopalong Cassidy says, that for a country where men can tote their hardware in plain sight, a shoulder lay-out ain't no good: you gotta reach too high. Adios."

He watched the silent, philosophical man-of-cards walk slowly toward the door, upright, dignified and calm. Then he turned and approached the piano. "Sister," he said, politely, "yore gamblin' friend is leavin' town on th' next train. He has pressin' business back east a couple of stations an' wonders if you'll join him at th' depot in time for th' next train."

She had stopped playing and was staring at him in amazement. "Why didn't he come an' tell me himself, 'stead of sneakin' away an' sendin' you over?" she at last demanded, angrily.

"Well, he wanted to, but he saw a man an' slipped out with his gun in his hand. Mebby there'll be trouble; but I dunno. I'm just tellin' you. Gee," he laughed, looking at the snoring youth in the chair, "he got *that* quick. Why, I saw him less'n two hours ago an' he was sober as a judge. Reckon I'll take him over to th' hotel an' put him to bed." He went over to the helpless Sammy, shook him and made him get on his feet. "Come along, Kid," he said, slipping his arm under the sagging shoulder. "We'll get along. Good-by, Sugar," and, supporting the feebly protesting cub, he slowly made his way to the rear door and was gone, a grin wreathing his face as he heard the chink of gold coins in his several pockets.

CHAPTER XII

Sammy Knows the Game

A CLEAN-CUT, good-looking young cow-puncher limped slightly as he passed the post office and found a seat on a box in front of the store next door. He sighed with relief and gazed cheerfully at the littered square as though it was something worth looking at. The night had not been a pleasant one because Sammy Porter had insisted upon either singing or snoring; and when breakfast was announced the youth almost had recovered his senses and was full of remorse and a raging thirst. Being flatly denied the hair of the dog that bit him he grew eloquently profane and very abusive. Hence Mr. Cassidy's fondness for the box.

Sounds obtruded. They were husky and had dimensions and they came from the hotel bar. After increasing in volume and carrying power they were followed to the street by a disheveled youth who kicked open the door and blinked in the sunlight. Espying the contented individual on the box he shook an earnest fist at that person

and tried next door. In a moment he followed a new burst
of noise to the street and shook the other fist. Trying the
saloon on the other side of the hotel without success he
shook both fists and once again tried the hotel bar, where
he proceeded along lines tactful, flattering and diplomatic.
Only yesterday he had owned a gun, horse and other personal belongings; he had possessed plenty of money, a
clear head and his sins sat lightly on his youthful soul. He
still had the sins, but they had grown in weight. Tact
availed him nothing, flattery was futile and diplomacy was
in vain. To all his arguments the bartender sadly shook
his head, not because Sammy had no money, which was
the reason he gave, but because of vivid remembrance of
the grimness with which a certain red-haired, straight-
lipped, two-gun cowpuncher had made known his request.
"Let him suffer," had said the gunman. "It'll be a good
lesson for him. Understand; not a drop!" And the bartender had understood. To the drink-dispenser's refusal
Sammy replied with a masterpiece of eloquence and during its delivery the bartender stood with his hand on a
mallet, but too spellbound to throw it. Wheeling at the
close of a vivid, soaring climax, Sammy yanked open the
door again and stood transfixed with amazement and hos-
tile envy. His new and officious friend surely knew the
right system with women. To the burning indignities of
the morning this added the last straw and Sammy bitterly
resolved not to forget his wrongs.

Had Mr. Cassidy been a kitten he would have purred
with delight as he watched his youthful friend's vain
search for the hair of the dog, and his grin was threatening to engulf his ears when the Cub slammed into the
hotel. Hearing the beating of hoofs he glanced around and
saw a trim, pretty young lady astride a trim, high-spirited
pony; and both were thoroughbreds if he was any judge.
They bore down upon him at a smart lope and stopped at
the edge of the walk. The rider leaped from the saddle

and ran toward him with her hand outstretched and her face aglow with a delighted surprise. Her eyes fairly danced with welcome and relief and her cheeks, reddened by the thrust of the wind for more than twenty miles, flamed a deeper red, through which streaks of creamy white played fascinatingly. "Dick Ellsworth!" she cried. "When did you get here?"

Mr. Cassidy stumbled to his feet, one hand instinctively going out to the one held out to him, the other fiercely gripping his sombrero. His face flamed under its tan and he mumbled an incoherent reply.

"Don't you remember *me*?" she chided, a roguish, half-serious expression flashing over her countenance. "Not little Annie, whom you taught to ride? I used to think I needed you then, Dick; but oh, how I need you now. It's Providence, nothing else, that sent you. Father's gone steadily worse and now all he cares for is a bottle. Joe, the new foreman, has full charge of everything and he's not only robbing us right and left, but he's—he's bothering *me*! When I complain to father of his attentions all I get is a foolish grin. If you only knew how I have prayed for you to come back, Dick! Two bitter years of it. But now everything is all right. Tell me about yourself while I get the mail and then we'll ride home together. I suppose Joe will be waiting for me somewhere on the trail; he usually does. Did you ever hate anyone so much you wanted to kill him?" she demanded fiercely, beside herself for the moment.

Hopalong nodded. "Well, yes; I have," he answered. "But you mustn't. What's his name? We'll have to look into this."

"Joe Worth; but let's forget him for awhile," she smiled. "I'll get the mail while you go after your horse."

He nodded and watched her enter the post office and then turned and walked thoughtfully away. She was

mounted when he returned and they swung out of the
town at a lope.

"Where have you been, and what have you been doing?" she asked as they pushed along the firm, hard trail.

"Punchin' for th' Bar-20, southwest of here. I wouldn't
'a' been here today only I let th' outfit ride on without me.
We just got back from Kansas City a couple of days back.
But let's get at this here Joe Worth prop'sition. I'm plumb
curious. How long's he been pesterin' you?"

"Nearly two years—I can't stand it much longer."

"An' th' outfit don't cut in?"

"They're his friends, and they understand that father
wants it so. You'll not know father, Dick: I never thought
a man could change so. Mother's death broke him as
though he were a reed."

"Hum!" he grunted. "You ain't carin' how this coyote is
stopped, just so he is?"

"No!" she flashed.

"An' he'll be waitin' for you?"

"He usually is."

He grinned. "Le's hope he is this time." He was silent a
moment and looked at her curiously. "I don't know how
you'll take it, but I got a surprise for you—a big one. I'm
shore sorry to admit it, but I ain't th' man you think. I
ain't Dick What's-his-name, though it shore ain't *my* fault.
I reckon I must look a heap like him; an' I hope I can *act*
like him in this here matter. I want to see it through like
he would. I can do as good a job, too. But it ain't nowise
fair nor right to pretend I'm him. I ain't."

She was staring at him in a way he did not like. "Not
Dick Ellsworth!" she gasped. "You are *not* Dick?"

"I'm shore sorry—but I'd like to play his cards. I'm honin'
for to see this here Joe Worth," he nodded, cheerfully.

"And you let me believe you were?" she demanded
coldly. "You deliberately led me to talk as I did?"

"Well, now; I didn't just know what to do. You shore

was in trouble, which was bad. I reckoned mebby I could get you out of it an' then go along 'bout my business. You ain't goin' to stop me a-doin' it, are you?" he asked anxiously.

Her reply was a slow, contemptuous look that missed nothing and that left nothing to be said. Her horse did not like to stand, anyway, and sprang eagerly forward in answer to the sudden pressure of her knees. She rode the high-strung bay with superb art, angry, defiant, and erect as a statue. Hopalong, shaking his head slowly, gazed after her and when she had become a speck on the plain he growled a question to his horse and turned sullenly toward the town. Riding straight to the hotel he held a short, low-voiced conversation with the clerk and then sought his friend, the Cub. This youthful grouch was glaring across the bar at the red-faced, angry man behind it, and the atmosphere was not one of peace. The Cub turned to see who the newcomer was and thereupon transferred his glare to the smiling puncher.

"Hullo, Kid," breezed Hopalong.

"You go to hell!" growled Sammy, remembering to speak respectfully to his elders. He backed off cautiously until he could keep both of his enemies under his eyes.

Hopalong's grin broadened. He dug into his pockets and produced a large sum of money. "Here, Kid," said he, stepping forward and thrusting it into Sammy's paralyzed hands. "Take it an' buy all th' liquor you wants. You can get yore gun off'n th' clerk, an' he'll tell you where to find yore cayuse an' other belongings. I gotta leave town."

Sammy stared at the money in his hand. "What's this?" he demanded, his face flushing angrily.

"Money," replied Hopalong. "It's that shiny stuff you buys things with. Spondulix, cash, mazuma. You spend it, you know."

Sammy sputtered. He might have frothed had his mouth not been so dry. "Is it?" he demanded with great sarcasm.

"I thought mebby it was cows, or buttons. What you handin' it to me for? I ain't no damned beggar!"

Hopalong chuckled. "That money's yourn. I pried it loose from th' tin-horn that stole it from you. I also, besides, pried off a few chunks more; but them's mine. I allus pays myself good wages; an' th' aforesaid chunks is plenty an' generous. Amen."

Sammy regarded his smiling friend with a frank suspicion that was brutal. The pleasing bulge of the pockets reassured him and he slowly pocketed his rescued wealth. He growled something doubtless meant for thanks and turned to the bar. "A large chunk of th' Mojave Desert slid down my throat las' night an' I'm so dry I rustles in th' breeze. Let's wet down a li'l." Having extracted some of the rustle he eyed his companion suspiciously. "Thought you was a stranger hereabouts?"

"You've called it."

"Huh! Then I'm goin' to stick close to you an get acquainted with th' female population of th' towns we hit. An' I had allus reckoned lightnin' was quick!" he soliloquized, regretfully. "How'd you do it?" he demanded.

Hopalong was gazing over his friend's head at a lurid chromo portraying the Battle of Bull Run and he pursed his lips thoughtfully. "That shore was some slaughter," he commented. "Well, Kid," he said, holding out his hand, "I'm leavin'. If you ever gets down my way an' wants a good job, drop in an' see us. Th' clerk'll tell you how to get there. An' th' next time you gambles, stay sober."

"Hey! Wait a minute!" exclaimed Sammy. "Goin' home now?"

"Can't say as I am, direct."

"Comin' back here before you do?"

"Can't say that, neither. Life is plumb on-certain an' gunplay's even worse. Mebby I will if I'm alive."

"Who you gunnin' for? Can't I take a hand?"

"Reckon not, Sammy. Why, I'm cuttin' in where I ain't

wanted, even if I am needed. But it's my duty. It's a hell of a community as waits for a total stranger to do its work for it. If yo're around an' I come back, why I'll see you again. Meanwhile, look out for tin-horns."

Sammy followed him outside and grasped his arm. "I can hold up my end in an argument," he asserted fiercely. "You went an' did me a good turn—lemme do *you* one. If it's anythin' to do with that li'l girl you met to-day I won't cut in—only on th' trouble end. I'm particular strong on th' trouble part. Look here: Ain't a friend got no rights?"

Hopalong warmed to the eager youngster—he was so much like Jimmy; and Jimmy, be it known, could bedevil Hopalong as much as any man alive and not even get an unkind word for it. "I'm scared to let you come, Kid; she'd fumigate th' ranch when you left. Th' last twenty-four hours has outlawed you, all right. You keep to th' brush trails in th' draws—don't cavort none on skylines till you lose that biled owl look." He laughed at the other's expression and placed his hands on the youth's shoulders. "That ain't it, Kid; I never apologizes, serious, for th' looks of my friends. They're my friends, drunk or sober, in hell or out of it. I just can't see how you can cut in proper. Better wait for me here—I'll turn up, all right. Meanwhile, as I says before, look out for tin-horns."

Sammy watched him ride away, and then slammed his sombrero on the ground and jumped on it, after which he felt relieved. Procuring his gun from the clerk he paused to cross-examine, but after a fruitless half hour he sauntered out, hiding his vexation, to wrestle with the problem in the open. Passing the window of a general store he idly glanced at the meager display behind the dusty glass and a sudden grin transfigured his countenance. He would find out about the girl first and that would help him solve the puzzle. Thinking thus he wandered in carelessly and he wandered out again gravely clutching a small package. Slipping behind the next building he tore off the paper and carefully crumpled and soiled with dust the purchase. Then he went down to the depot and followed the railroad tracks toward the other side of the square. Reaching the place where the south trail crossed the tracks he left them and walked slowly toward a small depression that was surrounded by hoofprints. He stooped quickly and straightened up with a woman's handkerchief dangling from his fingers. He grinned foolishly, examined it, sniffed at it and scratched his head while he cogitated. A decisive wave of his hand apprised the two spectators that he had arrived at a conclusion, which he bore out by heading straight for the post office, which was a part of the grocery store. The postmaster and grocer, in person one, watched his approach with frank curiosity.

Sammy nodded and went in the store, followed by the proprietor. "Howd'y," he remarked, producing the handkerchief. "Just picked this up over on th' trail. Know who dropped it?"

"Annie Allison, I reckon," replied the other. "She came in that way from th' Bar-U. Want to leave it?"

Sammy considered. "Why, I might as well take it to her—I'm going down there purty soon. Don't know any other ranch that might use a broncho-buster, do you?"

The proprietor shook his head. "No; most folks 'round here bust their own. Perfessional?"

Sammy nodded. "Yes. Here, gimme two-bits' worth of them pep'mint lozengers. Yes, it shore is fine; but it'll rain before long. Well, by-by."

The bartender of the "Retreat" sniffed suspiciously and eyed the open door thoughtfully, holding aloft the bar-mop while he considered. Then he put the mop on the bar and went to the door, where he peered out. "Huh!" he grunted. "Hogin' that?" he sarcastically inquired. Sammy held out the bag and led the way to the bar. "Where's th' Bar-U? Yes? Do their own broncho-bustin'? Who, me? Ain't nothin' on laigs can throw me, includin' humans an' bartenders. What? Well, what you want to get all skinned up for, for nothin'? Five dollars? If you must lose it I might as well have it. One fall? All right; come out here an' get it."

The bartender chuckled and vaulted the counter as advance notice of his agility and physical condition, and immediately there ensued a soft shuffling. Suddenly the building shook and dusted itself and Sammy arose and stepped back, smiling at his victim. "Thanks," he remarked. "Good money was spent on part of my education—boxin' bein' th' other half. Now, for five more, where can't I hit you?"

"Behind th' bar," grinned the other; "I got deadly weapons there. Look here!" he exclaimed hurriedly as a great idea struck him. "Everybody 'round here will back their wrastlin' reckless; le's team up an' make some easy money. I'll make th' bets an' you win 'em. Split even. What say?"

"Later on, mebby. What'd you say that Bar-U foreman's name was?"

The bartender's reply was supplemented by a pious suggestion. "An' if you wrastles *him*, bust his cussed neck!"

"Why this friendship?" queried Sammy, laughing.

"Oh, just for general principles."

Sammy bought cigars, left some lozenges and went out to search for his horse, which he duly found. Inwardly he was elated and he flexed his muscles and made curious motions with his arms, which caused the pie-bald to show the whites of its eyes wickedly and flatten its ragged ears. Its actions were justified, for a left hand darted out and slapped the wrinkling muzzle, deftly escaping the clicking teeth. Then the warlike pie-bald reflected judiciously as it chewed the lozenge. The eyes showed less white and the ears, moving forward and back, compromised by one staying forward. The candy was old and stale and the sting of the mint was negligible, but the sugar was much in evidence. When the hand darted out again the answering nip was playful and the ears were set rigidly forward. Sammy laughed, slipped several more lozenges into the ready mouth, vaulted lightly to the saddle and rode slowly toward the square. The pie-bald kicked mildly and reached around to nip at the stirrup, and then went on about its business as any well-broken cow pony should.

Reaching the square Sammy drew rein suddenly and watched a horseman who was riding away from the "Retreat." Waiting a few minutes Sammy spurred forward to the saloon and called the bartender out to him. "Who was that feller that just left?" he asked, curiously.

"Joe Worth, th' man yo're goin' to strike for that job. Why don't you catch him now an' mebby save yoreself a day's ride?"

"Good idea," endorsed Sammy. "See you later," and the youth wheeled and loped toward the trail, but drew rein when hidden from the "Retreat" by some buildings. He watched the distant horseman until he became a mere dot and then Sammy pushed on after him. There was a satisfied look on his face and he chuckled as he cogitated. "I shore got th' drift of this; I know th' game! Wonder how Cassidy got onto it?" He laughed contentedly. "Well, five hundred ain't too little to split two ways; an' mebby it *is* a two-man job. Mr. Joe Worth, who was once Mr. George Atkins, I wouldn't give a peso for yore chances after I get th' lay of th' ground an' find out yore habits. Yo're goin' back to Willow Springs as shore as 'dogies' hang 'round water holes. An' you'll shore dance their tune when you gets there."

Mr. Cassidy, arriving at the Bar-U, asked for the foreman and was told that the boss was in town, but would be back sometime in the afternoon. The newcomer replied that he would return later and, carefully keeping out of sight of the ranch house as well as he could, he wheeled

and rode back the way he had come, being very desirous
to have a good look at the foreman before they met. Arriving at an arroyo several miles north of the ranch he
turned into it, and, leaving his horse picketed on good
grass along the bottom, he climbed to a position where
he could see the trail without being seen. Having settled
himself comfortably he improved the wait by trying to
think out the best way to accomplish the work he had set
himself to do. Shooting was too common and hardly justifiable unless Mr. Worth forced the issue with weapons of
war.

The time passed slowly and he was relieved when a
horseman appeared far to the north and jogged toward
him, riding with the careless grace of one at home in the
saddle. Being thoroughly familiar with the trail and the
surrounding country the rider looked straight ahead as if
attention to the distance yet untraveled might make it
less. He passed within twenty feet of the watcher and went
on his way undisturbed. Hopalong waited until he was out
of sight around a hill and then, vaulting into the saddle,
rode after him, still puzzled as to how he would proceed
about the business in hand. He dismounted at the bunkhouse and nodded to those who lingered near the wash
bench awaiting their turn.

"Just in time to feed," remarked one of the punchers.
"Watch yore turn at th' basins—every man for hisself's th'
rule."

"All right," Hopalong laughed. "But is there any chance
to get a job here?" he asked, anxiously.

"You'll have to quiz th' Ol' Man—here he comes now,"
and the puncher waved at the approaching foreman. "Hey,
Joe! Got a job for this *hombre*?" he called.

The foreman keenly scrutinized the newcomer, as he
always examined strangers. The two guns swinging low
on the hips caught his eyes instantly but he showed no
particular interest in them, notwithstanding the fact that

they proclaimed a gunman. "Why I reckon I got a job for you," he said. "I been waitin' to keep somebody over on Cherokee Range. But it's time to eat: we'll talk later."

After the meal the outfit passed the time in various ways until bed-time, the foreman talking to the new member of his family. During the night the foreman awakened several times and looked toward the newcomer's bunk but found nothing suspicious. After breakfast he called Hopalong and one of the others to him. "Ned," he said, "take Cassidy over to his range and come right back. Hey, Charley! You an' Jim take them poles down to th' ford an' fence in that quicksand just south of it. Ben says he's been doin' nothin' but pullin' cows outen it. All right, Tim; comin' right away."

Ned and the new puncher lost no time but headed east at once with a packhorse carrying a week's provisions for one man. The country grew rougher rapidly and when they finally reached the divide a beautiful sight lay below them, stretching as far as eye could see to the east. In the middle distance gleamed the Cherokee, flowing toward the south through its valley of rocks, canyons, cliffs, draws and timber.

"There's th' hut," said Ned, pointing to a small gray blot against the dead black of a towering cliff. "Th' spring's just south of it. Bucket Hill, up north there, is th' north boundary; Twin Spires, south yonder is th' other end; an' th' Cherokee will stop you on th' east side. You ride in every Sat'day if you wants. Don't get lonesome," he grinned and, wheeling abruptly, went back the way they had come.

Hopalong shook his head in disgust. To be sidetracked like this was maddening. It had taken three hours of hard traveling over rough country to get where he was and it would take as long to return; and all for nothing! He regarded the pack animal with a grin, shrugged his shoulders and led the way toward the hut, the pack horse following obediently. It was another hour before he finally reached the little cabin, for the way was strange and rough. During this time he had talked aloud, for he had the tricks of his kind and when alone he talked to himself. When he reached the hut he relieved the pack horse of its load, carrying the stuff inside. Closing the door and blocking it with a rock he found the spring, drank his fill and then let the horses do likewise. Then he mounted and started back over the rough trail, thinking out loud and confiding to his horse and he entered a narrow defile close to the top of the divide, promising dire things to the foreman. Suddenly a rope settled over him, pinned his arms to his sides and yanked him from the saddle before he had time to think. He landed on his head and was dazed as he sat up and looked around. The foreman's rifle confronted him, and behind the foreman's feet were his two Colts.

"You talks too much," sneered the man with the drop. "I suspicioned you th' minute I laid eyes on you. It'll take a better man than you to get that five hundred reward. I reckon th' Sheriff was too scared to come hisself."

Hopalong shook his head as if to clear it. What was the man talking about? Who was the sheriff? He gave it up, but would not betray his ignorance. Yes: he had talked too much. He felt of his head and was mildly surprised to see his hand covered with blood when he glanced at it. "Five hundred's a lot of money," he muttered.

"Blood money!" snapped the foreman. "You had a gall tryin' to get me. Why, I been lookin' for somebody to try it for two years. An' I was ready every minute of all that time."

Slowly it came to Hopalong and with it the realization of how foolish it would be to deny the part ascribed to himself. The rope was loose and his arms were practically free; the foreman had dropped the lariat and was depending upon his gun. The captive felt of his head again and,

putting his hands behind him for assistance in getting up,
arose slowly to his feet. In one of the hands was a small
rock that it had rested upon during the effort of rising. At
the movement the foreman watched him closely and ordered him not to take a step if he wanted to live a little
longer.

"I reckon I'll have to shoot you," he announced. "I
dassn't let you loose to foller me all over th' country. Anyhow, I'd have to do it sooner or later. I wish you was
Phelps, damn him; but he's a wise sheriff. Better stand up
agin' that wall. I gotta do it; an' you deserve it, you Judas!"

"Meanin' yo're Christ?" sneered Hopalong. "Did you kill
th' other feller like that? If I'd 'a' knowed that I'd 'a' slapped
yo're dawg's face at th' bunkhouse an' made you take an
even break. Shore you got nerve enough to shoot straight
if I looks at you while yo're aimin'?" He laughed cynically.
"I don't want to close my eyes."

The foreman's face went white and he half lowered the
rifle as he took a step forward. Hopalong leaped sideways
and his arm straightened out, the other staggering under
the blow of the missile. Leaping forward Hopalong ran
into a cloud of smoke and staggered as he jumped to close
quarters. His hand smashed full in the foreman's face and
his knee sank in the foreman's groin. They went down,
the foreman weak from the kick and Hopalong sick and
weak from the bullet that had grazed the bone of his bad
thigh. And lying on the ground they fought in a daze, each
incapable of inflicting serious injury for awhile. But the
foreman grew stronger as his enemy grew weaker from
loss of blood and, wriggling from under his furious antag-
onist, he reached for his Colt. Hopalong threw himself
forward and gripped the gun wrist between his teeth and
closed his jaws until they ached. But the foreman, pounding ceaselessly on the other's face with his free hand, made
the jaws relax and drew the weapon. Then he saw all the
stars in the heavens as Hopalong's head crashed full

against his jaw and before he could recover the gun was
pinned under his enemy's knee. Hopalong's head crashed
again against the foreman's jaw and his right hand gripped
the corded throat while the left, its thumb inside the foreman's cheek and its fingers behind an ear, tugged and
strained at the distorted face. Growling like wild beasts
they strained and panted, and then, suddenly, Hopalong's
grip relaxed and he made one last, desperate effort to
bring his strength back into one furious attack; but in vain.
The battered foreman, quick to sense the situation, wrestled his adversary to one side long enough to grab the
Colt from under the shifting knee. As he clutched it a shot
rang out and the weapon dropped from his nerveless hand
before he could pull the trigger. An exulting, savage yell
roared in his ears and in the next instant he seemed to
leave the ground and soar through space. He dropped ten
feet away and lay dazed and helpless as a knee crashed
against his chest. Sammy Porter, his face working curiously with relief and rage, rolled him against the wall of
the defile and struck him over the head with a rifle, first
disarming him.

Hopalong opened his eyes and looked around, dazed
and sick. The foreman, bound hand and foot by a forty-
five foot lariat, lay close to the base of the wall and stared
sullenly at the sky. Sammy was coming up the trail with
a dripping sombrero held carefully in his hands and was
growling and talking it all over. Hopalong looked down
at his thigh and saw a heavy, blood-splotched bandage
fastened clumsily in place. Glancing at Sammy again he
idly noted that part of the youth's blue-flannel shirt was
missing. Curiously, it matched the bandage. He closed his
eyes and tried to think what it was all about.

Sammy ambled up to him, threw some water in the
bruised face and then grinned cheerfully at the language
he evoked. Producing a flask and holding it up to the light,
Sammy slid his thumb to a certain level and then shoved

the bottle against his friend's teeth. "Huh!" he chuckled, yanking the bottle away. "You'll be all right in a couple of days. But you shore are one hell of a sight—it's a toss-up between you an' Atkins."

It was night. Hopalong stirred and arose on one elbow and noticed that he was lying on a blanket that covered a generous depth of leaves and pine boughs. The sap-filled firewood crackled and popped and hissed and whistled under the licking attack of the greedy flames, which flared up and died down in endless alternation, and which grotesquely revealed to Hopalong's throbbing eyes a bound figure lying on another blanket. That, he decided, was the foreman. Letting his gaze wander around the lighted circle he made out a figure squatting on the other side of the fire, and concluded it was Sammy Porter. "What you doin', Kid?" he asked.

Sammy arose and walked over to him. "Oh, just watchin' a fool puncher an' five hundred dollars," he grinned. "How you feelin' now, you ol' sage hen?"

"Good," replied the invalid, and, comparatively, it was the truth. "Fine an' strong," he added, which was not the truth.

"That's the way to talk," cheered the Cub. "You shore had one fine séance. You earned that five hundred, all right."

Hopalong reflected and then looked across at the prisoner. "He can fight like the devil," he muttered. "Why, I kicked him hard enough to kill anybody else." He turned again and looked Sammy in the eyes, smiling as best he could. "There ain't no five hundred for me, Kid. I didn't come for that, didn't know nothin' about it. An' it's blood money, besides. We'll turn him loose if he'll get out of the country, hey? We'll give him a chance; either that or you take th' reward."

Sammy stared, grunted and stared again. "What you

ravin' about?" he demanded. "An' you didn't come after
him for that money?" he asked, sarcastically.

Hopalong nodded and smiled again. "That's right, Kid,"
he answered, thoughtfully. "I come down to make him
get out of th' country. You let him go after we get out of
this. I reckon I got yore share of the reward right here in
my pocket; purty near that much, anyhow. You take it an'
let him vamoose. What you say?"

Sammy rose, angry and disgusted. His anger spoke first.
"You go to hell with yore money! I don't want it!" Then,
slowly and wonderingly spoke his disgust. "He's yourn; do
what you want. But I here remarks, frank an' candid, open
an' so all may hear, that yo're a large, puzzlin' damned
fool. Now lay back on that blanket an' go to sleep afore I
changes my mind!"

Sammy drifted past the prisoner and looked down at
him. "Hear that?" he demanded. There was no answer
and he grunted. "Huh! You heard it, all right; an' it plumb
stunned you." Passing on he grabbed the last blanket in
sight, it was on the foreman's horse, and rolled up in it,
feet to the fire. His gun he placed under the saddle he had
leaned against, which now made his pillow. As he
squirmed into the most comfortable position he could find
under the circumstances he raised his head and glanced
across at his friend. "Huh!" he growled softly. "That's th'
worst of them sentimental fellers. That gal shore wrapped
him 'round her li'l finger all right. Oh, well," he sighed.
"Tain't none of my doin's, thank the Lord; I got sense!"
And with the satisfaction of this thought still warm upon
him he closed his eyes and went to sleep, confident that
the slightest sound would awaken him; and fully justified
in his confidence.

CHAPTER XIII

His Code

MR. "YOUBET" SOMES, erstwhile foreman of the Two-X-Two ranch, in Arizona, and now out of a job, rode gloomily toward Kit, a town between him and his destination.

Needless to say, he was a cowman through and through. More than that, he was so saturated with cowmen's traditions as to resent pugnaciously anything which flouted them.

He was of the old school, and would not submit quietly to two things, among others, which an old-school cowman hated—wire fences and sheep. To this he owed his present ride, for he hated wire fences cordially. They meant the passing of the free, open range, of straight trails across country; they meant a great change, an intolerable condition.

"Yessir, bronch! Things are gettin' damnabler every year, with th' railroads, tourists, nesters, barb' wire, an' sheep. Last year, it was a windmill, that screeched till our hair riz up. It wouldn't work when we wanted it to, an' we couldn't stop it when it once got started.

"It gave us no sleep, no peace; an' it killed Bob Cousins—swung round with th' wind an' knocked him off'n th' platform, sixty feet, to th' ground. Bob allus did like to monkey with th' buzz saw. I shore told him not to go up there, because th' cussed thing was loaded; but, bein' mule-headed, he knowed more'n me.

"But this year! Lord—but that was an awful pile of wire, bronch! Three strands high, an' over a hundred an' fifty miles round that pasture. That was a' insult, bronch; an' I never swaller 'em. That's what put me an' you out here, in th' middle of nowhere, tryin' to find a way out. G'wan, now! You ain't goin' to rest till I gets off you. G'wan, I told you!"

Mr. Somes was riding east, bound for the Bar-20, where he had friends. For a year or two, he had heard persistent rumors to the effect that Buck Peters had more cows than he knew what to do with; and he argued rightly that the Bar-20 foreman could find a place for an old friend, whose ability was unquestioned. Of one thing he was certain—there were no wire fences, down there.

It was dusk when he dismounted in front of Logan's, in Kit, and went inside. The bartender glanced up, reaching for a bottle on the shelf beside him.

Youbet nodded. "You got it first pop. Have one with me. I'm countin' on staying over in town tonight. Got a place for me?"

"Shore have—upstairs in th' attic. Want grub, too?"

"Well, I sorter hope to have somethin' to eat afore I pull out. Here's how!" And when Mr. Somes placed his empty glass on the bar, he smiled good-naturedly. "That's good stuff. Much goin' on in town?"

"Reckon you can get a game most anywhere."

"Where do I get that grub? Here?"

"No—down th' street. Ridin' far?"

"Yes—a little. Goin' down to th' Bar-20 for a job punch-in'. I hear Peters has got more cows than he can handle. Know anybody down there you wants to send any word to?"

"I'll be hanged if I know," laughed the bartender. "I know a lot of fellers, but they shift so I can't keep track of 'em, nohow."

A man in a far corner pushed back his chair, and approached the bar, scowling as he glanced at Youbet. "Gimme another," he ordered.

"Why, hullo, stranger!" exclaimed Youbet. "I didn't see you before. Have one with me."

The other looked him squarely in the eyes. "Ex-cuse me, stranger—I'm a sheepman, an' I don't drink with cowmen."

"Well, ex-cuse *me*!" retorted Youbet, like a flash. "If I'd 'a' knowed you was a sheepman, I wouldn't 'a' asked you!"

The sheepman drank his liquor and, returning to his corner, placed his elbows on the table, and his chin in his hands, apparently paying no further attention to the others.

"If I can't get a job with Peters, I can try th' C-80 or Double Arrow," continued Youbet, as he toyed with his glass. "If I can't get on with one of them, I reckons Waffles, of th' O-Bar-O, will find a place for me, though I don't like that country a whole lot."

The bartender hesitated for a moment. "Do you know Waffles?" he asked.

"Shore—know 'em all. Why? Do you know him, too?"

"No; but I've heard of him."

"That so? He's a good feller, he is. I've punched with both him an' Peters."

"I heard he wasn't," replied the bartender, slowly but carelessly.

"Then you heard wrong, all right," rejoined Youbet. "He's one of us old fellers—hates sheep, barb' wire, an'

nesters as bad as I do; an' sonny," he continued, warming
as he went on. "Th' cow country ain't what it used to be—
not no way. I can remember when there warn't no wires,
no nesters, an' no sheep. An', between you and me, I don't
know which is th' worst. Every time I runs up agin' one
of 'em, I says it's th' worst; but I guess it's just about a
even break."

"I heard about yore friend Waffles through sheep," replied the bartender. "He chased a sheep outfit out of a hill
range near his ranch, an' killed a couple of 'em, a-doin'
it."

"Served 'em right—served 'em right," responded
Youbet, turning and walking toward the door. "They ain't
got no business on a cattle range—not nohow."

The man in the corner started to follow, half raising his
hand, as though to emphasize something he was about to
say; but changed his mind, and sullenly resumed his
brooding attitude.

"Reckon I'll put my cayuse in yore corral, an' look th'
town over," Youbet remarked, over his shoulder. "Remember, yo're savin' a bed for me."

As he stepped to the street, the man in the corner lazily
arose and looked out of the window, swearing softly while
he watched the man who hated sheep.

"Well, there's another friend of yore business," laughed
the bartender, leaning back to enjoy the other's discomfiture. "*He* don't like 'em, neither."

"He's a fool of a mossback, so far behind th' times he
don't know who's President," retorted the other, still staring down the street.

"Well, he don't know that this has got to be a purty fair
sheep town—that's shore."

"He'll find out, if he makes many more talks like that—
an' that ain't no dream, neither!" snapped the sheepman.
He wheeled, and frowned at the man behind the bar. "You
see what he gets, if he opens his cow mouth in here to-

night. Th' boys hate this kind real fervent; an' when they finds out that he's a side pardner of that coyote Waffles, they won't need much excuse. You wait—that's all!"

"Oh, what's th' use of gettin' all riled up about it?" demanded the bartender easily. "He didn't know *you* was a sheepman, when he made his first break. An' lemme tell you somethin' you want to remember—them old-time cowmen can use a short gun somethin' slick. They've got 'em trained. Bet *he* can work th' double roll without shootin' hisself full of lead." The speaker grinned exasperatingly.

"Yes!" exploded the sheepman, who had tried to roll two guns at once, and had spent ten days in bed as a result of it.

The bartender laughed softly as he recalled the incident. "Have you tried it since?" he inquired.

"Go to th' devil!" grinned the other, heading for the door. "But he'll get in trouble, if he spouts about hatin' sheep, when th' boys come in. You better get him drunk an' lock him in th' attic, before then."

"G'wan! I ain't playin' guardian to nobody," rejoined the bartender. "But remember what I said—them old fellers can use 'em slick an' rapid."

The sheepman went out as Youbet returned; and the latter seated himself, crossing his legs and drawing out his pipe.

The bartender perfunctorily drew a cloth across the bar, and smiled. "So you don't like wire, sheep, or nesters," he remarked.

Mr. Somes looked up, in surprise, forgetting that he held a lighted match between thumb and finger. "Like 'em! Huh, I reckon not. I'm lookin' for a job because of wire. Hell!" he exclaimed, dropping the match, and rubbing his finger. "That's twice I did that fool thing in a week," he remarked, in apology and self-condemnation, and struck another match.

"I was foreman of my ranch for nigh onto ten years. It was a good ranch, an' I was satisfied till last year, when they made me put up a a windmill that didn't mill, but screeched awful. I stood for that because I could get away from it in th' daytime.

"But this year! One day, not very long ago, I got a letter from th' owners, an' it says for me to build a wire fence around our range. It went on to say that there was two carloads of barb' wire at Mesquite. We was to tote that wire home, an' start in. If two carloads wasn't enough, they'd send us more. We had one busted-down grub wag-gin, an' Mesquite shore was fifty miles away—which meant a whoppin' long job totin'.

"When I saw th' boys, that night, I told 'em that I'd got orders to raise their pay five dollars a month—which made 'em cheer. Then I told 'em that was so providin' they helped me build a barb' wire fence around th' range—which didn't make 'em cheer.

"Th' boundary lines of th' range we was usin' was close onto a hundred an' fifty miles long, an' three strands of wire along a trail like that is some job. We was to put th' posts twelve feet apart, an' they was to be five feet outen th' ground an' four feet in it—which makes 'em nine feet over all.

"There wasn't no posts at Mesquite. Them posts was supposed to be growin' freelike on th' range, just waitin' for us to cut 'em, skin 'em, tote an' drop 'em every twelve feet along a line a hundred an' fifty miles long. An' then there was to be a hole dug for every post, an' tampin', staplin', an' stringin' that hell-wire. An' don't forget that lone, busted-down grub waggin that was to do that totin'!

"There was some excitement on th' Two-X-Two that night, an' a lot of figgerin'; us bein' some curious about how many posts was needed, an' how many holes we was to dig to fit th' aforesaid posts. We made it sixty-six thousand. Think of it! An' only eight of us to tackle a job like that, an' ride range at th' same time!"

"Oh, ho!" roared the bartender, hugging himself, and trying to carry a drink to the narrator at the same time. "Go on! That's good!"

"Is, is it?" snorted Youbet. "Huh! You wouldn't 'a' thought so, if you was one of us eight. Well, I set right down an' writ a long letter—took six cents' worth of stamps—an' gave our views regardin' wire fences in general an' this one of ourn in particular. I hated fences, an' do yet; an' so'd my boys hate 'em, an' they do yet.

"In due time, I got a answer, which come for two cents. It says: 'Build that fence.'

"I sent Charley over to Mesquite to look over them cars of wire. He saw 'em, both of 'em. An' th' agent saw him.

"Th' agent was a' important man, an' he grabs Charley quick. 'Hey, you Two-X-Two puncher—you get that wire home quick. It went past here three times before they switched it, an' I've been gettin' blazes from th' company ever since. We needs th' cars.'

" 'Don't belong to me,' says Charley. 'I shore don't want it. I'm eatin' beans an' bacon instead.'

" 'You send for that wire!' yells th' agent, wild-like.

"Charley winks. 'Can't you keep it passin' this station till it snows hard? Have a drink.'

"Well, th' agent wouldn't drink, an' he wouldn't send that pore wire out into a cold world no more; an' so Charley comes home an' reports, him lookin' wanlike. When he told us, he looked sort of funny, an' blurts out that his mother went an' died in Laramie, an' he must shore 'nuff rustle up there an' bury her. He went.

"Then Fred Ball begun to have pains in his stomach, an' said it was appendix somethin', what he had been readin' about in th' papers. He had to go to Denver, an' get a good doctor, or he'd shore die. He went.

"Carson had to go to Santa Fé to keep some of his numerous city lots from bein' sold off by th' sheriff. He went.

"Th' rest, bein' handicapped by th' good start th' others had made in corrallin' all th' excuses, said they'd go for th' wire. They went.

"I waited four days, an' then I went after 'em. When I got to th' station, I sees th' agent out sizin' up our wire; an' when I hails, he jumps my way quick, an' grabs my laig tight.

"'You take that wire home!' he yells.

"'Shore,' says I soothingly. 'You looks mad,' I adds.

"'Mad! Mad!' he shouts, hoppin' round, but hangin' onto my laig like grim death. 'Mad! I'm goin' *loco*—crazy! I can't sleep! There's twenty letters an' messages on my table, tellin' me to get that wire off'n th' cars an' send th' empties back on th' next freight! You've got to take it—*got to*!'"

The bartender shocked his nervous system by drinking plain water by mistake, but he listened eagerly. "Yes? What then?"

"Well, then I asks him where I can find my men, an' team, an' waggin'. He tells me. Th' team an' waggin is in a corral down th' street, but he don't know where th' men are. They held a gun to his head, an' said they'd kill him if he didn't flag th' next train for 'em. Th' next train was a through express, carryin' mail. He wasn't dead.

"He showed me ten more letters an' messages, regardin' th' flaggin' of a contract-mail train for four fares; an' some of them letters must 'a' been written by a old-time cowman, they was that eloquent an' God-fearin'. Then I went.

"Why, Charley was twenty years old; an' we figgered that, when th' last staple was drove in th' last post, he'd 'a' been dead ten years! Where did I come in, the—?"

"Oh, Lord!" sighed the bartender, holding his sides, and

trying to straighten his face so that he could talk out of the middle of it. "That's th' best ever! Have another drink!"

"I ain't tellin' my troubles for liquor," snorted Youbet. "You have one with me. Here comes some customers down th' street, I reckon."

"Say!" exclaimed the bartender hurriedly. "You keep mum about sheep. This is a red-hot sheep town, an' it hates Waffles an' all his friends. Hullo, boys!" he called to four men, who filed into the room. "Where's th' rest of you?"

"Comin' in later. Same thing, Jimmy," replied Clayton, chief herder. "An' give us th' cards."

"Have you seen Price?" asked Towne.

"Yes; he was in here a few minutes ago. What'd you say, Schultz?" the bartender asked, turning to the man who pulled at his sleeve.

"I said dot you vas nod right aboud vat you said de odder day. Chust now I ask Glayton, und he said you vas nod."

"All right, Dutchy—all right!" laughed the bartender. "Then it's on me this time, ain't it?"

Youbet walked to the bar. "Say, where do I get that grub? It's about time for me to mosey off an' feed."

"Next building—and you'll take mutton if yo're wise," replied the bartender, in a low voice. "Th' hash is awful, an' the beef is tough," he added, a little louder.

"Mutton be damned!" snorted Youbet, stamping out. "I eat what I punch!" And his growls became lost in the street.

Schultz glanced up. "Yah! Und he shoot vat *I* eat, tam him, ven he gan!"

"Oh, put yore ante in, an' don't talk so much!" rejoined Towne. "He ain't going to shoot *you*."

"It'll cost you two bits to come in," remarked Clayton.

"An' two more," added Towne, raising the ante.

"Goot! I blay mit you. But binochle iss der game!"

"I'll tell you a good story about a barb' wire fence to-morrow, fellers," promised the bartender, grinning.

The poker game had been going for some time before further remarks were made about the cowman who had left, and then it was Clayton who spoke.

"Say, Jimmy!" he remarked, as Schultz dealt. "Who is yore leather-pants friend who don't like mutton?"

The bartender lifted a bottle, and replaced it with great care. "Oh, just a ranch foreman, out of a job. He's a funny old feller."

"So? An' what's so funny about him? Get in there, Towne, if you wants to do any playin' with us."

"Why, he was ordered to build a hundred an' fifty miles of wire fence around his range, an' he jumped ruther than do it."

"Yas—an' most of it government land, I reckon," interposed Towne.

"Pshaw! It's an old game with them," laughed Clayton. "Th' law don't get to them; an' if they've got a good outfit, nobody has got any chance agin 'em."

"Py Gott, dot's right!" grunted Schultz.

"Shore, it is," responded Towne, forgetting the game. "Take that Apache Hills run-in. Waffles didn't have no more right to that range than anybody else, but that didn't make no difference. He threw a couple of outfits in there, penned us in th' cabin, killed MacKay, an' shot th' rest of us up plenty. Then he threatened to slaughter our herd if we didn't pull out. By God, I'd like to get a cowman like him up here, where th' tables are turned around on th' friends proposition."

"Hullo, boys!" remarked the bartender to the pair who came in.

"Just in time. Get chairs, an' take hands," invited Clayton, moving over.

"Who's th' cowman yo're talkin' about?" asked Baxter, as he leaned lazily against the bar.

"Oh, all of 'em," rejoined Towne surlily. "There's one in town, now, who don't like sheep."

"That so?" queried Baxter slowly. "I reckon he better keep his mouth shut, then."

"Oh, he's all right! He's a jolly old geezer," assured the bartender. "He just talks to hear hisself—one of them old-timers what can't get right to th' way things has changed on th' range. It was them boys that did great work when th' range was wild."

"Yes, an' it's them bull-headed old fools what are raisin' all th' hell with th' sheep," retorted Towne, frowning darkly as he remembered some of the indignities he had borne at the hands of cowmen.

"I wish his name was Waffles." Clayton smiled significantly.

"Rainin' again," remarked a man in the doorway, stamping in. "Reckon it ain't never goin' to stop."

"Where you been so long, Price?" asked Clayton, as a salutation.

"Oh, just shiftin' about. That cow wrastler raised th' devil in th' hotel," Price replied. "Old fool! They brought him mutton, an' he wanted to clean out th' place. Said he'd as soon eat barb' wire. They're feedin' him hash an' canned stuff, now."

"He'll get hurt, if he don't look out," remarked Clayton. "Who is he, anyhow, Price?"

"Don't know his name; but he's from Arizona, on his way to th' Pecos country. Says he's a friend of Buck Peters an' Waffles. To use one of his own expressions, he's a old mosshead."

"Friend of Waffles, hey?" exclaimed Towne.

"Yumpin' Yimminy!" cried Oleson, in the same breath.

"Well, if he knows when he's well off, he'll stay away from here, an' keep his mouth closed," said Clayton.

"Aw, let him alone! He's one agin' th' whole town—an' a good old feller, at that," hastily assured the bartender. "It ain't his fault that Waffles buffaloed you fellers out of th' Hills, is it? He's goin' on early tomorrow; so let him be."

"You'll get yoreself in trouble, Jimmy, m' boy, if you inserts yoreself in this," warned Towne. "It was us agin' a whole section, an' we got ours. Let him take his, if he talks too much."

"Shore," replied Price. "I heard him shoot off his mouth, an hour ago, an' he's got altogether too much to say. You mind th' bar an' yore own business, Jimmy. We ain't kids."

"Go you two bits better," said Clayton, shoving out a coin. "Gimme some cards, Towne. It'll cost you a dollar to see our raises."

Baxter walked over to watch the play. "I'm comin' in next game. Who's winnin', now?"

"Reckon I am; but we ain't much more'n got started," Clayton replied. "Did you call, Towne? Why, I've got three little tens. You got anythin' better?"

"Never saw such luck!" exclaimed Towne disgustedly. "Dutchy, yo're a Jonah."

"Damn th' mutton, says I. It was even in that hash!" growled a voice, just outside the door.

A moment later, Youbet Somes entered, swinging his sombrero energetically to shake off the water.

"Damn th' rain, too, an' this wart of a town. A man can't get nothin' fit to eat for love or money, on a sheep range. Gimme a drink, sonny! Mebby it'll cut th' taste of that rank tallow out'n my mouth. Th' reason there is sheep on this earth of our'n is that th' devil chased 'em out 'n his place— an' no blame to him."

He drank half his liquor, and, placing the glass on the bar beside him, turned to watch the game. "Ah, strangers—that's th' only game, after all. I've dabbled in 'em all from faro to roulette, but that's th' boss of 'em all."

"See you an' call," remarked Clayton, ignoring the new-comer. "What you got, you Dutch pagan?"

"*Zwei Kaisers* und a bair of chackasses, mit a deuce."

"Kings up!" exclaimed Clayton. "Why, say—you bet th' worst of anybody I ever knew! You'll balk on bettin' two bits on threes, and plunge on a bluff. I reckoned you didn't have nothin'. Why ain't you more consistent?" he asked, winking at Towne.

"Gonsisdency iss no chewel in dis game—it means go broke," placidly grunted Schultz, raking in his winnings.

His friend Schneider smiled.

"Coyotes are gettin' too numerous, this year," Baxter remarked, shuffling.

Youbet pushed his sombrero back on his head. "They don't get numerous on a cow range," he said significantly.

"Huh!" snorted Baxter. "They've got too much respect to stay on one longer than they've got to."

"They'd ruther be with their woolly-coated cousins," re-joined the cowman quietly. It was beneath his dignity as a cowman to pay much attention to what sheepmen said, yet he could not remain silent under such a remark.

He regarded sheep herders, those human beings who walked at their work, as men who had reached the lowest rung in the ladder of human endeavors. His belief was not original with him, but was that of many of his school. He was a horseman, a mounted man, and one of the aristoc-racy of the range; they were, to him, the rabble, and al-most beneath his contempt.

Besides, it was commonly believed by cowmen that sheep destroyed the grass as far as cattle grazing was con-cerned—and this was the chief reason for the animosity against sheep and their herders, which burned so strongly in the hearts of cattle owners and their outfits.

Youbet drained his glass, and continued: "The coyote leaves th' cattle range for th' same good reason yore sheep leave it—because they are chased out, or killed. Naturally, blood kin will hang together in banishment."

"You know a whole lot, don't you?" snorted Clayton, with sarcasm. "Yo're shore wise, you are!"

"He is so vise as a—a gow," remarked Schultz, grinning.

"You'll know more, when you get as old as me," replied the ex-foreman, carefully placing the empty glass on the bar.

"I don't want to get as old as you, if I have to lose all my common sense," retorted Clayton angrily.

"An' be a damned nuisance generally," observed Towne.

"I've seen a lot of things in my life," Youbet began, trying to ignore the tones of the others. They were young men, and he knew that youth grew unduly heated in argument. "I saw th' comin' of th' Texas drive herds, till th' range was crowded where th' year before there was nothin'. I saw th' comin' of th' sheep—an' barb' wire, I'm sorry to say. Th' sheep came like locusts, leavin' a dyin' range behind 'em. Thin, half-starved cattle showed which way they went. You can't tell me nothin' I don't know about sheep."

"An *I*'ve seen sheep dyin' in piles on th' open range," cried Clayton, his own wrongs lashing him into a rage. "*I*'ve seen 'em dynamited, an' drowned and driven hell-to-split over canyons! I've had my men taunted, an' chased, an' killed—*killed*, by God!—just because they tried to make a' honest livin'! Who did it all? Who killed my men an' my sheep? *Who did it?*" he shouted, taking a short step forward, while an endorsing growl ran along the line of sheepmen at his side.

"Cowpunchers—they did it! They killed 'em—an' why? Because we tried to use th' grass that we had as much right to as they had—*that's* why!"

"Th' cows was here first," replied Youbet, keenly alert,

but not one whit abashed by the odds, long as they were. "It was theirs because they was there first."

"It was not theirs, no more'n th' sun was!" cried Towne, unable to allow his chief to do all the talking.

"You said you knowed Waffles," continued Clayton loudly. "Well, he's another of you old-time cowmen! He killed MacKay—murdered him—because we was usin' a hill range a day's ride from his own grass! He had twenty men like hisself to back him up. If we'd been as many as them, they wouldn't 'a' tried it—an' you know it!"

"I don't know anything of th' kind, but I do know—" began Youbet; but Schultz interrupted him with a remark intended to contain humor.

"Ven you say you doand know anyt'ing, you know somedings; ven you know dot you doand know noddings, den you know somedings. Und das iss so—yah."

"Who th' devil told you to stick yore Dutch mouth—" retorted Youbet; but Clayton cut him short.

"So yo're a old-timer, hey?" cried the sheepman. "Well, by God, yore old-time friend Waffles is a coward, a murderer, an'—"

"Yo're a liar!" rang out the vibrant voice of the cowman, his gun out and leveled in a flash. The seven had moved forward as one man, actuated by the same impulse; and their hands were moving toward their guns when the crashes of Youbet's weapon reverberated in the small room, the acrid smoke swirling around him as though to shield him from the result of his folly—a result which he had weighed and then ignored.

Clayton dropped, with his mouth still open. Towne's gun chocked back in the scabbard as its owner stumbled blindly over a chair and went down, never to rise. Schultz fired once, and fell back across the table.

The three shots had followed one another with incredible quickness; and the seven, not believing that one man would dare attack so many, had not expected his play.

Before the stunned sheepmen could begin firing, three were dead.

Price, badly wounded, fired as he plunged to the wall for support; and the other three were now wrapped in their own smoke.

Wounded in several places, with his gun empty, Youbet hurled the weapon at Price, and missed by so narrow a margin that the sheepman's aim was spoiled. Youbet now sprang to the bar, and tried to vault over it, to get to the gun which he knew always lay on the shelf behind it. As his feet touched the upper edge of the counter, he grunted and, collapsing like a jackknife, loosed his hold, and fell to the floor.

"Mein Gott!" groaned Schneider, as he tried to raise himself. He looked around in a dazed manner, hardly understanding just what had happened. "He vas mat; crazy mat!"

Oleson arose unsteadily to his feet, and groped his way along the wall to where Price lay.

The fallen man looked up, in response to the touch on his shoulder; and he swore feebly: "Damn that fool—that idiot!"

"Shut up, an' git out!" shouted the bartender, standing rigidly upright, with a heavy Colt in his upraised hand. There were tears in his eyes, and his voice broke from excitement. "He wouldn't swaller yore insults! He knowed he was a better man! Get out of here, every damned one of you, or I'll begin where he stopped. "G 'wan—*get out!*"

The four looked at him, befuddled and sorely hurt; but they understood the attitude, if they did not quite grasp the words—and they knew that he meant what he looked. Staggering and hobbling, they finally found the door, and plunged out to the street, to meet the crowd of men who were running toward the building.

Jimmy, choking with anger and with respect for the man who had preferred death to insults, slammed shut the door and, dropping the bar into place, turned and gazed at the quiet figure huddled at the base of the counter.

"Old man," he muttered, "now I understands why th' sheep don't stay long on a cattle range."

CHAPTER XIV

Sammy Hunts a Job

SAMMY PORTER, detailed by Hopalong, the trail-boss, rode into Truxton three days before the herd was due, to notify the agent that cars were wanted. Three thousand three-year-olds were on their way to the packing houses and must be sent through speedily. Sammy saw the agent and, leaving him much less sweeter in temper than when he had found him, rode down the dismal street kicking up a prodigious amount of dust. One other duty demanded attention and its fulfillment was promised by the sign over the faded pine front of the first building.

"Restaurant," he read aloud. "That's mine. Beans, bacon an' biscuits for 'most a month! But now I'm goin' to forget that Blinky Thompkins ever bossed a trail wagon an' tried to cook."

Dismounting, he glanced in the window and pulled at the downy fuzz trying to make a showing on his upper lip. "Purty, all-right. Brown hair an' I reckon brown eyes. Nice li'l girl. Well, they don't make no dents on *me* no more," he congratulated himself, and entered. His twenty years fairly sagged with animosity toward the fair sex, the intermittent smoke from the ruins of his last love affair still painfully in evidence at times. But careless as he tried to be he could not banish the swaggering mannerisms of Youth in the presence of Maid, or change his habit of speech under such conditions.

"Well, well," he smiled. "Here I 'are' again. Li'l Sammy in search of his grub. An' if it's as nice as you he'll shore have to flag his outfit an' keep this town all to hisself. Got any chicken?"

The maid's nose went up and Sammy noticed that it tilted a trifle, and he cocked his head on one side to see it better. And the eyes were brown, very big and very deep—they possessed a melting quality he had never observed before. The maid shrugged her shoulders and swung around, the tip-tilt nose going a bit higher.

Sammy leaned back against the door and nodded approval of the slender figure in spic-and-span white. "Li'l Sammy is a fer-o-cious cow-punch from a chickenless land," he observed, sorrowfully. "There ain't *no* kinds of chickens. Nothin' but men an' cattle an' misguided cooks; an' beans, bacon an' biscuits. Li'l Miss, have you a chicken for me?"

"No!" The head went around again, Sammy bending to one side to see it as long as he could. The pink, shell-like ear that flirted with him through the loosely-gathered, rebellious hair caught his attention and he leveled an accusing finger at it. "Naughty li'l ear, peekin' at Sammy that-a-way! Oh, you stingy girl!" he chided as the back of her head confronted him. "Well, Sammy don't like girls, no matter how pink their ears are, or turned up their noses, or wonderful their eyes. He just wants chicken, an' all th' fixin's. He'll be very humble an' grateful to Li'l Miss if she'll tell him what he can have. An' he'll behave just like a Sunday-school boy.

"Aw, you don't want to get mad at only me," he continued after she refused to answer. "Got any chicken? Got any—eggs? Lucky Sammy! An' some nice ham? Two lucky Sammies. An' some mashed potatoes? Fried? Good. An' will Li'l Miss please make a brand new cup of strong coffee? Then he'll go over an' sit in that nice chair an' watch an' listen. But you oughtn't get mad at him. Are you really-an'-truly mad?"

She swept down the room, into the kitchen partitioned off at the farther end and slammed the door. Sammy grinned, tugged at his upper lip and fancy-stepped to the table. He smoothed his tumbled hair, retied his neckerchief and dusted himself off with his red bandanna handkerchief. "Nice li'l town," he soliloquized. "*Fine* li'l town. Dunno as I ought to go back to th' herd—Hoppy didn't tell me to. Reckon I'll stick in town an' argue with th' agent. If I argue with th' agent I'll be busy; an' I can't leave while I'm busy." He leaned back and chuckled. "Lucky me! If Hoppy had gone an' picked Johnny to argue with th' agent for three whole days where would *I* be? But I gotta keep Johnny outa here, th' son-of-a-gun. He ain't like me—he *likes* girls; an' he ain't bashful."

He picked up a paper lying on a chair near him and looked it over until the kitchen door squeaked. She carried a tray covered with a snow-white napkin which looked like a topographical map with its mountains and valleys and plains. His chuckle was infectious to the extent of a smile and her eyes danced as she placed his dinner before him.

"Betcha it's fine," he grinned, shoveling sugar into the inky coffee. "Blinky oughta have a good look at *this* layout."

"Don't be too sure," she retorted. "Mrs. Olmstead is sick and I'm taking charge of things for her. I'm not a good cook."

"Nothin's th' matter with this," he assured her between

bites. "Lots better'n most purty girls can do. If Hopalong goes up against this he'll offer you a hundred a month an' throw Blinky in to wash th' dishes. But he'd have to 'point me guard, or you wouldn't have no time to do no cookin'.'"

"You'd make a fine guard," she retorted.

"Don't believe it, huh? Jus' wait till you know me better."

"How do you know I'm going to?"

"I'm a good guesser. Jus' put a li'l pepper right there on that yalla spot. Say, any chance to get a job in this town?"

"Why, I don't know."

"Goin' to stay long?"

"I can't stay. I won't go till Mrs. Olmstead is well."

"Not meanin' no harm to Mrs. Olmstead, of course—but you don't *have* to go, do you?"

"I do as I please."

"So I was thinkin'. Now, 'bout that job: any chance? Any ranches near here?"

"Several. But they want *men*. Are you a real cowboy?"

Sammy folded his hands and shook his head sorrowfully. "Huh! Want *men*! Now if I only had whiskers like Blinky. Why, 'course I'm a cowboy. Regular one—but I can outgrow it easy. I'm a sorta maverick an' I'm willin' to wear a nice brand. My name's Sammy Porter," he suggested.

"That's nice. Mine isn't nice."

"Easy to change it. Really like mine?"

"Coffee strong enough?"

"Sumptious. How long's Mrs. Olmstead going to be sick?"

Her face clouded. "I don't know. I hope it will not be for long. She's had *so* much trouble the past year. Oh, wait! I forgot the toast!" and she sped lightly away to rescue the burning bread.

The front door opened and slammed shut, the newcomer dropping into the nearest chair. He pounded on the table. "Hello, there! I want somethin' to eat, quick!"

Sammy turned and saw a portly, flashily dressed drummer whose importance was written large all over him. "Hey!" barked the drummer, "gimme something to eat. I can't wait all day!"

A vicious clang in the kitchen told that his presence was known and resented.

As Sammy turned from the stranger he caught sight of a pretty flushed face disappearing behind the door jamb, the brown eyes snapping and the red lips straight and compressed. His glance, again traveling to the drummer, began with the dusty patent leathers and went slowly upward, resting boldly on the heavy face. Sammy's expression told nothing and the newcomer, glaring at him for an instant, looked over the menu card and then stared at the partition, fidgeting in his chair, thumping meanwhile on the table with his fingers.

At a sound from the kitchen Sammy turned back to his table and smiled reassuringly as the toast was placed before him. "I burned it and had to make new," she said, the pink spots in her cheeks a little deeper in color.

"Why, th' other was good enough for me," he replied. "Know Mrs. Olmstead a long time?" he asked.

"Ever since I was a little girl. She lived near us in Clev—"

"Cleveland," he finished. "State of Ohio," he added, laughingly. "I'll get it all before I go."

"Indeed you won't!"

"Miss," interrupted the drummer, "if you ain't *too* busy, would you mind gettin' me a steak an' some coffee?" The tones were weighted with sarcasm and Sammy writhed in his chair. The girl flushed, turned abruptly and went slowly into the kitchen, from where considerable noise now emanated. In a short time she emerged with the drummer's order, placed it in front of him and started back again.

But he stopped her. "I said I wanted it rare an' it's well done. An' also that I wanted fried potatoes. Take it back."

The girl's eyes blazed: "You gave no instructions," she retorted.

"Don't tell me that! I know what I said!" snapped the drummer. "I won't eat it an' I won't pay for it. If you wasn't so *busy* you'd heard what I said."

Sammy was arising before he saw the tears of vexation in her eyes, but they settled it for him. He placed his hand lightly on her shoulder. "You get me some pie an' take a li'l walk. Me an' this here gent is goin' to hold a palaver. Ain't we, stranger?"

The drummer glared at him. "We ain't!" he retorted.

Sammy grinned ingratiatingly. "Oh, my; but we are." He slung a leg over a chair back and leaned forward, resting his elbow on his knee. "Yes, indeed we are—least-a-wise, *I* am." His tones became very soft and confiding. "An' I'm shore goin' to watch you eat that steak."

"What's that you're going to do?" the drummer demanded, half rising.

"Sit down," begged Sammy, his gun swinging at his knee. He picked up a toothpick with his left hand and chewed it reflectively. "These here Colts make a' awful muss, sometimes," he remarked. " 'Specially at close range. Why," he confided, "I once knowed a man what was shot 'most in two. He was a mosshead an' wouldn't do what he was told. Better sorta lead off at that steak, *hombre*," he suggested, chewing evenly on the toothpick. Noticing that the girl still lingered, hypnotized by fear and curiosity, he spoke to her over his shoulder. "Won't you please get me that pie, or somethin'? Run out an' borrow a pan, or somethin'," he pleaded. "I don't like to be handicapped when I'm feedin' cattle."

The drummer's red face paled a little and one hand stole cautiously under his coat—and froze there. Sammy hardly had moved, but the Colt was now horizontal and

glowered at the gaudy waistcoat. He was between it and
the girl and she did not see the movement. His smile was
placid and fixed and he spoke so that she should get no
inkling of what was going on. "Never drink on an empty
stomach," he advised. "After you eat that meal, then you
can fuss with yore flask all you wants." He glanced out of
the corner of his eye at the girl and nodded. "Still there!
Oh, I most forgot, stranger. You take off yore hat an' 'pol-
ogize, so she can go. Jus' say yo're a dawg an never did
have no manners. *Say* it!" he ordered, softly. The drummer gulped and muttered something, but the Colt, still
hidden from the girl by its owner's body, moved forward
a little and Sammy's throaty growl put an end to the muttering. "Say it plain," he ordered, the color fading from
his face and leaving pink spots against the white. "That's
better—now, Li'l Miss, you get me that pie—please!" he
begged.

When they were alone Sammy let the gun swing at his
knee again. "I don't know how they treats wimmin where
you came from, stranger; but out here we're plumb polite.
'Course you didn't know that, an' that's why you didn't
get all mussed up. Yo're jus' plain ignorant an' can't help
yore bringin' up. Now, you eat that steak, *pronto!*"

"It's too cold, now," grumbled the drummer, fidgeting
in the chair.

The puncher's left hand moved to the table again and
when it returned to his side there was a generous layer
of red pepper on the meat. "Easy to fix things when you
know how," he grinned. "If it gets any colder I'll fix it
some more." His tones became sharper and the words lost
their drawled softness. "You goin' to start ag'in that by
yoreself, or am I goin' to help you?" he demanded, lifting
his leg off the chair and standing erect. All the humor had
left his face and there was a grimness about the tight lips
and a menace in the squinting eyes that sent a chill rippling down the drummer's spine. He tasted a forkful of

the meat and gulped hastily, tears welling into his eyes. The puncher moved a little nearer and watched the frantic gulps with critical attention. " 'Course, you can eat any way you wants—yo're payin' for it; but boltin' like a coyote ain't good for th' stummick. Howsomever, it's yore grub," he admitted.

A cup of cold coffee and a pitcher of water followed the meat in the same gulping haste. Tears streamed down the drummer's red face as he arose and turned toward the door. "Hol' on, stranger!" snapped Sammy. "That costs six bits," he prompted. The coins rang out on the nearest table, the door slammed and the agonized stranger ran madly down the street, cursing at every jump. Sammy sauntered to the door and craned his neck. "Somebody's jus' naturally goin' to bust him wide open one of these days. He ain't got no sense," he muttered, turning back to get his pipe.

A cloud of dust rolled up from the south, causing Briggs a little uneasiness, and he scowled through the door at the long empty siding and the pens sprawled along it.

Steps clacked across the platform and a grinning cowpuncher stopped at the open window. "They're here," he announced. "How 'bout th' cars?"

Briggs looked around wearily. For three days his life had been made miserable by this pest, who carried a laugh in his eyes, a sting on his tongue and a chip on his shoulder. "They'll be here soon," he replied, with little interest. "But there's th' pens."

"Yes, there's th' pens," smiled Sammy. "They'll hold 'bout one-tenth of that herd. Ain't I been pesterin' you to get them cars?"

The agent sighed expressively and listened to the instrument on his table. When it ceased he grabbed the key and asked a question. Then he smiled for the first time that day. "They're passing Franklin. Be here in two hours. Now get out of here or I'll lick you."

"There's a nice place in one of them pens," smiled Sammy.

"I see you're eating at Olmstead's," parried the agent.

"Yea."

"Nice girl. Come up last summer when Mrs. Olmstead petered out. I ate there last winter."

Sammy grinned at him. "Why'd you stop?"

Briggs grew red and glanced at the nearing cloud of dust. "Better help your outfit, hadn't you?"

Sammy was thoughtful. "Say, that's a plumb favorite eatin' place, ain't it?"

Briggs laughed. "Wait till Saturday when th' boys come in. There's a dozen shinin' up to that girl. Tom Clarke is real persistent."

Sammy forsook the building as a prop. "Who's he? Puncher?"

"Yes; an' bad," replied the agent. "But I reckon she don't know it."

Sammy looked at the dust cloud and turned to ask one more question. "What does this persistent gent look like, an' where's he hang out?" He nodded at the verbose reply and strode to his horse to ride toward the approaching herd. He espied Red first, and hailed. "Cars here in two hours. Where's Hoppy?"

"Back in th' dust. But what happened to *you*?" demanded Red, with virile interest. Sammy ignored the challenge and loped along the edge of the cloud until he found the trail boss. "Them cars'll be here in two hours," he reported.

"Take you three days to find it out?" snapped Hopalong.

"Took me three days to get 'em. I just about unraveled that agent. He swears every time he hears a noise, thinkin' it's me."

"Broke?" demanded Hopalong.

Sammy flushed. "I ain't gambled a cent since I hit town. An' say, them pens won't hold a tenth of 'em," he replied, looking over the dark blur that heaved under the dust cloud like a fog-covered, choppy sea.

"I'm goin' to hold 'em on grass," replied the trail boss. "They ain't got enough cars on this toy road to move all them cows in less'n a week. I ain't goin' to let 'em lose no weight in pens. Wait a minute! You're on night herd for stayin' away."

When Sammy rode into camp the following morning he scorned Blinky's food, much to the open-mouthed amazement of that worthy and Johnny Nelson. Blinky thought of doctors and death; but Johnny, noticing his bunkmate's restlessness and careful grooming of his person, had grave suspicions. "Good grub in this town?" he asked, saddling to go on his shift.

Sammy wiped a fleck of dust off his boot and looked up casually. "Shore. Best is at the Dutchman's at th' far end of th' street."

Johnny mounted, nodded and departed for the herd, where Red was pleasantly cursing his tardiness. Red would eat Blinky's grub and gladly. Johnny was cogitating. "There's a girl in this town, an' he's got three days' head start. No wonder them cars just got here!" Red's sarcastic voice intruded. "Think I eat grass, or my stummick's made of rubber?" he snapped. "Think I feed onct a month like a snake?"

"No, Reddie," smiled Johnny, watching the eyebrows lift at the name. "More like a hawg."

Friday morning, a day ahead of the agent's promise, the cars backed onto the siding and by noon the last cow of the herd was taking its first—and last—ride. Sammy slipped away from the outfit at the pens and approached the restaurant from the rear. He would sit behind the partition this time and escape his friends.

The soft sand deadened his steps and when he looked in at the door, a cheery greeting on the tip of his tongue, he stopped and stared unnoticed by the sobbing girl bent over the table. One hand, outflung in dejected abandon, hung over the side and Sammy's eyes, glancing at it, narrowed as he looked. His involuntary, throaty exclamation sent the bowed head up with a jerk, but the look of hate and fear quickly died out of her eyes as she recognized him.

"An' all th' world tumbled down in a heap," he smiled. "But it'll be all right again, same as it allus was," he assured her. "Will Li'l Miss tell Sammy all about it so he can put it together again?"

She looked at him through tear-dimmed eyes, the sobs slowly drying to a spasmodic catching in the rounded throat. She shook her head and the tears welled up again in answer to his sympathy. He walked softly to the table and placed a hand on her bowed head. "Li'l Miss will tell Sammy all about it when she dries her eyes an' gets comfy. Sammy will make things all right again an' laugh with her. Don't you mind him a mite—jus' cry hard, an' when all th' tears are used up, then you tell Sammy what it's all about." She shook her head and would not look up. He bent down carefully and examined the bruised wrist—and his eyes glinted with rage; but he did not speak. The minutes passed in silence, the girl ashamed to show her reddened and tear-stained face; the boy stubbornly determined to stay and learn the facts. He heard his friends tramp past, wondering where he was, but he did not move.

Finally she brushed back her hair and looked up at him and the misery in her eyes made him catch his breath. "Won't you go?" she pleaded.

He shook his head.

"Please!"

"Not till I find out whose fingers made them marks," he replied. The look of fear flashed up again, but he checked it with a smile he far from felt. "Nobody's goin' to make you cry, an' get away with it," he told her. "Who was it?"

"I won't tell you. I can't tell you! I don't know!"

"Li'l Miss, look me in th' eyes an' say it again. I thought so. You mustn't say things that ain't true. Who did that?"

"What do you want to know for?"

"Oh, jus' because."

"What will you do?"

"Oh, I'll sorta talk to him. All I want to know is his name."

"I won't tell you; you'll fight with him."

He turned his sombrero over and looked gravely into its crown. "Well," he admitted, "he *might* not like me talkin' 'bout it. Of course, you can't never tell."

"But he didn't mean to hurt me. He's only rough and boisterous; and he wasn't himself," she pleaded, looking down.

"Uh-huh," grunted Sammy, cogitating. "So'm I. *I'm* awful rough an' boisterous, *I* am; only I don't hurt wimmin. What's his name?"

"I'll not tell you!"

"Well, all right; but if he ever comes in here again an' gets rough an' boisterous he'll lose a hull lot of future. I'll naturally blow most of his head off, which is frequent fatal. What's that? Oh, he's a bad man, is he? Uh-huh; so'm I. Well, I'm goin' to run along now an' see th' boss. If you won't tell, you won't. I'll be back soon," and he sauntered to the street and headed for Pete's saloon, where the agent had said Mr. Clarke was wont to pass his fretful hours.

As he turned the corner he bumped into Hopalong and Johnny, who grabbed at him, and missed. He backed off and rested on his toes, gingery and alert. "Keep yore dusty han's off'n me," he said, quietly. "I'm goin' down to palaver with a gent what I don't like."

Hopalong's shrewd glance looked him over. "What did this gent do?" he asked, and he would not be evaded.

"Oh, he insulted a nice li'l girl, an' I'm in a hurry."

"G'way!" exclaimed Johnny. "That straight?"

"Too damn straight," snapped Sammy. "He went an' bruised her wrists an' made her cry."

"Lead th' way, Kid," rejoined Johnny, readjusting his belt. "Mebby he's got some friends," he suggested, hopefully.

"Yes," smiled Hopalong, "mebby he has. An' anyhow, Sammy; you *know* yo're plumb careless with that gun. You might miss him. Lead th' way."

As they started toward Pete's Johnny nudged his bunkmate in the ribs: "Say; she ain't got no sisters, has she?" he whispered.

One hour later Sammy, his face slightly scratched, lounged into the kitchen and tossed his sombrero on a chair, grinning cheerfully at the flushed, saucy face that looked out from under a mass of rebellious, brown hair. "Well, I saw th' boss, an' I come back to make everythin' well again," he asserted, laughing softly. "That rough an' boisterous Mr. Clarke has sloped. He won't come back no more."

"Why, *Sammy*!" she cried, aghast. "What *have* you done?"

"Well, for one thing, I've got you callin' me Sammy," he chuckled, trying to sneak a hand over hers. "I told th' boss I'm goin' to get a job up here, so I'll know Mr. Clarke won't come back. But you know, he only thought he was bad. I shore had to take his ol' gun away from him so he wouldn't go an' shoot hisself, an' when las' seen he was feelin' for his cayuse, intendin' to leave these parts. That's what I *done*," he nodded, brightly. "Now comes what I'm goin' to do. Oh, Li'l Miss," he whispered, eagerly. "I'm jus' all mixed up an' millin'. My own feet plumb get in my way. So I jus' gotta stick aroun' an' change yore name, what you don't like. Uh-huh; that's jus' what I gotta do," he smiled.

She tossed her head and the tip-tilt nose went up indignantly. "Indeed you'll do nothing of the kind, Sammy Porter!" she retorted. "I'll choose my own name when the time comes, and it will not be Porter!"

He arose slowly and looked around. Picking up the pencil that lay on the shelf he lounged over to the partition and printed his name three times in large letters. "All right, Li'l Miss," he agreed. "I'll jus' leave a list where you can see it while you're selectin'. I'm now goin' out to get that job we spoke about. You have th' name all picked out when I get back," he suggested, waving his hand at the wall. "An' did anybody ever tell you it was plumb risky to stick yore li'l nose up thataway?"

"Sammy Porter!" she stormed, stamping in vexation near the crying point. "You get right out of here! I'll *never* speak to you again!"

"You won't get a chance to talk much if you don't sorta bring that snubby nose down a li'l lower. I'm plumb weak at times." He laughed joyously and edged to the door. "Don't forget that list. I'm goin' after that job. So-long, Li'l Miss."

"Sammy!"

"Oh, all right; I'll go after it later on," he laughed, returning.

CHAPTER XV

When Johnny Sloped

JOHNNY NELSON hastened to the corner of the bunkhouse and then changed his pace until he seemed to ooze from there to the cook shack door, where he lazily leaned against the door jamb and ostentatiously picked his teeth with the negative end of a match. The cook looked up calmly, and calmly went on with his work; but if there was anything rasping enough to cause his calloused soul to quiver it was the aforesaid calisthenics executed by Johnny and the match; for Cookie's blunt nature hated hints. If Johnny had demanded, even profanely and with large personal animus, why meals were not ahead of time, it would be a simple matter to heave something and en- large upon his short cut speech. But the subtleties left the cook floundering in a mire of rage—which he was very careful to conceal from Johnny. The youthful nuisance had been evincing undue interest in early suppers for nearly a month; and judging from the lightness of his re- pasts he was entirely unjustified in showing any interest at all in the evening meal. So Cookie strangled the biscuit in his hand, but smiled blandly at his tormentor.

"Well, all through?" he pleasantly inquired, glancing carelessly at Johnny's clothes.

"I'm hopin' to begin," retorted Johnny, and the tooth-pick moved rapidly up and down.

Cookie condensed another biscuit and gulped. "That's shore some stone," he said, enviously, eying the two-caret diamond in Johnny's new, blue tie. Johnny never had worn a tie before he became owner of the diamond, but with the stone came the keen realization of how lost it was in a neck-kerchief, how often covered by the wind-blown folds; so he had hastened to Buckskin and spent a dollar that belonged to Red for the tie, thus exhausting both the supply of ties and Red's dollars. The honor of wearing the only tie and diamond in that section of the cow-country brought responsibilities, for he had spoken hastily to several humorous friends and stood a good chance of being soundly thrashed therefor.

He threw away the match and scratched his back ec-statically on the door jamb while he strained his eyes try-ing to look under his chin. Fixed chins and short ties are trials one must learn to accept philosophically—and Johnny might have been spared the effort were it not for the fact that the tie had been made for a boy, and was awesomely shortened by encircling a sixteen-inch neck. Evidently it had been made for a boy violently inclined toward a sea-faring life, as suggested by the anchors em-broidered in white down its middle.

"Lemme see it," urged Cookie, sighing because its owner had resolutely refused to play poker when he had no cash. This had become a blighting sorrow in the life of a naturally exuberant and very fair cook.

"An' for how long?" demanded Johnny, a cold and cal-culating light glinting in his eyes.

"Oh, till supper's ready," replied Cookie with great carelessness.

"Nix; but you can wear it twenty minutes if you'll get my grub quick," he replied. "Got to meet Lucas at half-past five." He cautiously dropped the match he had thoughtlessly produced.

The cook tried to look his belief and accepted the offer. Johnny's remarkably clean face, plastered hair and general gala attire suggested that Lucas was a woman—which Lucas profanely would have denied. Also, Johnny had been seen washing Ginger, and when a puncher washes a cayuse it's a sign of insanity. Besides, Ginger belonged to Red, who also had owned that lone dollar. Red's clothes did not fit Johnny.

"Goin' to surprise Lucas?" inquired the cook.

"What you mean?"

Cookie glanced meaningly at the attire: "Er—you ain't in th' habit of puttin' on war paint for to see Lucas, are you?"

Johnny's mental faculties produced: "Oh, we're goin' to a dance."

"Where 'bouts?" exploded the cook.

"*Way* up north!" One's mind needs to be active as a flea to lie properly to a man like the cook. He had made a ghastly mistake.

"By golly! I'll give th' boys cold grub an' go with you," and the cook began to save time.

Johnny gulped and shook his head: "Got a invite?"

Cookie caught the pan on his foot before it struck the floor and gasped: "Invite? Ain't it free-fer-all?"

"No; this is a high-toned thing-a-bob. Costs a dollar a head, too."

"High-toned?" snorted the cook, derisively. "Don't they know you? An' I thought Red was broke. Show me that permit!"

"Lucas's got it—that's why I've got to catch him."

"Oh! An' is *he* goin' all feathered up, too?"

"Shore, he's got to."

"Huh! He wouldn't dress like that to see a *fight*. Has she got any sisters?" Cookie finished, hopefully.

"Now what you talkin' about?"

"Why, Lucas," answered the cook, placidly. "Lemme tell you something. When you want to lose me have a invite to a water-drinkin' contest. An' before you go, be shore to rub Hoppy's boots some more; that's such a pasty shine it'll look like sand-paper before you get to th'— dance. You want to make it hard an' slippery. An' I've read som'ers that only wimmin ought to smell like a drug-store. You better let her do th' fumigatin'."

Johnny surrendered and dolefully whiffed the crushed violets he had paid two bits a pint for at El Paso—it was not necessary to whiff them, but he did so.

"You ought to hone yore razor, too," continued the cook, critically.

"I told Buck it was dull, I ain't goin' to sharpen it for him. But, say, are you shore about th' perfumery?"

"Why, of course."

"But how'll I git it off?"

"Bury th' clothes," suggested Cookie, grinning.

"I like your gall! Which clothes are best, Pete's or Billy's?"

"Pete's would fit you like th' wide, wide world. You don't want blankets on when you go courtin'. Try Billy's. An' I got a pair of socks, though one's green—but th' boots'll hide it."

"I didn't put none on my socks, you chump!"

"How'd *I* know? But, say! Has she got any sisters?"

"No!" yelled Johnny, halfway through the gallery in search of Billy's clothes. When he emerged Cookie looked him over. "Ain't it funny, Kid, how a pipe'll stink up clothes?" he smiled. Johnny's retort was made over several yards of ground and when he had mounted Cookie yelled and waved him to return. When Johnny had obeyed and impatiently demanded the reason, Cookie pleasantly remarked: "Now, be shore an' give her my love, Kid."

Johnny's reply covered half a mile of trail.

Johnny rode alertly through Perry's Bend, for Sheriff Nolan was no friend of his; and Nolan was not only a discarded suitor of Miss Joyce, but a warm personal friend of George Greener, the one rival Johnny feared. Greener was a widower as wealthy as he was unscrupulous, and a power on that range: when he said "jump," Nolan soared. The sheriff was standing before the Palace saloon when Johnny rode past, and he could not keep quiet. His comment was so judiciously chosen as to bring white spots on Johnny's flushed cheeks. The Bar-20 puncher was not famed for his self-control, and, wheeling in the saddle, he pointed a quivering forefinger at Mr. Nolan's badge of office, so conspicuously displayed: "Better men than you have hid behind a badge and banked on a man's regard for th' law savin' 'em from their just deserts. Politics is a hell of a thing when it opens th' door to anything that might roll in on th' wind. You come down across th' line tomorrow an' see me, without th' nickel-plated ornament you disgraces," he invited. "Any dog can tell a lie in his kennel, but it takes guts to bark outside th' yard."

Mr. Nolan flushed, went white, hesitated, and walked away. To fight in defense of the law was his duty; but no sane man warred on the Bar-20 unless he must. Mr. Nolan was a man whose ideas of necessity followed strange curves, and not to his credit. One might censure Mr. Cassidy or Mr. Connors, or pick a fight with some of the others of that outfit and not get killed; but he must not harm their protégé. Mr. Nolan not only walked away but he sought the darkest shadows and held conversation with himself. If it were only possible to get the pugnacious and very much spoiled Mr. Nelson to fracture, smash, pulverize some law! This, indeed, would be sweet.

Meanwhile Johnny, having watched the sheriff slip away, loosed a few more words into the air and went on his way, whistling cheerfully. Reaching the Joyce cottage he was admitted by Miss Joyce herself and at sight of her blushing face his exuberant confidence melted and left him timid. This he was wont to rout by big words and a dashing air he did not feel.

"Oh! Come right in," she invited. "But you are late," she laughed, chidingly.

He critically regarded the dimples, while he replied that he had drawn rein to slay the sheriff but, knowing that it would cost him more valuable time, he had consented with himself to postpone the event.

"But you must not do that!" she cried. "Why, that's terrible! You shouldn't even think of such things."

"Well, of course—if yo're agin' it I wont."

"But what did he do?"

"Oh, I don't reckon I can tell that. But do you really want him to live?"

"Why, certainly! What a foolish question."

"But why do you? Do you—*like* him?"

"I like everybody."

"Yes; an' everybody likes you, too," he growled, the smile fading. "That's th' trouble. Do you like him very much?"

"I wish you wouldn't ask such foolish questions."

"Yes; I know. But do you?"

"I prefer not to answer."

"Huh! That's an answer in itself. You do."

"I don't think you're very nice tonight," she retorted, a little pout spoiling the bow in her lips. "You're awfully jealous, and I don't like it."

"Gee! Don't like it! I should think you'd want me to be

jealous. I only wish you was jealous of *me*. Norah, I've just
got to say it now, an' find out—"

"Yes; tell me," she interrupted eagerly. "What *did* he
do?"

"Who?"

"Mr. Nolan, of course."

"Nolan?" he demanded in surprise.

"Yes, yes; tell me."

"I ain't talking about *him*. I was goin' to tell you something that I've—"

"That you've done and now regret? Have you ever—
ever killed a man?" she breathed. "Have you?"

"No; *yes!* Lots of 'em," he confessed, remembering that
once she had expressed admiration for brave and daring
men. "Most half as many as Hopalong; an' I ain't near as
old as him, neither."

"You mean Mr. Cassidy? Why don't you bring him with
you some evening? I'd like to meet him."

"Not *me*. I went an' brought a friend along once, an'
had to lick him th' next day to keep him away from here.
He'd 'a' camped right out there in front if I hadn't. No,
ma'am; not any."

"Why, the idea! But Mr. Greener's very much like your
friend, Mr. Cassidy. He's very brave, and a wonderful shot.
He told me so himself."

"What! He told you so hisself! Well, well. Beggin' yore
pardon, he ain't nowise like Hoppy, not even in th' topics
of his conversation. Why, he's a child; an' blinks when he
shoots off a gun. Here—can he show a gun like mine?"
and forthwith he held out his Colt, butt foremost, and indicated the notches he had cut that afternoon. A fleeting
doubt went through his mind at what his outfit would say
when it saw those notches. The Bar-20 cut no notches. It
wanted to forget.

She looked at them curiously and suddenly drew back.
"Oh! Are they—*are* they?" she whispered.

He nodded: "They are. There is plenty of room for No-lan's, an' mebby his owner, too," he suggested. "Can't you see, Norah?" he asked in a swift change of tone. "Can't you see? Don't you know how much I—"

"Yes. It must be terrible to have such remorse," she quickly interposed. "And I sympathize with you deeply, too."

"Remorse nothin'! Them fellers was lookin' for it, an' they got just what they deserved. If I hadn't 'a' done it somebody else would."

"And *you* a murderer! I never thought that of *you*. I can hardly believe it of you. And you calmly confess it to me as though it were nothing!"

"Why, I—I—"

"Don't talk to me! To think you have human blood on your hands. To think—"

"Norah! Norah, listen; won't you?"

"—that you are that sort of a man! How dare you call here as you have? How dare you?"

"But I tell you they were tryin' to get *me*! I just *had* to. Why, I didn't do it for nothin'. I've got a right to defend myself, ain't I?"

"You *had* to? Is that true?" she demanded.

"Why, shore! Think I go 'round killin' men, like Greener does, just for th' fun of it?"

"He doesn't do anything of the kind," she retorted. "You know he doesn't! Didn't you just say he blinks when he shoots off a gun?"

"Yes; I did. But I didn't want you to think he was a murderer like Nolan," he explained. Even Cookie, he thought, would find it hard to get around that neat little effort.

"I'm so relieved," she laughed, delighted at her success in twisting him. "I am so glad he doesn't blink when he shoots. I'd hate a man who was afraid to shoot."

Johnny's chest arose a little. "Well, how 'bout me?"

"But you've killed men; you've shot down your fellow men; have ghastly marks on your revolver to brag about."

"Well—say—but how can I shoot without shootin' or kill without killin'?" he demanded. "An' I don't brag about 'em, neither; it makes me feel too sad to do any braggin'. An' Greener's killed 'em, too; an' he brags about it."

"Yes; but he doesn't blink!" she exclaimed triumphantly.

"Neither do *I*."

"Yes; but you shoot to kill."

"Lord pity us—don't *he*?"

"Y-e-s, but that's different," she replied, smiling brightly.

Johnny looked around the room, his eyes finally resting on his hat.

"Yes, I see it's different. Greener can kill, an' blink! I can't. If he kills a man he's a hero; I'm a murderer. I kinda reckon he's got th' trail. But I love you, an' you've got to pick my trail—does it lead up or down?"

"Johnny Nelson! What are you saying?" she demanded, arising.

"Something turrible, mebby. I don't know; an' I don't care. It's true—so there you are. Norah, can't you see I do?" he pleaded, holding out his hands. "Won't you marry me?"

She looked down, her cheeks the color of fire, and Johnny continued hurriedly: "I've loved you a whole month! When I'm ridin' around I sorta' see you, an' hear you. Why, I talk to you lots when I'm alone. I've saved up some money, an' I had to work hard to save it, too. I've got some cows runnin' with our'n—in a little while I'll have a ranch of my own. Buck'll let me use th' east part of th' ranch, an' there's a hill over there that'd look fine with a house on it. I can't wait no longer, Norah, I've got to know. Will you let me put this on yore finger?" He swiftly bent the pin into a ring and held it out eagerly: "Can I?"

She pushed him away and yielded to a sudden pricking

of her conscience, speaking swiftly, as if forcing herself to
do a disagreeable duty, and hating herself at the moment.
"Johnny, I've been a—a flirt! When I saw you were beginning to care too much for me I should have stopped it;
but I didn't. I amused myself—but I want you to believe
one thing; I never thought what it might mean to you. It
was carelessness with me. But I was flirting, just the
same—and it hurts to admit it. I'm not good enough for
you, Johnny Nelson; it's hard to say, but it's true. Can you,
will you forgive me?"

He choked and stepped forward holding out his hands
imploringly, but she eluded him. When he saw the shame
in her face, the tears in her eyes, he stopped and laughed
gently: "But we can begin right, now, can't we? I don't
care, not if you'll let me see you same as ever. You might
get to care for me. And, anyhow, it ain't yore fault. I
reckon it's me that's to blame."

At that moment he was nearer to victory than he had
ever been; but he did not realize it and opportunity died
when he failed to press his advantage.

"I *am* to blame," she said, so low he could hardly catch
the words. When she continued it was with a rush: "I am
not free—I haven't been for a week. I'm not free any
more—and I've been leading you on!"

His face hardened, for now the meaning of Greener's
sneering laugh came to him, and a seething rage swept
over him against the man who had won. He knew
Greener, knew him well—the meanness of the man's nature, his cold cruelty; the many things to the man's dis-
credit loomed up large against the frailty of the woman
before him.

Norah stepped forward and laid a pleading hand on his
arm, for she knew the mettle of the men who worked
under Buck Peters: "What are you thinking? Tell me!"

"Why, I'm thinking what Nolan said. An', Norah, listen.
You say you want me to forgive you? Well, I do, if there's

anything to forgive. But I want you to primise me that if Greener don't treat you right you'll tell me."

"What do you mean?"

"Only what I said. Do you promise?"

"Perhaps you would better speak to him about it!" she retorted.

"I will—an' plain. But don't worry 'bout me. It was my fault for bein' a tenderfoot. I never played this game before, an' don't know th' cards. Good-by."

He rode away slowly, and made the rounds, and by the time he reached Lacey's he was so unsteady that he was refused a drink and told to go home. But he headed for the Palace instead, and when he stepped high over the doorsill Nolan was seated in a chair tipped back against one of the side walls, and behind the bar on the other side of the room Jed Terry drummed on the counter and expressed his views on local matters. The sheriff was listening in a bored way until he saw Johnny enter and head his way, feet high and chest out; and at that moment Nolan's interest in local affairs flashed up brightly.

Johnny lost no time: "Nolan," he said, rocking on his heels, "tell Greener I'll kill him if he marries that girl. He killed his first wife by abuse an' he don't kill no more. Savvy?"

The sheriff warily arose, for here was the opportunity he had sought. The threat to kill had a witness.

"An' if you opens your toad's mouth about her like you did tonight, I'll kill you, too." The tones were dispassionate, the words deliberate.

"Hear that, Jed?" cried the sheriff, excitedly. "Nelson, yo're under ar—"

"Shut up!" snapped Johnny loudly, this time with feeling. "When yo're betters are talkin' you keep your face closed. Now, it ain't hardly healthy to slander wimmin in this country, 'specially *good* wimmin. You lied like a dog to me tonight, an' I let you off; don't try it again."

"I told th' truth!" snapped Nolan, heatedly. "I said she was a flirt an' by th' great horned spoon she is a flirt, an' you—"

The sheriff prided himself upon his quickness, but the leaping gun was kicked out of his hand before he knew what was coming; a chair glanced off Jed's face and wrapped the front window about itself in its passing, leaving the bartender in the throbbing darkness of interplanetary space; and as the sheriff opened his eyes and recovered from the hard swings his face had stopped, a galloping horse drummed southward toward the Bar-20; and the silence of the night was shattered by lusty warwhoops and a spurting .45.

When the sheriff and his posse called at the Bar-20 before breakfast the following morning they found a grouchy outfit and learned some facts.

"Where's Johnny?" repeated Hopalong, with a rising inflection. "Only wish I knowed!"

A murmur of wistful desire arose and Lanky Smith restlessly explained it: "He rampages in 'bout midnight an' wakes us up with his racket. When we asks what he's doin' with *our* possessions he suggests we go to hell. He takes *his* rifle, Pete's rifle, Buck's brand new canteen, 'bout eighty pounds of catridges an' other useful duffle, *all* th' tobacco, an' blows away quick."

"On my cayuse," murmured Red.

"Wearin' my *good* clothes," added Billy, sorrowfully.

"An' *my* boots," sighed Hopalong.

"I ain't got no field glasses no more," grumbled Lanky.

"But he only got one laig of my new pants," chuckled Skinny. "I was too strong for him."

"He yanked my blanket off'n me, which makes me steal Red's," grinned Pete.

"Which you didn't keep very long!" retorted Red, with derision.

"Which makes us all peevish," plaintively muttered Buck.

"Now ain't it a hell of a note?" laughed Cookie, loudly, forthwith getting scarce. He had nothing good enough to be taken.

"An' whichever was it run ag'in' yore face, Sheriff?" sympathetically inquired Hopalong. "Mighty good thing it stopped," he added thoughtfully.

"Never mind my face!" snorted the peace officer hotly as his deputies smoothed out their grins. "I want to know where Nelson is, an' damned quick! We'll search the house first."

"Hold on," responded Buck. "North of Salt Spring Creek yo're a sheriff; down here yo're nothin'. Don't search no house. He ain't here."

"How do I know he ain't?" snapped Nolan.

"My word's good; or there'll be another election stolen up in yore county," rejoined Buck ominously. "An' I wouldn't hunt him too hard, neither. We'll punish him."

Nolan wheeled and rode toward the hills without another word, his posse pressing close behind. When they entered Apache Pass one of them accidentally exploded his rifle, calling forth an angry tirade from the sheriff. Johnny heard it, and cared little for the warning from his friend Lucas; he waited and then rode down the rocky slope of the pass on the trail of the posse, squinting wickedly at the distant group as he caught glimpses of them now and again, and with no anxiety regarding backward glances. "Lot's wife'll have nothing on them if they look back," he muttered, fingering his rifle lovingly. At nightfall he watched them depart and grinned at the chase he would lead them when they returned.

But he did not see them again, although his friends reported that they were turning the range upside down to find him. One of his outfit rode out to him with supplies and information every few days and it was Pete who told him that six posses were in the hills. "An' you can't leave, 'cause one of th' cordon would get you shore. I had a hell of a time getting in today." Red reported that the sheriff had sworn to take him dead or alive. Then came the blow. The sheriff was at the point of death from lockjaw caused by complete paralysis of the curea-frend nerve just above the phlagmatic diaphragm, which Johnny had fractured. It was Hopalong who imparted this sad news, and withered Johnny's hope of returning to a comfortable bunkhouse and square meals. So the fugitive clung to the hills, shunned sky-lines and wondered if the sheriff would recover before snow flew. He was hungry most of the time now because the outfit was getting stingy with the food supplies—and he dared not shoot any game.

Four weeks passed, weeks of hunger and nervous strain, and he was getting desperate. He had learned that Greener and his fiancée were going down to Linnville soon, since Perry's Bend had no parson; and his cup of bitterness, overflowing, drove him to risk an attempt to leave that part of the country. He had seen none of Pete's "cordon" although he had looked for them, and he believed he could get away. So he rode cautiously down Apache Pass one noon, thoughtfully planning his flight. The sand, washed down the rock walls by the last rain, deadened all sounds of his progress, and as he turned a sharp bend in the cut he almost bumped into Greener and Norah Joyce. They were laughing at how they had eluded the crowd of friends who were eager to accompany them—but the laughter froze when Johnny's gun swung up.

" 'Nds up, Greener!" he snapped, viciously, remembering his promise to Sheriff Nolan. "Miss Joyce, if you make any trouble it'll cost him his life."

"Turned highwayman, eh?" sneered Greener, keenly alert for the necessary fraction of a second's carelessness on the part of the other. He was gunman enough to need no more.

"Miss Joyce, will you please ride along? I want to talk to him alone," said Johnny, his eyes fastened intently on those of his enemy.

"Yes, Norah; that's best. I'll join you in a few minutes," urged Greener, smiling at her.

Johnny had a sudden thought and his warning was grave and cold. "Don't get very far away an' don't make no sounds, or signals; if you do it'll be th' quickest way to *need* 'em. He'll pay for any mistakes like that."

"You coward!" she cried, angrily, and then delivered an impromptu lecture that sent the blood surging into the fugitive's wan cheeks. But she obeyed, slowly, at Greener's signal, and when she was out of sight Johnny spoke.

"Greener, yo're not going to marry her. You know what you are, you know how yore first wife died—an' I don't intend that Norah shall be abused as the other was. I'm a fugitive, hard pressed; I'm weak from want of food, and from hardships; all I have left is a slim chance of gettin' away. I've reached the point where I can't harm myself by shooting you an' I'm goin' to do it rather than let any trouble come to her. But you'll get an even break, because I ain't never going to shoot a man when he's helpless. Got anything to say?"

"Yes; yo're th' biggest fool I ever saw," replied Greener. "Yo're locoed through an' through; an' I'm goin' to take great pleasure in putting you away. But I want to thank you for one thing you did. You were drunk at the time an' may not remember it. When you hit Nolan for talking like he did I liked you for it, an' I'm goin' to tell you so. Now we'll get at th' matter before us so I can move along."

Neither had paid any attention to Norah in the earnestness and keen-eyed scrutiny of each other and the first sign they had of her actions was when she threw her arms around Greener's neck and shielded him. He was too much of a man to fire from cover and Johnny realized it while the other tried to get her to leave the scene.

"I won't leave you to be murdered—I *know* what it means, I *know* it," she cried. "My place is here, and you can't deny your wife's first request! What will I do without you! Oh, dear, let me stay! I *will* stay! What woman ever had such a wedding day before! Dear, dear, what can I do? Tell me what to do!"

Johnny sniffled and wished the posse had taken him. This was a side he had never thought of. His wife! Greener's wife! Then he was too late, and to go on would be a greater evil than the one he wished to eliminate. When she turned on him like a tigress and tore him to pieces word by word, tears rolling down her pallid cheeks and untold misery in her eyes, he shook his head and held up his hand.

"Greener, you win; I can't stop what's happened," he said slowly. "But I'll tell you this, an' I mean every word: If you don't treat her like she deserves, I'll come back some of these days and kill you *shore.* Nolan got his because he talked ill of her; an' you'll get yours if I die the next minute, if you ain't square with her."

"I don't need no instructions on how to treat my wife," retorted the other. "An' I'm beginnin' to see th' cause of yore insanity, and it pardons you as nothing else will. Put up yore gun an' get back to th' ranch, where you belong— an' *keep away from me.* Savvy?"

"Not much danger of me gettin' in yore way," growled Johnny, "when I'm hunted like a dog for doing what any man would 'a' done. When th' sheriff gets well, if he ever does, mebby I'll come back an' take my medicine. How was he, anyhow, when you left?"

"Dead tired, an' some under th' influence of liquor," replied Greener, a smile breaking over his frown. He knew the whole story well, as did the whole range, and he had laughed over it with the Bar-20 outfit.

"What's that? Ain't he near dead?" cried Johnny, amazed.

"Well, purty nigh dead of fatigue dancin' at our weddin' last night; but I reckon he'll be driftin' home purty soon, an' all recovered." Greener suddenly gave way and roared with laughter. There was a large amount of humor in his make-up and it took possession of him, shaking him from head to foot. He had always liked Johnny, not because he ever wanted to but because no one could know the Bar-20 protégé and keep from it. This climax was too much for him, and his wife, gradually recovering herself, caught the infection and joined in.

Johnny's eyes were staring and his mouth wide open, but Greener's next words closed the eyes to a squint and snapped shut the open mouth.

"That there paralysis of th' cure-a-friend nerve didn't last; an' when I heard why you licked him I said a few words that made him a wiser man. He didn't hunt you after th' first day. Now you go up an' shake han's with him. He knows he got what was coming to him and so does everybody else know it. Go home an' quit playin' th' fool for th' whole blamed range to laugh at."

Johnny stirred and came back to the scene before him. His face was livid with rage and he could not speak at first. Finally, however, he mastered himself and looked up: "I'm cured, all right, but *they* ain't! Wait till my turn comes! What a fool I was to believe 'em; but they usually tell th' truth. 'Cure-a-friend nerve'! They'll pay me dollar for cent before I'm finished!" He caught the sparkle of his diamond pin, the pin he had won, when drunk, at El Paso, and a sickly grin flickered over the black frown. "I'm a little late, I reckon; but I'd like to give th' bride a present to show there ain't no hard feelin's on my part, an' to bring her luck. This here pin ain't no fit ornament for a fool like me, so if it's all right, I'll be plumb tickled to see her have it. How 'bout it, Greener?"

The happy pair exchanged glances and Mrs. Greener, hesitating and blushing, accepted the gift: "You can bend it into a ring easy," Johnny hastily remarked, to cut off her thanks.

Greener extended his hand: "I reckon we can be friends, at that, Nelson. You squared up with me when you licked Nolan. Come up an' see us when you can."

Johnny thanked him and shook hands and then watched them ride slowly down the canyon, hand in hand, happy as little children. He sat silently, lost in thought, his anger rising by leaps and bounds against the men who had kept him on the anxious seat for a month. Straightening up suddenly, he tore off the navy blue necktie and, hurling it from him, fell into another reverie, staring at the canyon wall, but seeing in his mind's eye the outfit planning his punishment; and his eyes grew redder and redder with fury. But it was a long way home and his temper cooled as he rode; that is why no one knew of his return until they saw him asleep in his bunk when they awakened at daylight the following morning. And no one ever asked about the diamond, or made any explanations—for some things are better unmentioned. But they paid for it all before Johnny considered the matter closed.

Turn the page
for an excerpt from
the exciting sequel to
*The Coming of
Cassidy:*

BAR-20

Buckskin

THE TOWN lay sprawled over half a square mile of alkali plain, its main street depressing in its width, for those who were responsible for its inception had worked with a generosity born of the knowledge that they had at their immediate and unchallenged disposal the broad lands of Texas and New Mexico on which to assemble a grand total of twenty buildings, four of which were of wood. As this material was scarce, and had to be brought from where the waters of the Gulf lapped against the flat coast, the last-mentioned buildings were a matter of local pride, as indicating the progressiveness of their owners. These creations of hammer and saw were of one story, crude and unpainted; their cheap weather sheathing warped and shrunken by the pitiless sun, curled back on itself and allowed unrestricted entrance to alkali dust and air. The other shacks were of adobe and owned by Indians and Mexicans.

It was an incident of the Cattle Trail, that most unique and stupendous of all modern migrations, and its founders must have been inspired with a malicious desire to perpetrate a crime against geography, or else they reveled in a perverse cussedness, for within a mile on every side lay broad prairies, and two miles to the east flowed the indolent waters of the Rio Pecos itself. The distance separating the town from the river was excusable, for at certain seasons of the year the placid stream swelled mightily and swept down in a broad expanse of turbulent, yellow flood.

Buckskin was a town of one hundred inhabitants, located in the valley of the Rio Pecos fifty miles south of the Texas-New Mexico line. The census claimed two hundred, but it was a well-known fact that it was exaggerated. One instance of this is shown at the name of Tom Flynn. Those who once knew Tom Flynn, alias Johnny Redmond, alias Bill Sweeney, alias Chuck Mullen, by all four names, could find them in the census list. Furthermore, he had been shot and killed in the March of the year preceding the census, and now occupied a grave in the young but flourishing cemetery. Perry's Bend, twenty miles up the river, was cognizant of this and other facts, and, laughing in open derision at the padded list, claimed to be the better town in all ways, including marksmanship.

One year before this tale opens, Buck Peters, an example for the more recent Billy the Kid, had paid Perry's Bend a short but busy visit. He had ridden in at the north end of Main Street and out at the south. As he came in he was fired at by a group of ugly cowboys from a ranch known as the C-80. He was hit twice, but he unlimbered his artillery, and before his horse had carried him, half dead, out on the prairie, he had killed one of the group. Several citizens had joined the cowboys and added their bullets against Buck. The deceased had been the best bartender in the country, and the rage of the suffering citizens can well be imagined. They swore vengeance on Buck, his ranch, and his stamping ground.

The difference between Buck and Billy the Kid is that the former never shot a man who was not trying to shoot him, or who had not been warned by some action against Buck that would call for it. He minded his own business, never picked a quarrel, and was quiet and pacific up to a certain point. After that had been passed he became like a raging cyclone in a tenement house, and storm-cellars were much in demand.

"Fanning" is the name of a certain style of gun play and was universal among the bad men of the West. While Buck was not a bad man, he had to rub elbows with them frequently, and he believed that the sauce for the goose was the sauce for the gander. So he had removed the trigger of his revolver and worked the hammer with the thumb of the "gun hand" or the thumb of the unincumbered hand. The speed thus acquired was greater than that of the more modern double-action weapon. Six shots in three seconds was his average speed when that number was required, and when it is thoroughly understood that at least five of them found their intended billets it is not difficult to realize that fanning was an operation of danger when Buck was doing it.

He was a good rider, as all cowboys are, and was not afraid of anything that lived. At one time he and his chums, Red Connors and Hopalong Cassidy, had successfully routed a band of fifteen Apaches who wanted their scalps. Of these, twelve never hunted scalps again, nor anything else on this earth, and the other three returned to their tribe with the report that three evil spirits had chased them with "wheel guns" (cannons).

So now, since his visit to Perry's Bend, the rivalry of the two towns had turned to hatred and an alert and eager readiness to increase the inhabitants of each other's graveyard. A state of war existed, which for a time resulted in nothing worse than acrimonious suggestions. But the time came when the score was settled to the satisfaction of one side, at least.

Four ranches were also concerned in the trouble. Buckskin was surrounded by two, the Bar-20 and the Three Triangle. Perry's Bend was the common point for the C-80 and the Double Arrow. Each of the two ranch contingents accepted the feud as a matter of course, and as a matter of course took sides with their respective towns. As no better class of fighters ever lived, the trouble assumed Homeric proportions and insured a danger zone well worth watching.

Bar-20's northern line was C-80's southern one, and Skinny Thompson took his turn at outriding one morning after the season's round-up. He was to follow the boundary and turn back stray cattle. When he had covered the greater part of his journey he saw Shorty Jones riding toward him on a course parallel to his own and about long revolver range away. Shorty and he had "crossed trails" the year before and the best of feelings did not exist between them.

Shorty stopped and stared at Skinny, who did likewise at Shorty. Shorty turned his mount around and applied the spurs, thereby causing his indignant horse to raise both heels at Skinny. The latter took it all in gravely and, as Shorty faced him again, placed his left thumb to his nose, wiggling his fingers suggestively. Shorty took no apparent notice of this but began to shout:

"Yu wants to keep yore busted-down cows on yore own side. They was all over us today afore yisterday. I'm goin' to salt any more what comes over, and don't yu fergit it, neither."

Thompson wigwagged with his fingers again and shouted in reply: "Yu c'n salt all yu wants to, but if I ketch yu adoin' it yu won't have to work no more. An' I kin say right here thet they's more C-80 cows over here than they's Bar-20's over there."

Shorty reached for his revolver and yelled, "Yore a liar!"

Among the cowboys in particular and the Westerners in general at that time, the three suicidal terms, unless one was an expert in drawing quick and shooting straight with one movement, were the words "liar," "coward," and "thief." Any man who was called one of these in earnest, and he was the judge, was expected to shoot if he could and save his life, for the words were seldom used without a gun coming with them. The movement of Shorty's hand toward his belt before the appellation reached him was enough for Skinny, who let go at long range—and missed.

The two reports were as one. Both urged their horses nearer and fired again. This time Skinny's sombrero gave a sharp jerk and a hole appeared in the crown. The third shot of Skinny's sent the horse of the other to its knees and then over on its side. Shorty very promptly crawled behind it and, as he did so, Skinny began a wide circle, firing at intervals as Shorty's smoke cleared away.

Shorty had the best position for defense, as he was in a shallow coulée, but he knew that he could not leave it until his opponent had either grown tired of the affair or had used up his ammunition. Skinny knew it, too. Skinny also knew that he could get back to the ranch house and lay in a supply of food and ammunition and return before Shorty could cover the twelve miles he had to go on foot.

Finally Thompson began to head for home. He had carried the matter as far as he could without it being murder. Too much time had elapsed now, and, besides, it was before breakfast and he was hungry. He would go away and settle the score at some time when they would be on equal terms.

He rode along the line for a mile and chanced to look back. Two C-80 punchers were riding after him, and as they saw him turn and discover them they fired at him and yelled. He rode on for some distance and cautiously drew his rifle out of its long holster at his right leg. Suddenly he turned around in the saddle and fired twice. One of his pursuers fell forward on the neck of his horse, and his comrade turned to help him. Thompson wigwagged again and rode on, reaching the ranch as the others were finishing their breakfast.

At the table Red Connors remarked that the tardy one had a hole in his sombrero, and asked its owner how and where he had received it.

"Had a argument with C-80 out'n th' line."

"Go 'way! Ventilate enny?"

"One."

"Good boy, sonny! Hey, Hopalong, Skinny perforated C-80 this mawnin'!"

Hopalong Cassidy was struggling with a mouthful of beef. He turned his eyes toward Red without ceasing, and grinning as well as he could under the circumstances managed to grunt out "Gu—," which was as near to "Good" as the beef would allow.

Lanky Smith now chimed in as he repeatedly stuck his knife into a reluctant boiled potato, "How'd yu do it, Skinny?"

"Bet he sneaked up on him," joshed Buck Peters; "did yu ask his pardin, Skinny?"

"Ask nothin'," remarked Red, "he jest nachurly walks up to C-80 an' sez, 'Kin I have the pleasure of ventilatin' yu?' and' C-80 he sez, 'If yu do it easy like,' sez he. Didn't he, Thompson?"

'They'll be some ventilatin' under th' table if yu fellows don't lemme alone; I'm hungry," complained Skinny.

"Say, Hopalong, I bets yu I kin clean up C-80 all by my lonesome," announced Buck, winking at Red.

"Yah! Yu onct tried to clean up the Bend, buckie, an' if Pete an' Billy hadn't afound yu when they come by Eagle Pass that night yu wouldn't be here eatin' beef by th' pound," glancing at the hard-working Hopalong. "It was plum' lucky fer yu that they was acourtin' that time, wasn't it, Hopalong?" suddenly asked Red. Hopalong nearly strangled in his efforts to speak. He gave it up and nodded his head.

"Why can't yu git it straight, Connors? I wasn't doin' no courtin', it was Pete. I runned into him on th' other side o' th' pass. I'd look fine acourtin', wouldn't I?" asked the downtrodden Williams.

Pete Wilson skillfully flipped a potato into that worthy's coffee, spilling the beverage of the questionable name over a large expanse of blue flannel shirt. "Yu's all right, yu are. Why, when I meets yu, yu was lost in th' arms of yore ladylove. All I could see was yore feet. Go an' git tangled up with a two hundred and forty pound half-breed squaw an' then try to lay it onter me! When I proposed drownin' yore troubles over at Cowan's, yu went an' got mad over what yu called th' insinooation. An' yu shore didn't look any too blamed fine, neither."

"All th' same," volunteered Thompson, who had

taken the edge from his appetite, "we better go over
an' pay C-80 a call. I don't like what Shorty said about
saltin' our cattle. He'll shore do it, unless I camps on
th' line, which same I hain't hankerin' after."

"Oh, he wouldn't stop th' cows that way, Skinny; he
was only afoolin'," exclaimed Connors meekly.

"Foolin' yore gran'mother! That there bunch'll do
anything if we wasn't lookin'," hotly replied Skinny.

"That's shore nuff gospel, Thomp. They's sore fer
mor'n one thing. They got aplenty when Buck went on
th' warpath, an' they's hankerin' to git square," remarked Johnny Nelson, stealing the pie, a rare treat,
of his neighbor when that unfortunate individual was
not looking. He had it halfway to his mouth when its
former owner, Jimmy Price, a boy of eighteen, turned
his head and saw it going.

"Hi-yi! Yu clay-bank coyote, drap thet pie! Did yu
ever see such a son-of-a-gun fer pie?" he plaintively
asked Red Connors, as he grabbed a mighty handful of
apples and crust. "Pie'll kill yu some day, yu bobtailed
jack! I had an uncle that died onct. He et too much pie
an' he went an' turned green, an' so'll yu if yu don't let
it alone."

"Yu ought'r seed th' pie Johnny had down in Eagle
Flat," murmured Lanky Smith reminiscently. "She had
feet that'd stop a stam*pede*. Johnny was shore loco
about her. Swore she was the finest blossom that ever
growed." Here he choked and tears of laughter coursed
down his weather-beaten face as he pictured her. "She
was about fifteen han's high an' about sixteen han's
around. Johnny used to chalk off when he hugged her,
usen't yu, Johnny? One night when he had got purty
well around on th' second lap he run inter a man jest
startin' out on his fust. They hain't caught that Mexican
yet."

Nelson was pelted with everything in sight. He slowly wiped off the pie crust and bread and potatoes. "Anybody'd think I was a busted grub wagon," he grumbled. When he had fished the last piece of beef out of his ear he went out and offered to stand treat. As the round-up was over, they slid into their saddles and raced for Cowan's saloon at Buckskin.

The Rashness of Shorty

BUCKSKIN WAS very hot; in fact it was never anything else. Few people were on the streets and the town was quiet. Over in the Houston hotel a crowd of cowboys was lounging in the barroom. They were very quiet— a condition as rare as it was ominous. Their mounts, twelve in all, were switching flies from their quivering skins in the corral at the rear. Eight of these had a large C-80 branded on their flanks; the other four, a Double Arrow.

In the barroom a slim, wiry man was looking out of the dirty window up the street at Cowan's saloon. Shorty was complaining, "They shore oughter be here now. They rounded up last week." The man nearest assured him that they would come. The man at the window turned and said, "They's yer now."

In front of Cowan's a crowd of nine happy-go-lucky, dare-devil riders were sliding from their saddles. They threw the reins over the heads of their mounts and filed in to the bar. Laughter issued from the open door and the clink of glasses could be heard. They stood in picturesque groups, strong, self-reliant, humorous, virile. Their expensive sombreros were pushed far back on their heads and their hairy chaps were covered with the alkali dust from their ride.

Cowan, bottle in hand, pushed out several more glasses. he kicked a dog from under his feet and looked at Buck. "Rounded up yet?" he inquired.

"Shore, day afore yisterday," came the reply. The rest were busy removing the dust from their throats, and gradually drifted into groups of two or three. One of these groups strolled over to the solitary card table, and found Jimmy Price resting in a cheap chair, his legs on the table.

"I wisht yu'd extricate yore delicate feet from off'n this hyar table, James," humbly requested Lanky Smith, morally backed up by those with him.

"Ya-as, they shore is delicate, Mr. Smith," responded Jimmy, without moving.

"We wants to play draw, Jimmy," explained Pete.

"Yore shore welcome to play if yu wants to. Didn't I tell yu when yu growed that mustache that yu didn't have to ask me any more?" queried the placid James, paternally.

"Call 'em off, sonny. Pete sez he kin clean me out. Anyhow, yu kin have the fust deal," compromised Lanky.

"I'm shore sorry fer Pete if he cayn't. Yu don't reckon I has to have fust deal to beat yu fellers, do yu? Go way an' lemme alone; I never seed such a bunch fer buttin' in as yu fellers."

Billy Williams returned to the bar. Then he walked along it until he was behind the recalcitrant possessor of the table. While his aggrieved friends shuffled their feet uneasily to cover his approach, he tiptoed up behind Jimmy and, with a nod, grasped that indignant individual firmly by the neck while the others grabbed his feet. They carried him, twisting and bucking, to the middle of the street and deposited him in the dust, returning to the now vacant table.

Jimmy rested quietly for a few seconds and then slowly arose, dusting the alkali from him. "Th' wall-eyed piruts," he muttered, and then scratched his head for a way to "play hunk." As he gazed sorrowfully at the saloon he heard a snicker from behind him. He, thinking it was one of his late tormentors, paid no attention to it. Then a cynical, biting laugh stung him. He wheeled, to see Shorty leaning against a tree, a sneering leer on his flushed face. Shorty's right hand was suspended above his holster, hooked to his belt by the thumb—a favorite position of his when expecting trouble.

"One of yore reg'lar habits?" he drawled.

Jimmy began to dust himself in silence, but his lips were compressed to a thin white line.

"Does they hurt yu?" pursued the onlooker.

Jimmy looked up. "I heard tell that they make glue outen cayuses, sometimes," he remarked.

Shorty's eyes flashed. The loss of the horse had been rankling in his heart all day.

"Does they git yu frequent?" he asked. His voice sounded hard.

"Oh, 'bout as frequent as yu lose a cayuse, I reckon," replied Jimmy hotly.

Shorty's hand streaked to his holster and Jimmy followed his lead. Jimmy's Colt was caught. He had bucked too much. As he fell Shorty ran for the Houston House.

Pistol shots were common, for they were the universal method of expressing emotions. The poker players grinned, thinking their victim was letting off his indignation. Lanky sized up his hand and remarked half audibly, "He's a shore good kid."

The bartender, fearing for his new beveled, gilt-framed mirror, gave a hasty glance out the window. He turned around, made change and remarked to Buck, "Yore kid, Jimmy, is plugged." Several of the more credulous craned their necks to see, Buck being the first. "Hell!" he shouted, and ran out to where Jimmy lay coughing, his toes twitching. The saloon was deserted and a crowd of angry cowboys surrounded their chum—a boy. Buck had seen Shorty enter the door of the Houston House and he swore. "Chase them damn cayuses behind th' saloon, Pete, an' git under cover."

Jimmy was choking and he coughed up blood. "He's shore—got me. My—gun stuck," he added apologetically. He tried to sit up, but was not able and he looked surprised. "It's purty—damn hot—out here," he suggested. Johnny and Billy carried him in the saloon and placed him by the table, in the chair he had previously vacated. As they stood up he fell across the table and died.

Billy placed the dead boy's sombrero on his head and laid the refractory revolver on the table. "I wonder who th' shooter was." He looked at the slim figure and started to go out, followed by Johnny. As he reached the threshold a bullet zipped past him and thudded into the frame of the door. He backed away and looked surprised. "That's Shorty's shootin'—he allus misses 'bout that much." He looked out and saw Buck standing behind the live oak that Shorty had leaned against, firing at the hotel. Turning around he made for the rear, remarking to Johnny that "they's in th' Houston."

Johnny looked at the quiet figure in the chair and swore softly. He followed Billy. Cowan, closing the door and taking a .60-caliber buffalo gun from under the bar, went out also and slammed the rear door forcibly.

The Argument

U<small>P</small> <small>THE</small> street two hundred yards from the Houston House Skinny and Pete lay hidden behind a bowlder. Three hundred yards on the other side of the hotel Johnny and Billy were stretched out in an arroyo. Buck was lying down now, and Hopalong, from his position in the barn belonging to the hotel, was methodically dropping the horses of the besieged, a job he hated as much as he hated poison. The corral was their death trap. Red and Lanky were emitting clouds of smoke from behind the store, immediately across the street from the barroom. A .60 caliber buffalo gun roared down by the plaza and several Sharps cracked a protest from different points. The town had awakened and the shots were dropping steadily.

Strange noises filled the air. They grew in tone and volume and then dwindled away to nothing. The hum of the buffalo gun and the sobbing *pi-in-in-ing* of the

Winchesters were liberally mixed with the sharp whines of the revolvers.

There were no windows in the hotel now. Raw furrows in the bleached wood showed yellow, and splinters mysteriously sprang from the casings. The panels of the door were producing cracks and the cheap door handle flew many ways at once. An empty whisky keg on the stoop boomed out mournfully at intervals and finally rolled down the steps with a rumbling protest. Wisps of smoke slowly climbed up the walls and seemed to be waving defiance to the curling wisps in the open.

Pete raised his shoulder to refill the magazine of his smoking rifle and dropped the cartridges all over his lap. He looked sheepishly at Skinny and began to load with his other hand.

"Yore plum' loco, yu are. Don't yu reckon they kin hit a blue shirt at two hundred?" Skinny cynically inquired. "Got one that time," he announced a second later.

"I wonder who's got th' buffalo," grunted Pete. "Mus' be Cowan," he replied to his own question and settled himself to use his left hand.

"Don't yu git Shorty; he's my meat," suggested Skinny.

"Yu better tell Buck—he ain't got no love fer Shorty," replied Pete, aiming carefully.

The panic in the corral ceased and Hopalong was now sending his regrets against the panels of the rear door. He had cut his last initial in the near panel and was starting a wobbly "H" in its neighbor. He was in a good position. There were no windows in the rear wall, and as the door was a very dangerous place he was not fired at.

He began to get tired of this one-sided business and crawled up on the window ledge, dangling his feet on the outside. He occasionally sent a bullet at a different part of the door, but amused himself by annoying Buck.

"Plenty hot down there?" he pleasantly inquired, and as he received no answer he tried again. "Better save some of them cartridges fer some other time, Buck."

Buck was sending .45 Winchesters into the shattered window with a precision that presaged evil to any of the defenders who were rash enough to try to gain the other end of the room.

Hopalong bit off a chew of tobacco and drowned a green fly that was crawling up the side of the barn. The yellow liquid streaked downward a short distance and was eagerly sucked up by the warped boards.

A spurt of smoke leaped from the battered door and the bored hopalong promptly tumbled back inside. He felt of his arm, and then, delighted at the notice taken of his artistic efforts, shot several times from a crack on his right. "This yer's shore gittin' like home," he gravely remarked to the splinter that whizzed past his head. He shot again at the door and it sagged outward, accompanied by the thud of a falling body. "Pies like mother used to make," he announced to the empty loft as he slipped the magazine full of .45's. "An' pills like popper used to take," he continued when he had lowered the level of the liquor in his flask.

He rolled a cigarette and tossed the match into the air, extinguishing it by a shot from his Colt.

"Got any cigarettes, Hoppy?" said a voice from below.

"Shore," replied the joyous puncher, recognizing Pete; "how'd yu git here?"

"Like a cow. Busy?"

"None whatever. Comin' up?"

"Nope. Skinny wants a smoke too."

Hopalong handed tobacco and papers down the hole. "So long."

"So long," replied the daring Pete, who risked death twice for a smoke.

The hot afternoon dragged along and about three o'clock Buck held up an empty cartridge belt to the gaze of the curious Hopalong. That observant worthy nodded and threw a double handful of cartridges, one by one, to the patient and unrelenting Buck, who filled his gun and piled the few remaining ones up at his side. "Th' lives of mice and men gang aft all wrong," he remarked at random.

"Th' son-of-a-gun's talkin' Shakespeare," marveled Hopalong.

"Satiate any, Buck?" he asked as that worthy settled down to await his chance.

"Two," he replied, "Shorty an' another. Plenty damn hot down here," he complained. A spurt of alkali dust stung his face but the hand that made it never made another. "Three," he called. "How many, Hoppy?"

"One. That's four. Wonder if th' others got any?"

"Pete said Skinny got one," replied the intent Buck.

"Th' son-of-a-gun, he never said nothin' about it, an' me a fillin' his ornery paws with smokin'." Hopalong was indignant.

"Bet yu ten we don't git 'em afore dark," he announced.

"Got yu. Go yu ten more I gits another," promptly responded Buck.

"That's a shore cinch. Make her twenty."

"She is."

"Yu'll have to square it with Skinny, he shore wanted Shorty plum' bad," Hopalong informed the unerring marksman.

"Why didn't he say suthin' about it? Anyhow, Jimmy was my bunkie."

Hopalong's cigarette disintegrated and the board at his left received a hole. He promptly disappeared and Buck laughed. He sat up in the loft and angrily spat the soaked paper out from between his lips.

"All that trouble fer nothin', th' white-eyed coyote," he muttered. Then he crawled around to one side and fired at the center of his "C." Another shot hurtled at him and his left arm fell to his side. "That's funny— wonder where th' damn pirut is?" He looked out cautiously and saw a cloud of smoke over a knothole which was situated close up under the eaves of the barroom; and it was being agitated. Some one was blowing at it to make it disappear. He aimed very carefully at the knot and fired. He heard a sound between a curse and a squawk and was not molested any further from that point.

"I knowed he'd git hurt," he explained to the bandage, torn from the edge of his kerchief, which he carefully bound around his last wound.

Down in the arroyo Johnny was complaining.

"This yer's a no good bunk," he plaintively remarked.

"It shore ain't—but it's th' best we kin find," apologized Billy.

"That's th' sixth that feller sent up there. He's a damn poor shot," observed Johnny; "must be Shorty."

"Shorty kin shoot plum' good—tain't him," contradicted Billy.

"Yas—with a six-shooter. He's off'n his feed with a rifle," explained Johnny.

"Yu wants to stay down from up there, yu ijit," warned Billy as the disgusted Johnny crawled up the bank. He slid down again with a welt on his neck.

"That's somebody else now. He oughter a done better'n that," he said.

Billy had fired as Johnny started to slide and he smoothed his aggrieved chum. "He could onct, yu means."

"Did yu git him?" asked the anxious Johnny, rubbing his welt.

"Plum' center," responded the businesslike Billy. "Go up agin, mebby I kin git another," he suggested tentatively.

"Mebby you kin go to hell. I ain't no gallery," grinned the now exuberant owner of the welt.

"Who's got th' buffalo?" he inquired as the .60 caliber roared.

"Mus' be Cowan. He's shore all right. Sounds like a bloomin' cannon," replied Billy. "Lemme alone with yore fool questions, I'm busy," he complained as his talkative partner started to ask another. "Go an' git me some water—I'm alkalied. An' git some .45's, mine's purty near gone."

Johnny crawled down the arroyo and reappeared at Hopalong's barn.

As he entered the door a handful of empty shells fell on his hat and dropped to the floor. He shook his head and remarked, "That mus' be that fool Hopalong."

"Yore shore right. How's business?" inquired the festive Cassidy.

"Purty fair. Billy's got one. How many's gone?"

"Buck's got three, I got two and Skinny's got one. That's six, an' Billy's is seven. They's five more," he replied.

"How'd yu know?" queried Johnny as he filled his flask at the horse trough.

"Because they's twelve cayuses behind th' ho*tel*. That's why."

"They might git away on 'em," suggested the practical Johnny.

"Can't. They's all cashed in."

"Yu said that they's five left," ejaculated the puzzled water carrier.

"Yah; yore a smart cuss, ain't yu?"

Johnny grinned and then said, "Got any smokin'?"

Hopalong looked grieved. "I ain't no store. Why don't yu git generous and buy some?"

He partially filled Johnny's hand, and as he put the sadly depleted bag away he inquired, "Got any papers?"

"Nope."

"Got any matches?" he asked cynically.

"Nope."

"Kin yu smoke 'em?" he yelled, indignantly.

"Sure nuff," placidly replied the un Johnny. "Billy wants some .45's."

Hopalong gasped. "Don't he want my gun, too?"

"Nope. Got a better one. Hurry up, he'll git mad."

Hopalong was a very methodical person. He was the only one of his crowd to carry a second cartridge strap. It hung over his right shoulder and rested on his left hip, holding one hundred cartridges and his second Colt. His waist belt held fifty cartridges and all would fit both the rifle and revolvers. He extracted twenty from that part of the shoulder strap hardest to get at, the back, by simply pulling it over his shoulder and plucking out the bullets as they came into reach.

"That's all yu kin have. I'm *Buck's* ammernition jackass," he explained. "Bet yu ten we gits 'em afore dark"—he was hedging.

"Any fool knows that. I'll take yu if yu bets th' other way," responded Johnny, grinning. He knew Hopalong's weak spot.

"Yore on," promptly responded Hopalong, who would bet on anything.

"Well, so long," said Johnny as he crawled away.

"Hey, yu, Johnny!" called out Hopalong, "don't yu go an' tell anybody I got any pills left. I ain't no ars'nal."

Johnny replied by elevating one foot and waving it. Then he disappeared.

Behind the store, the most precarious position among the besiegers, Red Connors and Lanky Smith were ensconced and commanded a view of the entire length of the barroom. They could see the dark mass they knew to be the rear door and derived a great amount of amusement from the spots of light which were appearing in it.

They watched the "C" (reversed to them) appear and be completed. When the wobbly "H" grew to completion they laughed heartily. Then the hardwood bar had been dragged across their field of vision and up to the front windows, and they could only see the indiscriminate holes which appeared in the upper panels at frequent intervals.

Every time they fired they had to expose a part of themselves to a return shot, with the result that Lanky's forearm was seared its entire length. Red had been more fortunate and only had a bruised ear.

They laboriously rolled several large rocks out in the open, pushing them beyond the shelter of the store with their rifles. When they had crawled behind them they each had another wound. From their new position they could see Hopalong sitting in his window. He promptly waved his sombrero and grinned.

They were the most experienced fighters of all except Buck, and were saving their shots. When they did shoot they always had some portion of a man's body to aim at, and the damage they inflicted was considerable. They said nothing, being older than the rest and more taciturn, and they were not reckless. Although Hopalong's antics made them laugh, they grumbled at his recklessness and were not tempted to emulate him. It was noticeable, too, that they shoved their rifles out simultaneously and, although both were aiming, only one fired. Lanky's gun cracked so close to the enemy's that the whirr of the bullet over Red's head was merged in the crack of his partner's reply.

When Hopalong saw the rocks roll out from behind the store he grew very curious. Then he saw a flash, followed instantly by another from the second rifle. He saw several of these follow shots and could sit in silence no longer. He waved his hat to attract attention and then shouted, "How many?" A shot was sent straight up in the air and he notified Buck that there were only four left.

The fire of these four grew less rapid—they were saving their ammunition. A pot shot at Hopalong sent that gentleman's rifle hurtling to the ground. Another tore through his hat, removing a neat amount of skin and hair and giving him a lifelong part. He fell back inside and proceeded to shoot fast and straight with his revolvers, his head burning as though on fire. When he had vented the dangerous pressure of his anger he went below and tried to fish the rifle in with a long stick. It was obdurate, so he sent three more shots into the door, and, receiving no reply, ran out around the corner of his shelter and grasped the weapon. When half way back he sank to the ground. Before another shot could be fired at him with any judgment a ripping, spitting rifle was being frantically worked from the barn. The bullets tore the door into seams and gaps; the lowest panel, the one having the "H" in it, fell inward in chunks. Johnny had returned for another smoke.

Hopalong, still grasping the rifle, rolled rapidly around the corner of the barn. He endeavored to stand, but could not. Johnny, hearing rapid and fluent swearing, came out.

"Where'd they git yu?" he asked.

"In th' off leg. Hurts like hell. Did yu git him?"

"Nope. I jest come fer another cig; got any left?"

"Up above. Yore gall is shore appallin'. Help me in, yu two-laigged jackass."

"Shore. We'll shore pay our 'tentions to that door. She'll go purty soon—she's as full of holes as th' Bad Lan's," replied Johnny. "Git aholt an' hop along, Hopalong."

He helped the swearing Hopalong inside, and then the lead they pumped into the wrecked door was scandalous. Another panel fell in and Hopalong's "C" was destroyed. A wide crack appeared in the one above it and grew rapidly. Its mate began to gape and finally both were driven in. The increase in the light caused by these openings allowed Red and Lanky to secure better aim and soon the fire of the defenders died out.

Johnny dropped his rifle and, drawing his six-shooter, ran out and dashed for the dilapidated door, while Hopalong covered that opening with a fusilade.

As Johnny's shoulder sent the framework flying inward he narrowly missed sudden death. As it was he staggered to the side, out of range, and dropped full length to the ground, flat on his face. Hopalong's rifle cracked incessantly, but to no avail. The man who had fired the shot was dead. Buck got him immediately after he had shot Johnny.

Calling to Skinny and Red to cover him, Buck sprinted to where Johnny lay gasping. The bullet had entered his breast, just missed his lungs and had passed out his back. Buck, Colt in hand, leaped through the door, but met with no resistance. He signaled to Hopalong, who yelled, "They's none left."

The trees and rocks and gullies and buildings yielded men who soon crowded around the hotel. A young doctor, lately graduated, appeared. It was his first case, but he eased Johnny and saved his life. Then he went over to Hopalong, who was now raving, and attended to him. The others were patched up as well as possible and the struggling young physician had his pockets crammed full of gold and silver coins.

The scene of the wrecked barroom was indescribable. Holes, furrows, shattered glass and bottles, the liquor oozing down the walls of the shelves and running over the floor; the ruined furniture, a wrecked bar, seared and shattered and covered with blood; bodies as they had been piled in the corners; ropes, shells, hats; and liquor everywhere, over everything, met the gaze of those who had caused the chaos.

Perry's Bend had failed to wipe out the score.